**KU-415-767**

Bella Andre has always been a writer. Songs came first, and then non-fiction books, but as soon as she started her first romance novel, she knew she'd found her perfect career. Since selling her first book in 2003, she's written sixteen "sensual, empowered stories enveloped in heady romance" (*Publisher's Weekly*) about sizzling alpha heroes and the strong women they'll love forever.

She is the author of: *Wild Heat, Hot as Sin* and *Never Too Hot*, all available from *Rouge*.

www.bellaandre.com

# Also by Bella Andre:

*Wild Heat*
*Hot As Sin*
*Never Too Hot*

# BELLA ANDRE

# HOT AS SIN

1 3 5 7 9 10 8 6 4 2

First published in the United States in 2009 by Bantam Dell,
a Division of Random House, Inc. New York

Published in the UK in 2012 by Rouge, an imprint of Ebury Publishing
A Random House Group Company

The Random House Group Limited Reg. No. 954009

Addresses for companies within the Random House Group can be
found at www.randomhouse.co.uk

A CIP catalogue record for this book is available from the British Library

The Random House Group Limited supports The Forest Stewardship
Council (FSC®), the leading international forest certification organisation.
Our books carrying the FSC label are printed on FSC® certified paper.
FSC is the only forest certification scheme endorsed by the
leading environmental organisations, including Greenpeace.
Our paper procurement policy can be found at:
www.randomhouse.co.uk/environment

Printed and bound in Great Britain by Clays Ltd, St Ives PLC
ISBN 9780091949075

To buy books by your favourite authors and register for offers visit
www.randomhouse.co.uk

For Julia, Hunter, & Paul.
I love you!

# ACKNOWLEDGMENTS

FIRST AND foremost, I want to thank my agent, Jessica Faust. Best. Agent. Ever.

A big thank-you to Shauna Summers and Jessica Sebor for your excellent editing and enthusiasm for what I do.

As always, huge thanks go to my Nor Cal crew: Monica McCarty, Jami Alden, Barbara Freethy, Anne Mallory, Veronica Wolff, Carol Grace Culver, Tracy Grant, Penelope Williamson, and Poppy Reiffin. Great company, lots of laughs, and incredible brainstorming. A perfect combination!

Again, thank you to my parents, Louisa and Alvin, and my mother-in-law Elaine for wearing my kids out every Monday. When I tell them they're spending the day with you, they always cheer!

And to everyone who wrote me to say how much you loved Logan and Maya's story, thanks so much for taking the time to drop me a note. I hope you love Sam and Dianna's story just as much!

Enjoy!
Bella Andre

# ACKNOWLEDGEMENTS

# HOT
## AS SIN

# CHAPTER ONE

COMING TO Colorado had been a mistake.

Dianna Kelley slammed the door of her rental car shut and turned the heat on full blast, then wrapped her hands around her upper arms as she shivered on the cold leather seat.

Earlier that day when she'd flown into the small Vail airport, the breeze had been cool and steady, but the sky had been blue and clear. Tonight, however, wind howled through the trees while black, ominous clouds spat out sheets of rain all over the quickly flooding sidewalk.

She closed her eyes and fought back a heavy wave of sorrow at the emotionally charged blowout she'd just had with her younger sister in a bustling café. Dianna knew better than to expect too much from April, but she'd never stopped hoping that the two of them would finally connect.

Growing up, Dianna had longed for a baby brother or sister, so when she was eight and April had been born, she'd showered her baby sister with love. Until the horrible day when their easily overwhelmed, usually broke single mother had decided there were too many mouths to feed and gave four-year-old April up to the state.

As soon as Dianna turned eighteen, she began her fight to pull April out of the foster system, but it took four years to bring her sister home.

In the decade that they'd been apart, April had changed. The innocent, cheerful, inquisitive girl she'd once been was long gone. In her place was a hardened, foulmouthed fourteen-year-old who'd seen and experienced way too much.

Dianna's hands tightened on the steering wheel as she remembered the way April used to lash out at her, accusing her of ruining her life, of trying to control her every move like a jail warden. All through April's high school years, Dianna had tried to protect her sister. From the mean girls in her classes who thrived on picking on the new girl, from the cute boys who would break her heart just because they could, and from the teachers who didn't understand that April needed more patience and attention than kids with normal upbringings.

But it had proved impossible to protect her little sister.

As the years ticked by and she grew from a lanky teen into a knockout young woman, April retreated further and further into herself. She refused to share any details about her various foster homes with not only Dianna, but a series of therapists as well. By the time April eked out a high school diploma, they were nothing more than two strangers who passed each other at the fridge a couple of times a week.

In the two years since graduation, April had bounced from part-time job to part-time job and boyfriend to boyfriend, and Dianna worried that April was going to get pregnant and end up marrying one of the losers she was dating. Or not marrying him and becoming a broke single mother in a trailer park, just as their own mother had been.

Dianna blinked hard through the windshield wipers into the driving rain as she replayed the moment when she came home from work three months ago and found April's key on the kitchen table. Running into April's room, she'd realized her sister's favorite ratty jeans and tops were gone along with her duffel bag. At least she'd taken her toothbrush.

For seven horribly long days, she'd waited for some word as to where her sister had gone, and when—*if*— she was coming back. Finally, April left a message on Dianna's cell phone when she was taping her live television show and couldn't possibly answer it. She was in Colorado and she was fine. She didn't leave a new number or address.

Again and again during the past three months, Dianna had tried to tell herself that her little sister was simply going through a patch of self-discovery. After all, normal twenty-year-old girls tried things out and learned from their mistakes and moved on, didn't they?

But nothing about April's life was normal. Not after ten years bouncing from family to family in the state foster system. Dianna hated not being able to keep watch over her sister, hated knowing she couldn't keep her safe.

So when April finally called and asked if Dianna could come to Vail to meet with her, although it wasn't easy to shift all of her interviews on such short notice, Dianna couldn't miss her chance to connect with April.

But instead of connecting, they'd fought. And April had stormed out of the café. Leaving Dianna to helplessly wonder how she could possibly save her sister this time.

The rental car's windows were covered with condensation, so Dianna hit the defrost button, but it didn't work. Reaching into her large leather tote for a package of Kleenex, she wiped a clear circle on the windshield and slowly pulled into the street, inching forward as marble-sized hail battered her car. Every few seconds, she hit the brakes and wiped the moisture off of the windshield.

Prudence told her to turn back, but all she wanted was to be back home in San Francisco, wrapped up in a soft blanket on her couch with a novel. As it was, she was cutting it close to get to the airport in time for her flight.

The two-lane road that led from Vail to the airport was narrow and winding, and she seriously considered pulling over, turning around, and finding a nearby hotel to wait out the storm. Instead, she took a deep breath and forcefully shook off the sick sense of foreboding she'd carried with her ever since April had moved to Colorado, turning the radio on to a pop station.

I'm pulling out windows and taking down the doors
I'm looking under the floorboards
In the hopes of finding something more

Listen to me now 'cause I'm calling out
Don't hold me down 'cause I'm breaking out
Holding on I'm standing here
Outstretched
Outstretched
Outstretched for more

Her throat grew tight as she realized that this was one of the songs April had played over and over in her bedroom. How sensitive her little sister obviously was beneath her thick armor if she liked a heartbreaking song like this . . . and how hard she must be trying to hide her true feelings from everyone. Especially her big sister, who loved her more than anyone or anything.

But it had already been an emotional enough day

without some song making her cry, so she shifted her gaze to the stereo for a split second to turn it off. Lifting her eyes back to the road, she was startled by bright headlight beams from an oncoming car. Temporarily blinded, she swerved away from the light.

Too late, she realized that the only thing between her and the headlights was a wall of rock.

Dianna screamed as the oncoming car clipped the front bumper of her rental, instinctively bracing for further impact as she spun around and around in circles. The airbags exploded in a burst of white powder and thick, sticky material. Despite her seat belt, she flew into the tight bags of air, the breath knocked out of her lungs as she hit them hard.

Oh God, she was suffocating!

Ripping, grabbing, pulling, she tried to shove the airbag away from her mouth and nose, but she couldn't escape. Sharp pains ran through her, top to bottom. And yet, she didn't pass out, couldn't seem to find that numb place where everything would be all right.

Finally, after what seemed like hours, someone found her: a firefighter-paramedic, with jet-black hair and beautiful blue eyes.

"Everything's going to be all right," he said. "I'm going to take care of you."

Looking up at him, his features and coloring were close enough to Sam MacKenzie's that his words twisted up in her head, in her heart, and she was thrown back to another car crash, one that had taken everything from her.

*She'd been desperately craving Chinese food, so she'd driven into town for takeout. But after throwing up all morning, she'd been so starved that she couldn't make it out of the parking lot without dipping into the mu-shu pork.*

*She'd mixed the plum sauce into the cabbage and meat with her fingers and pretty much inhaled it, barely having any time to appreciate the sweet-salty combination before heartburn got her, right under her ribs.*

*Her obstetrician said it was normal, that the morning sickness would ease as soon as next week, when she hit her second trimester, but that the heartburn would probably get worse, along with possible constipation from the iron pills and being kept awake all night by a kicking baby.*

*The doctor had grinned and said, "Quite a lot to look forward to, isn't there?" and Dianna hadn't wanted to admit that she was still trying to get her head around being pregnant.*

*And the amazing fact that she was going to be Mrs. Sam MacKenzie in a week.*

*The Chinese restaurant was in a trailer right off Highway 50, and knowing the road was busy year-round with tourists, Dianna carefully backed out into traffic, putting her turn signal on to make a U-turn from the center lane. When the coast looked clear, she hit the gas pedal.*

*From out of nowhere, a large white limo careened toward her. She could see it coming, could see the driver's horrified ex-*

*pression, but no matter how hard she pressed on the gas, she couldn't get out of the way in time.*

*She was thrown into the steering wheel, and as her skull hit the glass all she could think about was her baby . . . and the sudden realization of how desperately she wanted it.*

*Going in and out of consciousness as fire engines and ambulances came on the scene, she felt someone move her onto a stretcher. She tried to speak, but she couldn't get her lips to move.*

*Her stomach cramped down on itself just as she heard somebody say, "There's blood. Between her legs."*

*She felt a hand on her shoulder. "Ma'am, can you hear me? Can you tell me if you are pregnant?"*

*But she couldn't nod, couldn't move or talk or do anything to tell him he had to save her baby.*

*And then a new voice came, its deep, rich tones so near and dear to her.*

*"Yes, she's pregnant."*

*Sam. He'd found her. He'd make everything all right, just like he always did.*

*Somehow she managed to open her eyes, but when she looked up she saw Connor MacKenzie, Sam's younger brother, kneeling over her, speaking into his radio.*

*"Tell Sam he needs to get off the mountain now! Dianna was in a car accident on Highway 50."*

*More cramps hit her one after the other and she felt thick, warm liquid seep out between her legs.*

*She screamed, "Sam!"*

*But it was too late for him to help her. Their baby was gone.*

"Can you hear me, ma'am?"

She opened her eyes and saw that the firefighter's eyebrows were furrowed with concern.

"Can you tell me if you're pregnant?"

Dianna blinked at him, belatedly realizing that she'd instinctively moved her hands to her abdomen.

Reality returned as she realized that the hero who had come to her rescue wasn't Sam. Her failed pregnancy was nothing but a distant memory she usually kept locked away, deep in the recesses of her heart.

Feeling the wet sting of tears in her eyes, she whispered, "No, I'm not pregnant," and then everything faded to black.


"I'm sorry," the doctor said softly. "Your brother didn't make it."

Dark eyes blinked in disbelief. This wasn't happening. His twin couldn't be dead. Not when they were together just that afternoon. Sharing a couple of beers in companionable silence until Jacob brought the meth lab up again, saying that they had enough money already, that they should shut the business down before they got caught and ended up in jail. Only hours ago, he'd told Jacob to go to hell, said he was the brains of the business and knew what was best for the both of them.

According to the paramedics, Jacob had been driving

down Highway 70 when his tires slipped on some black ice. He'd crashed head-on into another vehicle and the paramedics had rushed Jacob to Vail General Hospital.

For two hours, Jacob had been fighting for his life.

He wasn't fighting anymore.

The man's body rejected the news, head to toe, inside and out. Bile rose in his throat and he made it across the blue and green linoleum tiles in time to hurl into a garbage can.

More than just fraternal twins, he and Jacob had been extensions of each other. Losing his brother was like being cleaved in two straight down the middle, through his bones and guts and organs.

He needed air, needed to get out of the ICU waiting room, away from all of the other people who still had hope that their loved ones would recover from heart attacks and blood clots. He pushed open the door to the patio, just in time to see a loud group of reporters harassing anyone wearing scrubs.

"Do you have an update on Dianna Kelley?" one of the reporters asked a passing nurse in a breathless voice.

Another rushed up to a doctor, lights flashing, camera ready. "We've been told that Dianna Kelley was in a head-on collision on Highway 70. Could you confirm that for us, Doctor?"

*Dianna Kelley?*

Was she the other driver? Was she the person whose worthless driving had ended Jacob's life?

He'd only seen her cable TV show a handful of times

over the years, but her face was on the cover of enough newspapers and magazines for him to know what she looked like.

Blond. Pampered. Rich. Without a care in the world.

"Please," another reporter begged the doctor, "if you could just tell us how she is, if she's been badly hurt, or if she's going to be all right?"

None of the reporters had even acknowledged that there was another person involved in the crash. All they cared about was Dianna, Dianna, Dianna.

Knowing that no one gave a shit about Jacob was a big enough blow to send him completely over the edge.

"Would you like to come back and say good-bye?"

The doctor who had delivered the bad news was still waiting for him just inside the door. Her voice was kind and yet he knew his brother was just one more stranger who'd died on her shift.

Before he could respond, a tall blond girl ran past him and into the waiting room. For a minute he couldn't believe his eyes.

If Dianna Kelley had been in the crash with his brother, how was she running by him now?

It took him a few moments to realize that this girl in her dirt-streaked jeans and oversized raincoat was barely out of her teens. Although she bore a striking resemblance to the famous face he'd seen dozens of times, there was no way she could be the "important" woman the reporters were climbing over themselves to get a scoop on.

"I'm Dianna Kelley's sister," the girl said to the doctor in a breathless voice, her cheeks streaked with tears. "I saw on TV that Dianna was in a crash." She grabbed the doctor's arm. "I need to see her!"

The doctor looked between the two of them, and even in his fog of pain, he could see that she was torn between the guy with the dead brother and the girl with the hurt sister. But they both knew the famous sister would win.

"Excuse me, Jeannie, could you come help me?"

A moment later, a young nurse came around the corner and the doctor explained, "This is Dianna Kelley's sister."

"Come with me," the nurse said to the girl, whose raincoat was dripping a puddle on the carpet. "I'll need to see your ID first."

"She's not going to die, is she?" Dianna's sister asked in a shaking voice.

"I don't know, honey," the nurse said in a soothing voice. "You'll have to ask her doctor."

"I'm so sorry about all of this," the doctor said to him as she ran her badge in front of the locked ICU door. "I know how hard this is for you."

He wanted to use the doctor as a punching bag, to scream that she didn't know a damn thing about him, about the hole in his chest that was growing bigger by the second. Instead, he silently followed her down the hall into the busy ICU.

The overhead lights had been dimmed in his brother's

small room and a white sheet had been placed over his body. The doctor peeled back the cloth to reveal his brother's lifeless face, and before he could brace himself, pain unlike anything he'd ever felt before ripped through him. He felt dizzy and light-headed. As if he could drop to the floor at any second.

Moving closer and gently touching his brother's unmoving face, so similar to his own, he felt warm tears streak down his face.

"Would you like me to leave you for a few minutes?"

It was abundantly clear how much the doctor wanted to get away from him and his soul-sucking grief.

He nodded, taking his brother's stiff hand in his own. All their lives he'd looked out for Jacob, who had been the reckless one, the one who could never hold down a job, the twin who could never keep his fists in his pockets. Jacob was the reason he'd gotten into the drug trade. Manufacturing and selling methamphetamines had seemed like an easy way to support them both.

If only they hadn't fought that afternoon, then maybe Jacob would have hung out a little longer, would have realized the roads were too icy to drive and spent the night.

If only Dianna Kelley had swerved out of the way, or better yet, never got on the road at all.

It was all *her* fault.

"I'll make her pay for what she did to you, I swear it," he promised his brother.

Bending over, he pressed a kiss to Jacob's forehead.

Wiping his tears away with the back of his hand, he let go of Jacob's hand and was slowly walking out of the ICU when he saw her.

In a room a dozen feet from the exit, Dianna Kelley was lying in a bed behind a glass wall, hooked up to an IV, her blond hair fanning out behind her on the pillow. A nurse was busy dealing with a phone call just outside the room and she didn't pay him any notice as he stood there and stared.

Seeing the bitch still alive, breathing and blinking, the blood still pumping through her veins—while his brother was dead—only confirmed that she was to blame.

No jury would ever convict her of wrongdoing. She was too famous, too pretty for anyone to think she could have possibly done anything wrong. She'd killed his brother and she was going to get away with it.

Continuing to stare at her, rage and grief built up and up inside of him until there was no room left for anything else. The nurse finally noticed him and when she gave him a strange look, he turned to leave.

Just then, Dianna's sister burst in through the ICU doors, her shoulder knocking into his in her haste.

And that was when he realized that he already had the perfect weapon.

Dianna Kelley had killed his brother.

He would kill her sister.

Everything hurt like crazy, especially her head, Dianna thought as she slowly woke up. What was wrong with her? Why was she having such trouble moving her arms and legs?

She struggled to open her eyes. They felt dry, almost like they were filled with soot, and she blinked hard to try to clear them. She quickly realized she was in a hospital bed, but how could that be? The last thing she remembered, she was driving to the airport, heading back to San Francisco after arguing with her sister in the café.

She had the strange feeling that someone was standing nearby, watching her, but her vision was still too fuzzy for her to see the person's features. The only thing she could tell for sure was that it was a man, tall with broad shoulders and short-cropped hair.

Her fatigued brain instantly plopped Sam's face on the man's head. She'd spent ten years trying to forget him, but tonight she was too damn weary, too sore and achy to make much headway in dislodging her memories of a gorgeous firefighter, six foot two with midnight-black hair and sizzling blue eyes.

Was it really Sam? Had he come to see her? Or was this just another hallucination? Another vision she was manufacturing out of desperation?

Her heart rate soared, as did the faint beeping of the machines behind her.

With every breath she took, her discomfort grew. She'd never allowed herself to take more than a couple of Advil—given her mother's history of addiction—but right now, she needed more of whatever they'd put in the IV in her left arm.

Soon, a nurse moved beside her, murmuring something about another dose of Vicodin. Before Dianna could find out if Sam was really there, or merely a hallucination of her deepest desires, a cool rush of liquid settled into her veins and she fell back into painless oblivion.

# CHAPTER TWO

SAM MACKENZIE stood on a peak in the Sierra Nevadas and surveyed the rolling mountains for smoke and flames. He was covered head to toe in a thick layer of ash and dirt from digging fire lines and knocking his chain saw through endless mounds of dry brush for the past twenty-four hours.

Being a hotshot meant little to no sleep for days on end, a hundred and fifty pounds on your back while you ran miles to reach the fires nothing else could. It meant shoving nasty-tasting, high-calorie food that a dog would refuse into your mouth at regular intervals. And it meant the unpredictability of fire herself, capable of grinding up and destroying even the toughest men.

But saving lives and homes and old-growth forests

made it all worth it. Not to mention the undeniable rush he got from kicking a wildfire's ass.

He'd never wanted to be anything but a hotshot. He still didn't.

His radio crackled and Logan Cain, his squad boss, checked in. "You up for a helicopter ride? Looks like we've got a handle on this fire, but I need you to scan it from the air to make sure."

"Give me thirty to get out into the open for pickup," he said, giving Logan his coordinates before signing off.

Quickly packing up his tools, he threw his heavy bag over his shoulders and headed back up the deer trail he and his four-man crew had taken down the mountain a day earlier.

"You did good work, boys," he told them as they finished up their breakfast.

After a series of wildfires this week, he figured they were all looking forward to a six-pack of beer and a day of lazy fishing on the lake to recharge their batteries before the next call.

"You all can head on back to the anchor point. I'm going up with Joe in the chopper for a quick scan. Once we've got the all clear you can take showers at the station and get some rest."

The rookie of the bunch smiled at him, his white teeth breaking apart the black mask of ash and soot covering his face.

"Dude, you forgot what comes between the shower and rest." Zach looked around at the other guys, his eyebrows moving up and down comically. "Getting some ass."

Sam laughed. Zach was right. Used to be, he couldn't wait to get off the mountain and go home to the warm, soft body waiting for him in bed. A lifetime ago, when he was a rookie just like Zach, and was young and stupid enough to think he'd found "the one."

Joe, the helitack pilot, was waiting for him when he crested the hill. As soon as Sam climbed into the helicopter, the rotors started whirring and they lifted into the air.

After working together on wildfires for the past six years, they didn't bother with small talk. Flying slowly over the dry landscape, Sam carefully surveyed the mountains for any telltale signs of new fires. The lookout towers that ringed the region were useful, but they didn't catch everything. Especially in the densely forested valleys.

About to give the all clear, Sam saw a flicker of smoke emerge from behind the next ridge.

"Let's head west."

Joe shot him a concerned glance. "You see something?"

"A smoke column is rising up, just past that redwood grove."

Joe kicked the helicopter's blades up a notch and they soon spotted a fire blazing at the base of the hill beside a stream. Thank God they'd gone in to take one last look.

After radioing the fire's coordinates, Logan said, "I'm sending a support crew up the fire road. ETA is thirty minutes." He paused and Sam knew what was coming, the same thing his squad boss had been telling them since last summer. "Don't go in if it's too dangerous."

The previous summer's wildfire in Desolation Wilderness had turned from a routine job to a disaster in a matter of moments. The two of them, along with Sam's younger brother, Connor, had gotten caught in a blowup. Although Logan and Sam had emerged unscathed from their run up the mountain to safety, the wildfire had chewed Connor up and spit him out, and he'd ended up with serious burns on his arms, hands, and chest.

This was the first year in almost a decade that Sam had run these trails without his brother beside him. Every day, Sam missed Connor's company out in the forests. They were all adrenaline junkies—even the hotshots who denied it—but Connor had always been more reckless than most.

In the past few years, Sam had felt that he wasn't all that far behind his brother on the recklessness scale. Without a wife or kids to go back to at the end of a fire, he had no reason not to go all the way to the edge. Especially if the chances he took meant saving a life.

So even though this was a potentially deadly situation, Sam couldn't turn back.

"I'm heading in on foot to verify whether the area is populated," Sam informed Logan before shoving the radio back into his turnouts.

He was going in with his Pulaski, an ax-hoe combination, his chain saw, his "shake and bake" emergency fire tent, and his first-aid supplies. Hopefully, he'd need only the first two to cut a fire line through the brush and light a backfire. But until he knew what awaited him down below, he'd make damn certain he was prepared for a worst-case scenario.

"Drop me in, Joe."

A strong breeze shoved the helicopter a half-dozen feet closer to the mountain and Joe shot Sam a concerned glance. "The winds are really picking up. You sure you don't want to wait for backup?"

The breeze blew the flames away for a split second, just long enough for Sam to see a structure.

"There's a cabin down below. I have to check it out."

"I don't know if this is such a great idea," Joe said as he maneuvered the helicopter so that it hovered directly over a flat part of the roof, just out of reach of the highest flames. "I can't get any closer. It's going to be a long way down."

Sam looked out the bubble-front window to assess the risk. By rough calculations, he figured that the distance was a little less than ten feet. One measly story. No problem.

"It's close enough."

Sam pulled the emergency ladder out from beneath his seat, then opened the passenger door and latched the ladder onto the metal rim. Carefully climbing out of the hovering helicopter, he was halfway down the ladder when Joe shifted position so that the distance from the ladder to the roof closed in from ten feet to eight.

Sam let go and dropped. The fall was faster than he'd expected, but he managed to land on the peeling roofing tiles with both feet and hands like a spider.

The helicopter pulled up and away, leaving an eerie stillness all around the remote mountain cabin. Sam understood why people liked living deep in the woods. Who wouldn't want to listen to the wind through the trees and the rushing river, rather than traffic and neighbors? A cabin like this was the perfect place to get away from it all.

The only downside was that when danger struck, it usually meant there was no one around to help.

Suddenly, the silence was replaced by the sound of a child crying. Moving quickly across the roof, Sam found a rock cropping at the rear of the house. Using the rocks as natural steps to the ground, he headed in the direction of the cries toward an outbuilding.

A little girl with tear-streaked cheeks barreled into his legs. She was crying too hard for him to understand what she was saying, so he knelt down and gently brushed the hair out of her eyes. She was a skinny little thing and he wasn't exactly sure how old she was, but he guessed she wasn't quite in the double digits yet.

"Everything's going to be okay," he told her in a gentle voice. When her wild gaze finally locked onto his and her sobs receded, he asked, "Are your parents here?"

This time he was able to make out the words, "My dad's away at work. My mom is sick."

"Anyone else here with you?"

The girl shook her head.

"A dog or cat or iguana?"

Her lips almost curved up at his reptilian reference and he knew she was going to be just fine. Children were the first ones to forget their fear. He'd been just like that as a kid. So had his brother.

"I'm Sam. What's your name?"

"Piper."

"Can you show me where your mom is, Piper?"

The girl started running and Sam jogged behind her into the house. A woman was lying on the couch in a fetal position. Her hands were on her rounded stomach. She wasn't crying, but her eyes were wide and he could see that she was frightened.

She was tall and blond and slim, and her features were close enough to those of a woman Sam used to know that something splintered apart in his chest before he could shut it down.

*Dianna.*

Forcefully pushing thoughts of his ex aside, he knelt beside the woman. "I'm a firefighter and I've come to help you. What's your name?"

Her lips trembled slightly and her cheeks were wet from tears. "Tammy."

"Your daughter tells me you're not feeling well."

"I'm cramping," she whispered. "It's too soon for the baby to come. And I've miscarried before."

Every word was a knife in his gut. He knew, firsthand, how painful miscarriage was. His chest squeezed and his throat grew tight before he managed to take his emotions out of the picture.

After ten years as a hotshot, he knew better than to let anything get in the way of the job he had to do.

From the window above the couch, he could see the treetops bending in the mounting breeze. Within minutes, flames would roll over this house.

Joe was going to have a hell of a time getting down here to pick them up, and Sam found himself wondering if the three of them were going to make it out alive.

"Our phones went out and my husband has our car," Tammy said in a frantic voice. "I didn't think anyone was going to find us." She started crying again. "I don't want to lose my baby or let anything happen to my little girl."

Damn it, he didn't have time for doubt, for second-guessing himself. He had to get them out.

"Can you walk?"

She tried to stand up, then sank back into the cushions.

"It hurts too much," she said, her cramps obviously far too intense for her to stay upright.

With the fire raging, there was no way Joe could drop low enough to the cabin in the helicopter to get near them. Besides, in her condition, Tammy couldn't climb a ladder, which meant Sam needed to get them to an open patch where Joe could land.

Pulling out his radio, he said, "Joe, I'm heading northwest with a pregnant woman and her daughter. First open spot you can land, we'll need pickup for transport to the nearest hospital. Radio me when you choose your spot. And keep it close."

Reaching under Tammy's knees and shoulders, he hoisted her into his arms. "Wrap your arms around my neck and hold on tight." Turning to Piper he said, "You look like you're pretty fast."

"I am."

He smiled at the pretty little girl. "Good. Let's get out of here. We're going to hitch a ride on a helicopter."

Moving as fast as he could without jarring Tammy, they eventually made it past the cabin to the stream that ran adjacent to the property. The acrid smell of fresh smoke hung in the air, and he instructed them to cover their mouths with their shirts.

Joe radioed with news that he'd found a meadow a half mile up from the cabin. It was a steady slope to get from the valley to the meadow, but even pregnant, Tammy didn't weigh much.

As they began their ascent, he checked in with the brave little girl. "How are you doing, Piper?"

"Good. I'm going fast, aren't I?"

"You sure are, Piper. Tammy? Am I moving too fast? Am I hurting you?"

She had stopped crying and he sensed that she had

turned her entire focus to making it to the clearing, to getting up in the helicopter and flying to the hospital.

"Please, just hurry," was her reply.

He hadn't seen blood on her clothes or the couch when he'd picked her up, and he was praying that her cramping hadn't yet turned into a full-blown miscarriage.

He'd been too late with his own child. He had to save this one.

"Everything's going to be all right," he promised, hoping like hell that he was telling the truth.

He couldn't hear the helicopter yet, though, only the sound of hot flames already feasting on outbuildings. Could he get the three of them off the hill before they were next?

And then, thank God, he heard the whir of the helicopter's blades above them.

"Joe's coming to get us now," he said, and a couple of minutes later, when they crested the hill, the helicopter was already on the ground, waiting for them. Together, the two men lifted Tammy into the aircraft.

On the way to the hospital, another helicopter was heading in with a full load of water. Squeezing Tammy's hand, he smiled and said, "If the crew works fast, the fire may not move beyond your outbuildings and they'll be able to save your house."

"I don't care about my house," she said, her voice even weaker. "All I want is a healthy baby."

It was all he'd wanted for himself, too. "I know," he

told her. "We just need you to hold on a little longer, okay?"

Piper was holding tightly to her mother's hand. "You're going to be okay, Mama. And so will my baby sister."

He swallowed hard, the ache in his chest threatening to split wide open. If things had turned out differently for him, he would have had a kid Piper's age.

Seconds later they arrived at the hospital and Sam was incredibly glad to see that there was still no bleeding. A nurse came to wheel Tammy away, but Piper remained standing beside him.

"You saved my mom. And the baby sister I'm going to have, too."

Her smile was a ray of sunshine and then, suddenly, her skinny arms were around his legs and her face was pressing hard into him. Just as quickly, she released him and was gone, running down the hospital hallway after her mother and the nurse.

Everything was going to be all right. Tammy and her husband would be the proud parents of a new baby girl. Piper would be a great big sister.

But still, something dark and hard squeezed his chest, the dull pain he'd never been able to crush completely.

He found Joe chain-smoking in the smoking area in the side parking lot.

"I can't decide if what you did today was incredibly brave or mind-numbingly stupid," Joe said. "That fire was moving fast. What if it'd run right over you before I could land and get you out?"

The truth was, in all his years as a hotshot, while Sam had been in equally dangerous situations, he'd never dealt with one so close to his heart.

And he'd never had to work so hard to keep his shit together and stay on task.

Not planning to admit a damn thing to his friend, he simply said, "I did what I had to do."

Joe took a few quick puffs on his cigarette, then dropped it onto the cement and lit another. "Doesn't mean it wasn't nerve-racking as all hell knowing you were out there in the middle of a firestorm." His mouth moved into a half grin. "Would have sucked if you died on my watch."

"Yeah," Sam agreed, trying to shake off the lingering tension still weighing down his shoulders. "You would have never lived it down if you flew back to the station minus one."

After confirming via radio that they'd caught the last of the fires, Joe flew Sam back to the Tahoe Pines station. Flying over Lake Tahoe, Sam stared down into the bright blue water and reflected on the fact that coming to Lake Tahoe had changed his whole life.

He'd been a fenced-in suburban kid with a tagalong little brother, a mom who tried too hard to act like her marriage didn't suck, and a dad who was never around if he could help it. By the time Sam hit his teens, his mother's veneer had finally cracked wide open and the fights began. Endless, self-obsessed screaming matches between his mother and father that he tried to block out by turning his stereo speakers up as loud as they would go.

Sam didn't know what to do with his growing anger, his frustration, the fact that the adults clearly didn't have any answers. So he drank. He partied. He cut class. And then he got busted for driving with a six-pack of beer.

Thank God his football coach had stepped into his father's empty shoes and dragged his ass up into the Sierras for community service. Coach Rusmore had pretty much saved his life by showing him another way to let out his aggressions, how to consistently hit the level of adrenaline he needed to survive.

Very quickly, Sam had become a capable outdoorsman. All year long, the huge lake was cold and wild. When Sam wasn't deep in the mountains—for work or pleasure—he was on the water. Fishing, boating, kayaking, river rafting, kiteboarding. Despite the huge surge of tourists every winter and summer, and the more unsavory aspects of the casinos, Sam still couldn't believe he'd considered leaving Lake Tahoe behind ten years ago.

For a woman.

Chalk another one up to being young and stupid.

"Looks like Connor's here," Joe said as they flew over the station's parking lot and saw Connor's truck near the helipad.

Sam was glad his brother had dropped by the station.

He didn't come by nearly often enough. Of course, it wasn't hard to guess why he was keeping his distance.

After a series of painful skin grafts and ongoing physical therapy to regain the full use of his hands and fingers, Connor was well on his way to recovery, but the big question remained: Would he ever fight fire again?

Because no matter how hard Connor worked, regardless of how much he wanted to get back out there on the mountain, his future as a hotshot wasn't entirely up to him. The Forest Service had the final say. And the last thing they wanted was a crippled firefighter out in the middle of a wildfire.

Joe shook Connor's hand in greeting, then headed back for the showers, but when Sam caught his brother's troubled expression, he instantly knew something was wrong.

"Hit me with it."

Connor put a hand on his arm in warning. "Sit down, Sam."

Hell no, he wasn't going to sit down. He'd seen Connor look this way only once before: When Dianna's car had been hit on Highway 50 ten years ago.

When she'd lost the baby.

"It's Dianna, isn't it?"

When he didn't get an answer quickly enough, Sam got in his brother's face and grabbed a fistful of his shirt. Connor mirrored Sam in weight and height—both of them broad-shouldered, slim-hipped, and muscular— but Sam had fear on his side.

If his little brother didn't start talking fast he was going to start beating the information out of him.

"Tell me what the hell has happened to her."

"She was in another car accident. Last night, in Colorado. Vail. I just saw it on the news. I didn't want to hit you with it over the radio. I needed to tell you in person."

Sam dropped Connor's shirt, stumbling back against a row of metal storage cabinets. "Is she . . ."

He swallowed the word "dead." His brain wouldn't let him think it. His mouth wouldn't let him say it.

"The reporter didn't say how she was doing, just that the cars were totaled."

Sam would have given anything not to care about Dianna, to be able to hear what Connor had said about her and just get on with his day—with the rest of his goddamned life—as if it were business as usual. But the image of Dianna lying helpless in a hospital bed was like a stake shoved straight into his gut.

He couldn't erase it, couldn't stuff it down, couldn't walk away from it and pretend she didn't mean anything to him anymore.

"I've got to get to Colorado."

Connor shook his head. "That's why I'm here telling you in person. To make sure you don't do something stupid."

Every last instinct told Sam to go to Dianna. To be there to hold her. To help her.

"I don't need your advice," he growled.

"Fine, how about I jog your memory instead? Remember what happened to you after she left you?"

Ignoring his brother, Sam headed to his locker and stripped out of his turnouts. Connor followed behind him, like a dog intent on annoying its owner. As Sam changed into a clean pair of cargo pants and a T-shirt, Connor kept at it.

"When she dumped your ass and moved to San Francisco you fell apart. I never thought I'd see the day you'd skip out on your job. The job you used to love. But there you were, glued to the bar stool when you should have been out fighting fires."

The days and weeks after Dianna left were as fresh in Sam's mind as if they had happened yesterday. He didn't need Connor to remind him of the black hole he'd fallen into. How dark it had been. How deep. His high school problems had been rebellion. But the darkness he sought after Dianna left had nothing to do with mutiny, with revolt.

Instead, it had been despair. Bone deep and, he'd thought at the time, incurable.

"I know you thought she was the one," Connor insisted, "but the truth is, she was bad for you, man. You were royally fucked-up after she left. I don't want to see you like that again."

Sam couldn't refute any of his brother's statements. They were all true.

And yet, not going to her was unthinkable.

Moving to the phone, information connected him through to Vail General Hospital.

"I'm a," he paused, searching for the right word, "friend of Dianna Kelley's. Could you give me some information on her condition?"

"I'm sorry, sir," a woman replied politely. "I'm afraid we can't discuss patients with anyone except their family."

He hung up just as Logan stepped into the kitchen.

"Dianna's hurt," he told his closest friend, her name rasping out of his throat.

He cleared it, worked to get a grip. Jesus, he hadn't seen her for ten years, so why was he losing it now?

Connor quickly filled Logan in on the details of Dianna's accident. Of the twenty men currently on the Tahoe Pines crew, only Logan and Connor had been around ten years ago when Dianna was still in the picture. None of the other seventeen hotshots knew a damn thing about her, other than the fact that she was a gorgeous woman they sometimes drooled over when they were flipping through the channels.

"Tell him, Logan," Connor urged. "Tell him he can't go running after her."

Logan was newly married to an arson investigator who'd come to Tahoe last year to nail him to the wall as her prime arson suspect. Instead, Maya and Logan had caught the real arsonist and fallen in love.

Sam didn't need Logan's approval. He was going anyway.

"I'll buzz you when I know my time line," he told his squad boss.

Logan nodded. "You've been building up too much vacation on the books, anyway. It's a good time for you to take a few days." Logan grabbed a Coke out of the fridge, then clapped him on the shoulder. "Give Dianna my best."

Connor shoved his car keys into his jeans. "I can't let you do something this stupid alone. I'm coming with you."

"No thanks," Sam said as he headed to his car.

Making a fool of himself by going to see the woman who'd dumped his ass cold and walked out of his life was a big enough pill to swallow. He wasn't going to have the big reunion in front of his brother.

His foot was lead on the gas pedal of his truck as he headed to the nearest airport, four hours away in San Francisco. For ten years, he'd pushed thoughts of Dianna out of his head, but now he could no longer stop the floodgates from opening.

# CHAPTER THREE

*Ten years ago . . .*

IT WAS an early fire season and he'd been sent out to check on a trailer park that bordered state land. An evacuation order had been given, but for one reason or another, people didn't always leave. Sometimes they foolishly thought they'd be better off guarding their things. Sometimes they were just plain stupid and lazy.

Sam quickly confirmed that twenty-nine of the thirty beaten-up trailers were empty. Only one was left, a ratty hunk of metal that barely looked habitable.

The fire was blowing closer, a plume of fresh smoke spiraling up into the sky to the west. He needed to finish evacuations and get back to the station with the sure knowledge that no lives would be at stake if the fire rolled down the hill.

He parked his truck in front of the trailer and got out, immediately disliking what he saw. Very few vehicles were left in front of the other trailers, but there was an old convertible parked outside this one.

On his way to the door, he heard a woman's voice. He couldn't make out what she was saying, but he could tell she was pleading with someone. He knocked hard.

"Fire service. I need you to open up."

The door didn't open. He looked into the mountains, knew the flames were moving closer by the minute. He didn't have the luxury of reasoning with the trailer's resident. It was go or die.

"Move away from the door," he commanded, kicking it hard once, then twice with a heavy steel-toed boot. Using one shoulder for leverage, he leaned his weight into the door until the lock broke open.

Moments later, he was inside the trailer and saw that the voice he'd heard belonged to a young girl who was trying to drag her mother's limp body out of a back room and down the dark, narrow hallway to the door.

Thank God he'd muscled his way inside. The kid needed his help.

And then she looked up at him, clearly startled by his intrusion, and the air was knocked straight out of his guts.

She wasn't a kid at all. Instead, she was the prettiest woman he'd ever seen. Tall and fair, he couldn't tell much about her body beneath the baggy jeans and T-shirt she had on. But her eyes held him captive, big and green with flecks of gold and purple. He stood and stared at her, the wildfire almost forgotten.

"I'm sorry we're not out yet," she apologized. "As soon as I heard about the mandatory evacuation, I tried to wake her up. But when she's like this, it's impossible."

She blushed, clearly embarrassed, her high cheekbones highlighted in pink against her pale skin.

The carpet was ratty, the furniture even worse, but everything was reasonably clean. He suspected the girl, not her mother, was responsible for that.

He crossed the length of the trailer in a handful of strides. "Let me take over from here. Let me help."

In the back room of the trailer with the girl, the smell of body odor and beer was overpowering.

"It's horrible in here. You shouldn't come in."

Shit, he hadn't meant to let his reaction to the rank smell show on his face.

"I'm not going to judge you. I promise. I just want to help."

Moving past her, he bent over and easily shifted her mother's dead weight over his left shoulder.

Her beautiful eyes grew wide. "Thank you."

He'd been complimented plenty of times during his two years as a hotshot, but somehow praise from this pretty green-eyed woman made him feel like he was walking on water.

"She doesn't weigh much," he replied modestly as he

laid her mother in the extended cab of his Forest Service truck, then strapped her lifeless body in with the seat belt as securely as he could.

"They've set up an evacuation station at the high school. Do you know where that is?"

Her face flamed. "I do, but I can't take her there." At his silent question, she said, "I just can't."

Knowing firsthand how rough it was to have difficult parents, he made a split-second decision. "Follow me in your car to the station. She can sleep it off in my bunk."

He'd have to burn the sheets, but it was worth it to help out a beautiful damsel in distress.

And her appreciative expression was worth any price.

The rest of the hotshot crew was already out on the mountain fighting the fire by the time they arrived at the Tahoe Pines station thirty minutes later. He carried her mother to the sleeping quarters, and when he came back into the kitchen, the beautiful daughter was standing there, looking awkward and unsure of herself.

"You don't have to let her stay here," she said. "I can find another place for her to sleep it off and get both of us out of your hair."

"It's no problem. I don't want you to worry about it."

Her lips turned up slightly at the edges, a shy little smile that made his breath come faster, and he realized he wanted to see her again. Soon.

"I'm Sam," he said, holding out his hand to shake hers.

Her grip was cool and strong, and in that moment, he

knew how good it would be between them, that he'd never find anyone like her in a bar on a Saturday night.

"What's your name?"

"Dianna," she said. "With two n's."

"I've got to go out to the fire right now, Dianna-with-two-n's," he said, glad to see her smile again, "but I'm hoping you'll consider giving me your phone number."

She hesitated. "Why?"

Her simple question threw him for a loop. For the first time since early adolescence, Sam felt off his game. Hadn't she felt the sparks between them? He'd been with girls who were more put together than Dianna, but none of them made his blood rush hard and fast like this with only a smile. What, he wondered, had happened to her to make her so suspicious of men?

"I'd like to take you out. On a date."

Her green eyes connected with his, and as he held her gaze, he silently asked her to trust him.

*I'm not going to hurt you. I promise.*

At last, she nodded. Pulling a small notebook from her purse, she wrote down her telephone number in neat handwriting, then ripped out the page and handed it to him.

He put the note in his pocket, but he couldn't head out into the fire without doing one more thing: He had to kiss her.

Their kiss was nothing fancy, just lips pressing together for the first time, but Sam felt like someone had launched a series of rockets straight through his veins.

When he pulled back, her eyes were wide with surprise—but there was pleasure there, too. He forced himself to step away, even though all he wanted was to taste her with his tongue, to pull her hard against him and explore the curves she was hiding beneath all those clothes.

"I'll call you. Soon."

Walking out of the station, knowing all that heat and sexy-as-hell innocence was going to be waiting for him at the wildfire's end, made him more ready to kick ass than ever before.

Four days later, when the wildfire was finally put to rest, he took her to a drive-in. She seemed nervous sitting in the passenger seat of his Jeep, not touching the extra-large box of popcorn he'd bought.

As the opening credits started running, Sam reached across the gearshift for her hand. She was slow to respond, wide-eyed and silent for a long moment before she curled her cold fingers into his.

It wasn't hard to guess that she hadn't been out with many guys. He needed to go slow with her, ease her in to how much he wanted her, but now that she was sitting close enough for him to smell the faint scent of vanilla coming off her shiny blond hair and see the pulse point moving fast in the hollow of her neck, it was all he could do not to drag her onto his lap.

Reaching into the container of popcorn with his free hand, he picked up a piece and held it up to her lips. He watched her think about taking it from him, biting her lip in indecision, before she opened her mouth and let him feed her.

Sam had lost his virginity at fifteen to a hot senior cheerleader. In the past five years, he'd slept with plenty of girls, even dated a few of them for a month or two before breaking it off when things got too serious. But simply feeding Dianna—feeling her lips move softly around his fingers, watching her throat as she swallowed—was by far the most erotic experience of his life.

No longer able to control himself, he shoved the full container of popcorn into the backseat and took her face in his hands, kissing her with all of the desire he'd been holding back since the moment he met her. She met his kiss with just as much passion, her tongue swirling with his, a low moan of pleasure emerging from her throat.

He didn't know much more about Dianna than her name, her phone number, and where she lived, but based on how much he wanted her—and how hot this kiss was—he knew he was going to lay his claim to her that night in the most elemental of ways.

Abruptly, he broke their kiss, turned the key in the ignition, and burned rubber getting the heck out of the crowded outdoor theater.

They didn't speak as he pulled off the freeway onto a bumpy dirt road and drove through the woods. When the casino lights had fallen away and the moon shone bright through the tall pines, he shut down his engine and held out his hand.

"Come here, Dianna."

He was amazed when she didn't hesitate and crawled onto his lap to boldly straddle him. And then her mouth was on his and she was kissing his lips, his cheeks, his neck, pulling at his shirt and nipping at his chest. He wanted to tell her to slow down, that they had all night to explore each other's bodies, but he was already too far gone to get the words out.

A red light blinked in the back of his mind, a warning that she was too innocent, that she didn't know what she was asking him for, but instead of stopping and making sure he was doing the right thing, he reached for the snap on her jeans and yanked down the zipper.

Her eyes flew open as he slid in a finger. Oh shit, she was so wet.

She stilled on his lap. "Sam?"

"Baby, I want you so bad," was the only thing he could think to say.

And then they were kissing again and he was sliding his finger in and out, slowly at first and then faster as she bucked her pelvis against his hand. He rocked his palm against her clitoris, and her breath came out in quick pants accompanied by little moans and whimpers.

It was all he could do not to lose it behind his zipper. He wanted to blow inside her, not into blue-striped cotton boxers.

Ripping at the button fly on his jeans, he freed his erection and wrapped Dianna's hand around it. Her eyes flew open again and she stopped moving against him.

Somehow he managed to say, "I need to be inside you, but only if you want it," and thank God, she nodded and gently started stroking him.

"I want it, Sam."

He forgot to be gentle as he shoved her jeans and panties off. And then she was naked from the waist down and he was putting on a condom as fast as he could in the dark. Placing his hands on her slim waist, moving them to cup her perfect ass, he positioned her over his erection.

Barely breathing, he suddenly realized he couldn't just plunge into her. She was too tight. A virgin, just as he'd suspected.

"What's wrong?" she whispered.

"Nothing's wrong. You're perfect."

"I've never done this before," she admitted with a nervous catch in her voice as she slowly lowered herself back down onto his lap.

The head of his penis pressed into her folds, and Sam cupped her face to kiss her as he guided his thick shaft into her heat. She gasped against his lips as he filled her.

"Will you trust me?"

The "Yes" was barely out of her mouth before he drove into her, all the way to the hilt. She stiffened and he said "Trust me" again against her lips and then they were kissing, softly, sweetly as he found her clit with his thumb and pressed light circles against the hard nub. It didn't take long before he felt her muscles relax around him and a new wave of her arousal coat his shaft.

Moving as slow as he could manage, he slid out, then back in to her tight passage. Dianna's tall curves were a perfect fit, and she was so innately sensual that a part of him was amazed this was her first time.

And then, she was crying out and he could feel her inner muscles pulling and pushing against him and he was coming inside her, the sensation so much better than it had ever been with anyone else.

They held on to each other, panting, until she moved off his lap and sat back down on the passenger seat to pull on her panties and jeans. He tried to think of something to say that would lighten the mood and make her realize that having sex wasn't that big of a deal.

Instead, he suddenly realized that something had gone wrong. Really wrong.

The condom had broken, a big gaping hole right in the middle of the latex.

And the reservoir tip was completely empty.

Sam couldn't believe it. Dianna's first time making love and the condom had busted. He wasn't sure what was going on in her head right about now, but he had a feeling she wouldn't be too thrilled to find out that she was wet with more than just her own arousal.

The station tested the men for VD every six months and he'd just gotten back his latest clean report, so he knew he wasn't going to give her anything. And because she was a virgin—or had been a virgin until tonight, anyway—he knew he was safe.

What were the odds that she would get pregnant? Low, right? One of the older guys on the crew had been trying unsuccessfully to get his wife pregnant for months.

Before she could see the damage, he quickly removed the busted condom and shoved it into his pocket. Everything would be okay. There was no point in freaking her out for no reason.

That first incredibly hot date turned into another, then another, until all of Sam's free nights when he wasn't out on a mountain somewhere were spent with Dianna.

At first, they mostly made love, with small breaks to eat, but it didn't take too long for him to want to be more than a physical part of her life.

He'd never felt the urge to learn much about the girls he was dating, never wanted to know what they liked to eat for breakfast, never cared about their dreams or aspirations. But even though he refused to look too far into the future, he couldn't deny that the way he felt about Dianna was just plain different.

During the day she worked part-time at the downtown library along with taking business classes at the local junior college. He teased her about hiding such big brains behind such a knockout body, but he was incredibly proud of her. It wasn't hard to guess why she pushed herself so hard, even though they'd never really talked about it: She didn't want to end up like her mother, getting stuck in a trailer park with a baby at eighteen and no skills or money to fall back on.

And then, one night, he woke up and realized she wasn't in bed. He found her sitting at his kitchen table poring over paperwork. At first he thought it was homework, but when he got close enough to read the small print, he realized they were state documents.

"Guardianship forms and instructions? What's all this about?"

She'd been a virgin, so he knew she couldn't have a kid stashed away somewhere.

Dianna rubbed a hand over her eyes. "It's a long story."

"I'm not going anywhere."

It was an off-the-cuff response, but somehow, in that moment, they both knew he meant far more than he'd originally intended. In the far back of Sam's mind, a warning light began blinking, pictures of his parents' crap-ass marriage flashing before his eyes. But it was easy to shut that door, to tell himself that he and Dianna were merely having a good time together, that they were miles away from ever getting married.

"I have a sister," she finally said, explaining that her younger sister, April, had been sent away at four. "I won't stop until I get April out of the foster system and home with me."

Sam knew firsthand how important siblings were. The more your parents dropped the ball, the more you needed a brother or sister to hold things together. Connor was his real family. So he got that even though she hadn't seen her sister in six years, April meant just as much to Dianna.

He joined the battle that night, wanting to help her try to push through the reams of bureaucratic red tape that stood in her way. And when all she heard from the state was, "You don't have enough money or a job or a real home for your sister," when they claimed April was better off in the foster system living with a "stable" family, he held Dianna as she cried. But it was never long until her tears dried and she was back at it, chipping away at the system with more focus than ever.

Since becoming a hotshot, people had said again and again how tough he was. But for the first time in twenty years he knew what real strength was; he saw it every time he looked at his girlfriend filling out paperwork or arguing on the phone with a caseworker. She continually surprised him with her resiliency. He hadn't expected such a pretty package to be filled with steely determination.

All the while, every time they made love again, he pushed the broken condom to the back of his mind. After a few weeks passed, he figured they were out of the danger zone and pretty much forgot about it.

Until the day she walked into the station with red, puffy eyes. He'd just come in from a wildfire and the adrenaline was still pumping through him when he saw her. His stomach twisted with dread as he instantly guessed what she was going to tell him.

The secret that he'd been keeping had just come back to bite him in the ass.

His first thought was that he needed a stiff drink.

His second that he wasn't ready to be a father.

He was a twenty-year-old firefighter. He was supposed to be banging everything that moved. And even though he liked being with Dianna, he sure as hell didn't believe in happy families.

"I need to talk to you, Sam."

"You're pregnant," he said, his words coming out harder than he'd intended.

Her eyes widened in surprise and she covered her stomach with both hands. "How'd you know?"

He knew telling her about the condom wouldn't have made any difference for whether or not she got pregnant, but at least she wouldn't have been totally caught off guard.

He was used to being the hero. Not the villain who took the heroine's virginity and knocked her up all at the same time.

Tamping down on the urge to cut bait and run back into the hills to fight a fire, any fire he could find, he met her gaze.

"The condom broke."

She inhaled sharply, her eyes round with disbelief. "When?"

"The first time."

"Why didn't you tell me?"

Jesus, he didn't know what to say to her. Didn't know what to do. Especially since neither of them were ready to get married.

As it was, they hadn't even officially moved in together. She'd been careful not to leave clothes at his apartment, and he hadn't exactly offered up one of his dresser drawers.

The truth was, he was more than a little freaked out by how much he enjoyed being with her. By how important she was becoming to him. By the number of times he'd wanted to tell her that he loved her and barely managed to catch himself.

"I know I should have told you," he admitted, hating how guilty he felt, "but I just didn't think anything was going to come of it."

She almost looked angry now, the fiercest he'd ever seen her outside of her fight for April.

"You mean like a baby? You didn't think for one second that I might get pregnant? You didn't think I'd want to know that?"

He let her rail at him. Sure, it had taken two to tango, and getting pregnant wasn't entirely his fault, but he hadn't exactly played the aftermath well.

And that was when it hit him: She was going to have a baby.

He was going to be a father.

Sam looked at her again, for the first time seeing her as more than the hot woman he was falling for.

She was going to be the mother of his child.

In an instant, everything shifted. He knew exactly what he had to do. There was only one option.

"We're going to get married."

She took a step away from him, dropping her head so that her blond hair covered her face. But before she could hide her expression from him, he saw pain move across her striking features.

Shit. He was screwing everything up. Again.

Instead of showing her that he wasn't going to leave her in a lurch, that he was going to support her and the baby from here on out, he'd just proposed to her in the worst possible way. Like some sort of half-brained caveman.

Wanting to do it right, he dropped onto one knee on the gravel lot and reached for her hand.

She shook her head in dismay. "No, Sam, don't."

"Dianna, I want to marry you. I want to take care of you and our baby. Please let me be there for you."

She closed her eyes, tried to pull her hand away. "You don't need to do this. I can take care of—"

"No!"

The word boomed from his chest before she could finish her sentence. He wasn't going to let her bring up a baby alone in a trailer park, or, God forbid, have an abortion.

"Listen to me, Dianna. I know this is happening sooner

than either of us planned, but," he had to stop and clear his throat, "will you do me the honor of becoming my wife?"

"We can't get married just because I'm pregnant. It won't work out. It never does."

He knew she was thinking about her mother, who had gotten pregnant with her at eighteen. Obviously, her father hadn't stuck around. April's dad hadn't, either.

"You are not your mother," he told her in a firm voice, hating to see her look so defeated. "The first time I met you, I thought you were like any other beautiful woman. But when I saw how you were hell-bent on getting April back, that was when I knew that you were special. You're tougher than anyone would guess. Dianna, I don't even think you realize how strong you are, how smart you are."

Her cheeks had gone pink at his praise, but she refused to believe him so easily. "If I'm so smart, then tell me why the stick I peed on today turned blue? All my life I swore this was the one thing that was not going to happen to me." She gestured to the hotshot station with one hand. "Turns out all it took was one hot firefighter to knock me up."

She laughed, but there was no joy behind it, rather a self-derision that Sam refused to let stick.

"Okay, so you're pregnant. We can't change that. But we can try and make it work."

Honestly, he didn't know much about good marriages or about happy families, but he'd faced down enough deadly wildfires to know that he was as stubborn as Dianna.

"We're going to make it work."

"You mean like your parents made it work?" Dianna countered, still not ready to give in.

Until Dianna, Sam had never told anyone that his parents had gotten married when his mother got pregnant with him her freshman year at college—and that twenty years later, his mom and dad could barely stand to be in the same room with each other. But he'd known that Dianna wouldn't judge him.

It was one of the things he loved about her.

*I love her,* he suddenly realized, knowing in his heart that it had been true since the start.

"We are not my parents," he told her in a firm voice, even though the raw data—a surprise baby and shotgun wedding—sure looked a hell of a lot the same. "And you have to know how much I care for you."

Her eyes bore into his and he could feel the four-letter word hanging on the tip of his tongue. It was time to bite the bullet and say it already.

"I love you, Dianna."

A single tear slid down her cheek. "I've wanted to hear you say it, but not like this." Her voice broke. "Not because you have to."

He reached for her cold hands and pulled her against him, glad when she didn't fight him, when she let her body relax into his.

"I've never done anything because I have to. From the

moment I saw you, I wanted you. Now you're going to be the mother of my child, and our baby is going to grow up with a father and a mother who loves it. We're going to stay together and be a happy family."

He didn't know how he knew all of those things, but as he said them, he believed every last one of them.

He'd thought that Dianna was just a sexy summer fling. But she'd become more than that. Way more.

"Marry me, Dianna, and I promise you, I'll always be there for you. I'll never leave you. No matter what."

He knew he'd never forget the way her eyes looked after he'd said that. So green and clear he could almost see through them into her soul.

No one had ever really cared about her before. No one but him.

And as she said, "Yes, Sam, I'll marry you," he vowed to never, ever let her down.

## CHAPTER FOUR

BETWEEN THE long drive to the airport and the flight into Vail, Sam had plenty of time for playbacks of their three-month-long relationship. For ten years, he'd tried to convince himself that he'd forgotten her.

But the truth was that he hadn't forgotten one single moment.

Things moved at warp speed after his quick-and-dirty proposal—and her very reluctant acceptance. The next day he'd moved her clothes and books from her mother's trailer to his apartment. Eight weeks later the limo hit her and she miscarried. They postponed their wedding and six weeks later she disappeared, leaving her engagement ring on the kitchen table.

No warning. No fights. No giving things another shot.

Just gone.

And getting over her had been nearly impossible.

He'd known better than to trust a woman, but in the heat of the "I'm pregnant" moment, he'd actually thought their relationship was going to be the exception, not the rule.

He hadn't made that same mistake since.

It didn't matter how pretty or laid-back the girls he dated were about his crazy schedule. Commitment wasn't in the cards for him, simple as that. Although he hadn't exactly turned into a monk, he made damn sure that the women he went out with knew the score. He wasn't looking for anything serious. And he was religious about birth control, using two methods whenever possible.

Just after seven p.m., the Vail General Hospital parking lot was pretty well emptied out, apart from a throng of reporters smoking and waiting by the entrance. As he paid the driver, he suddenly wondered if they were here to see Dianna.

How could he have forgotten that she was famous now, that she had a whole new life that he knew nothing about? They were no longer on the same playing field. She was a star. And he was still just a firefighter.

But as he moved past the reporters and pushed through the tall glass entry doors into the lobby, none of that mattered. Not when the possibility of Dianna being injured and in pain had his heart racing and his hands sweating. Replaying the past had been nothing more than a convenient way to push away his fears regarding Dianna's current situation.

Sam hadn't spent much time in church, but it didn't stop him from praying now. *Please, God, let her be okay* was what he sent up as he headed to the reception desk.

A young redheaded woman was watching a soap opera on the TV hanging from the far corner of the room. A half-dozen people were slumped tiredly in their seats waiting to be called in to see the next available doctor.

"I'm looking for Dianna Kelley."

She stopped watching the TV and gave him her full attention, smiling up at him flirtatiously. "I'll bet you are. I swear, some women have all the luck."

He frowned. She wouldn't be flirting with him if Dianna was in a coma, would she? Or was this just her regular m.o. with every reasonably good-looking guy without a ring who walked into the hospital?

"How is she?"

The woman shrugged. "I don't know. But I heard it was a pretty bad crash. Head-on. That road she was on can be dangerous when it's icy."

Air whooshed out of his lungs. That wasn't what he wanted to hear. She was supposed to tell him that Dianna was all right, that she was the one in a million who walked away just fine. He'd tended to enough car crash survivors to know how bad her injuries probably were, that she was most likely fighting for her life that very second.

"I need to see her."

The woman studied him more carefully, looking at his left hand again. "Are you her husband?"

"No." *Hell, no,* he wasn't her husband. That ship had sailed a long time ago.

"You're not a reporter, are you?"

"No, I'm a firefighter."

"Oh, that's so much better," she said with a smile. "We've been given express instructions not to let any more of the reporters past the front desk. They're like vultures. It's kind of creepy," she said with a feigned shiver. "But firemen are *always* welcome here."

She quirked her head to the side, even more flirtatious than she'd been at first. "So who are you?"

It was a good question. He wasn't Dianna's boyfriend. Wasn't even a friend. And yet he'd flown all the way to Colorado to see her. Because he needed to see for himself that she was all right.

Sidestepping the woman's question with a charming grin, he said, "Sam MacKenzie."

Blushing furiously beneath his gaze, the woman immediately picked up the phone. "I'll let Ms. Kelley's nurse know that you'd like to pay her a visit."

Dianna woke up to bright light bouncing off the framed picture of wildflowers on the wall across from her bed. She squinted out the window, surprised to see that the sun was already setting over the mountains, but glad to realize that she finally felt reasonably alert after dozing off and on all day while the sedatives they'd given her during the night slowly left her system.

Her heart squeezed as she recalled the conversation she'd had with the doctor that morning.

"Please," she'd said, "I'd like to know if the people in the other car are okay."

The doctor hadn't taken her eyes off of her chart for a long moment. Too long. Something in the lines of her face had warned Dianna to prepare herself for bad news.

"I'm afraid the driver of the other vehicle died. There were no other passengers."

Every time Dianna thought about it, she had to fight back a thick wave of nausea.

Why was she lucky enough to be alive when the other driver had died?

What had she done to deserve such luck?

And what was she supposed to do with this incredible second chance?

Her life was pretty simple, really. She loved her job, wished she had a better relationship with her sister, and hadn't yet met the right man to settle down with. But even as she ran through the list, a voice in the back of her head told her she wasn't being totally honest.

Later. She'd take a hard look at herself and her life. When she wasn't so tired.

A nurse bustled into the hospital room and asked Dianna to try to sit up. Slowly shifting her weight with the woman's assistance, she was extremely happy to note that the throbbing in the back of her skull didn't get any worse.

She felt a little achy all over, kind of like when she had the flu, but apart from that she was surprised by how good she felt. Almost as if she'd simply had a little too much to drink the night before, rather than being rushed from a totaled car to the hospital in an ambulance.

Still, she didn't really feel up to making small talk with the small, dark-haired woman who took her temperature and blood pressure, then tentatively asked for an autograph.

Knowing the past four years as host of *West Coast Update* had made her a bit of a celebrity, Dianna played her part as best she could. With her job, there was no downtime. She always had to be on. And even though she was in the hospital, she still felt that she had an image to uphold. People—including this nurse—expected to see the "perfect" Dianna Kelley. She didn't want to disappoint them.

Not when she'd worked so hard to create that illusion.

As soon as the nurse closed the door behind her, Dianna pushed back the blanket and slowly swung her legs out over the edge of the bed.

So far, so good.

She slid her feet onto the floor and made sure to hold on to the side table as she stood up, just in case. Fortunately, she was only the slightest bit dizzy. Taking her large purse into the bathroom, she closed the door and stared at herself in the mirror.

She looked a sight!

For the past decade, she hadn't let anyone see her looking less than her best. But as she stared into the mirror, she saw right through the successful twenty-eight-year-old woman to the confused eighteen-year-old girl whom she feared was never far below the surface.

In the small shower, she scrubbed her skin with the industrial pump soap by the sink. After drying off with a tiny, thin towel that was a far cry from the ultrasoft, over-sized ones hanging in her bathroom at home, she stood naked in front of the mirror.

Looking at herself with a critical eye, she found herself wondering—not for the first time—how long it would be until she'd need to book an appointment with a plastic surgeon. Thus far, her breasts and stomach and thighs were still okay, but okay wasn't even close to good enough for TV.

She hated the thought of someone cutting her apart. Was there any other option? she wondered as she opened her makeup bag and brushed some color onto her pale skin. Could she grow old gracefully and not lose her viewership?

*Not likely,* she thought with a sigh. Not with a hundred—more like a thousand or more, actually—women waiting in the wings to take her place if she ever started slipping.

Giving silent thanks that the makeup artists she'd

worked with over the years had taught her everything they knew about doing professional hair and makeup on her own, fifteen minutes later the face staring back at her looked like the woman everyone recognized from *West Coast Update*.

The paramedics had retrieved her luggage from the trunk of her rental car and she changed into a pale yellow, long-sleeved cashmere shirt and her favorite form-fitting jeans. As a finishing touch, she spritzed herself with a tiny travel bottle of her signature scent, which she'd found in a tiny town in the south of France.

Realizing her legs were beginning to quiver, she made her way back to the bed. Scooting onto the mattress, she was pulling the blankets back up when a line from a song suddenly ran through her brain: *"Listen to me now 'cause I'm calling out. Don't hold me down 'cause I'm breaking out."*

In the rental car, she'd thought the lyrics had only applied to April's life, to the emotional hurdles that her sister was leaping as she became a woman. But suddenly, Dianna could no longer hide from the chilling truth: That song could have been about her own long days on a set with the crew and her guests, her dates with men she didn't care one fig about, even the girls' nights out where she was afraid to reveal too much in case she seemed too high maintenance. For years, she'd gone out of her way to make sure people had no reason to abandon her.

Her hands stilled on the blanket, halfway up her legs. For so long, she'd pushed forward with her career, with her façade of perfection, willing to do anything if it meant proving to the state that she would be a good guardian for April. Wasn't it time to stop covering up her true feelings with false smiles, with perfect makeup and hair and the latest designer clothes?

Feeling terribly shaken, this time from the inside, rather than from any surface injuries, she reached into her purse for her cell phone. She'd distract herself with work.

She couldn't remember the last time she'd gone this long without her phone in hand. Pulling it out, she wasn't surprised to see that there were a dozen messages. She settled back against the pillows with a pen and pad of paper to take notes for Ellen Ligurski, her best friend and producer, who was supposed to be dropping by the hospital within the hour.

But instead of someone from her staff calling with a problem at the studio, the first message was from her sister.

"Oh my God, Dianna, I just found out about your accident. I know you probably can't get this message, but just in case you can, I want you to know that I'm coming to the hospital right away."

Dianna pulled the phone away from her ear and stared at it. April had been at the hospital?

She hit the nurses' call button, and when the woman poked her head in, Dianna said, "I'm sorry to bother you again, but was my sister here earlier when I was sleeping?"

The nurse looked confused. "No. I don't think so."

Dianna's brain raced. "Could she have seen me in the ICU?"

"I could call over there to ask, if you'd like."

Using the phone beside Dianna's bed, the nurse quickly confirmed that April had, indeed, visited Dianna in the ICU when she was sedated. One of the nurses recalled seeing her sleeping on a chair in the waiting room a couple of hours earlier.

When the nurse left, Dianna called April's cell phone and left her a message saying she was all right and that she'd love to see her. But why, she wondered anxiously as she hung up, hadn't her sister come back for another visit?

Just then, her friend Ellen came rushing into the room. A ball of energy who never walked when she could run, and never ran when she could sprint, Ellen was a big reason that *West Coast Update* was such a success. Were it not for her friend's recommendation to the network's producers, Dianna might have remained just another green-eyed blonde waiting in the wings.

"Oh honey, how are you feeling?" Ellen asked mid-hug. "I wish I could have been here sooner, but I couldn't get a flight back out of San Francisco until late this morning." Not stopping for a breath, she said, "Oh boy, I have to tell you about a simply breathtaking man sitting across the aisle from me. Big shoulders, wounded eyes. What I wouldn't give to make things all better for him."

It was so nice to have Ellen's soft, warm arms around her that Dianna felt tears coming. Taking a deep breath, she blinked them away before sitting back against her pillows.

Smiling at her friend, she teased, "Did you take a covert picture of him on your cell phone?"

Ellen snapped her fingers. "No picture, darn it, but do the words 'tall,' 'dark,' and 'gorgeous' mean anything to you?"

Dianna felt her smile wobble. Tall, dark, and gorgeous sounded like Sam. Exactly like Sam.

She hadn't thought about him this much in years. Hadn't let herself. She must really be feeling bad if she was letting a bunch of old feelings about an ancient relationship get to her.

Wanting to change the subject, she said, "I can hardly believe I was in such a bad crash. Honestly, I feel more hungover than anything."

Ellen sat down on the edge of the bed and held Dianna's hands in both of hers. "Oh my gosh, honey, I shouldn't be talking about a man. What's important is that you're feeling better. We were all so worried about you. No one wanted to stay in San Francisco at the studio. They all wanted to come here to be with you."

Her staff at *West Coast Update* were as close as she got to family. Well, she had April, but they didn't exactly hang out and joke around. She was godmother to three new babies, and attended every birthday party she was invited to, even though she was usually the only childless, husbandless woman there. Years ago, she'd been on the verge of becoming a sleepless, but radiantly happy, new mother. Now she was resolutely single, without a family anywhere on the horizon.

At least she'd found a place where she belonged, where no one questioned where she'd come from. Her coworkers assumed Dianna had always been confident. Beautiful.

No one knew how hard she'd worked to transform herself.

Ten years ago, she'd come to San Francisco with just enough money to rent a crappy apartment. She'd needed to find a job. Fast.

She'd done surprisingly well in her communications course at Tahoe Junior College, given how shy she'd always been, so after carefully studying the morning newscasters and realizing she could probably do what they did, she went to a training salon. For ten dollars they gave her a cut and color, transforming her dirty-blond locks into golden waves.

They also told her about clothing resale shops, where she soon found a couple of beautiful outfits in her size with the tags still on them. She'd marveled over the fact that some people had so much money that they would give things away without ever using them, but she was thankful, too, because she no longer looked like a hick from the mountains. She looked like a young professional, ready to make her mark on the world.

That morning when she'd walked into the local news

station, she'd felt utterly out of place. A total imposter. All she wanted to do was turn tail and run. Instead, she planted a wide smile on her face and made sure they knew she was willing to work hard. She wasn't afraid of sweeping floors or cleaning toilets or filing endless piles of papers.

Amazingly, she got the job, and one day when someone on set was sick, they actually let her help out onstage. Even more remarkable, at twenty-four, after six years of giving every spare moment she wasn't fighting for April to the network, they'd accepted her proposal for a brand-new show.

Her vision of a positive, fun show that highlighted all the West Coast had to offer, from restaurants and shops to local stars, quickly became a hit. And she loved it. Even though sometimes she didn't feel like smiling or sitting still for two hours while the stylist touched up her highlights and perfected her makeup.

All that mattered was that she was making an excellent living doing exactly what she wanted to do—and that her success had allowed her to pull April out of the foster system. Even better, unlike her mother, she didn't have to rely on a man to take care of her . . . and she wouldn't be left with nothing after he'd gone.

"I shouldn't have let you go meet April by yourself," Ellen said, breaking into her thoughts.

Dianna squeezed her friend's hand, wanting to reassure her. "The accident could have happened anywhere. I shouldn't have been driving in that storm."

But Ellen knew too much about Dianna's difficult relationship with April to think that their meeting in the coffee shop was just a friendly chat between loving sisters.

"It was more than the storm, wasn't it? What did April say this time to upset you?"

Dianna's chest tightened as she thought about their conversation in the Vail coffee shop. "She has a new boyfriend. That's why she's decided to stay in Colorado."

In truth, there was much more to the situation, but Dianna wasn't ready to talk to anyone about what April had told her just yet. Not until she figured out what she was going to do about it.

A pretty middle-aged doctor whom Dianna hadn't met yet knocked lightly on the door before entering the room.

"It is a pleasure to meet you, Ms. Kelley. You are a very lucky lady to have survived that crash in such good condition. I've never seen anyone moved out of the ICU so quickly. Good for you. From what I can see on your X-rays you've got no broken bones and no internal injuries, although I'm sure you still feel pretty banged up."

The doctor flipped through the chart from the previous night. "How are you feeling today?"

"Pretty good, actually."

The doctor slipped her chart back into the slot on the side of the bed. "I'm glad to hear it. I'd like you to spend another couple of hours with us so that we can continue to monitor you. But if you feel up to it, and everything looks good, I'm prepared to discharge you tonight."

After shaking her hand and getting an autograph for her daughter, the doctor exited the room and the nurse stuck her head back inside.

"Ms. Kelley, I wanted to check with you about another visitor who'd like to say hello."

Quick to protect Dianna against reporters looking to get the first sound bite on the accident, Ellen replied, "She isn't ready to make a statement yet."

The nurse shook her head. "Oh no, this man says he's a firefighter, not a reporter."

Dianna's heart practically stopped beating. "A firefighter?"

"Swear to God he's one of the best-looking guys I've ever seen," the young nurse said innocently.

"What's his name?" Ellen asked, impatience ringing out in her tone.

"Oh, sorry, his name is Sam MacKenzie." The woman looked nervous now. "Should I tell him you don't feel well, Ms. Kelley?"

Dianna's heart and mind rebelled at the thought of seeing him exactly at the same time that she realized how badly she *wanted* to see him.

How badly she *needed* to see him.

Having the nurse tell him to go away would be the easiest thing to do. The smartest thing to do.

It didn't take a genius to know that a reunion with Sam wasn't a good idea. He'd been the reason for her greatest heartache, and regardless of the lies she'd told herself, the truth was, it had taken her years to get over him.

But Sam had obviously come all this way to see her and she knew Ellen wouldn't let up until she explained.

Most important, though, she refused to act like a coward.

"I'd be happy to see him," she lied to the nurse, a false smile from her arsenal of pretend smiles plastered on her face.

"Send him in."

# CHAPTER FIVE

THANK GOD, Sam thought as he stood in the doorway, *she's alive.*

Relief at seeing her sitting up in bed flooded through him a millisecond before his next thought caught him unaware.

*She's even more beautiful than the day I met her.*

Even with a bruise on her cheekbone, even ten years older, she was still the most stunning woman he'd ever seen. In a matter of seconds, he took in the details of her face, her bright green eyes, her soft red lips, her high cheekbones, and her long, graceful neck.

The beautiful girl he'd been in love with had been transformed into a hell of a woman.

In the time they'd been apart, he'd never allowed himself to give in to the ridiculously powerful urge to watch her show, but there had been times he'd been unable to avoid seeing *West Coast Update* when he was waiting in the airport or sitting in a bar drinking a beer with the guys.

Six years after she'd left Tahoe, he still remembered the day he saw her interviewing a pop star. Her smile had been so big, so wide, her eyes so shiny and bright, he felt like he'd been shot straight through the heart.

All along, he'd assumed that she'd been torn to pieces by losing the baby, because that's how he'd felt. As the camera zoomed in on her thousand-watt smile, he suddenly realized a baby would have held her back from the flashy life she'd really wanted.

Staring at her now on the hospital bed, he supposed he shouldn't be surprised to see her look so glossy, so polished, but he'd always assumed she looked that way because of the cameras, or the lights, or that maybe the TV screen was distorting the truth.

In his head she had always been the same Dianna, the pretty girl who'd changed his world with a smile. But this woman was blonder, slicker, a thousand times more sophisticated-looking than the girl he used to know. People in hospitals never looked good. And yet, somehow, she did.

Dianna was in the middle of saying something to a thin woman with a severe black haircut who was sitting on a chair beside the bed when she looked up and saw him. Breaking off in the middle of her sentence, she sucked in a deep breath, her face flushing beneath his scrutiny.

And yet, even as he mentally dissected all the ways she'd changed, all the reasons they were more different than ever, his body was telling him to get over there, to pull her tight against him and kiss her until they were both gasping for air.

What the hell was he thinking?

Her friend moved first, standing up and holding out her hand. "Hello, I'm Ellen Ligurski, Dianna's best friend. Her producer, too."

One of the woman's eyebrows was raised in question. She had to be wondering who the hell he was.

"Sam MacKenzie," he said. "Dianna's ex-fiancée."

Ellen's eyes went round like saucers, and she mouthed, "Oh my," at the same time that Dianna gasped.

Well, that confirmed what he'd suspected all along; Dianna had completely buried her past when she'd moved to San Francisco. Especially the part about him.

But before latent anger could get the best of him, he told himself to get over it. They'd both started fresh. They'd both come out of the relationship just fine. He still had his wildfires. And she had the whole world at her feet. Neither of them had a damn thing to complain about—apart from her car accident, of course.

"I saw you on the airplane," her friend said. "If I'd known that you were coming to see Dianna, I would have given you a ride."

She turned to Dianna and whispered, *"This is the guy I was telling you about,"* loud enough for him to overhear.

Dianna and her friend had been talking about him? Interesting.

He let one side of his mouth quirk into a charming half smile. Ellen responded as expected, her eyes and mouth growing soft, an answering smile on her lips.

She was clearly still trying and failing to cover her shock at hearing that he and Dianna had once been an item. Practically husband and wife, with a white picket fence and everything.

"I heard Dianna was in a car accident," he said to the woman. "And I wanted to see for myself that she was all right."

"I'm fine," Dianna said, her warm, slightly husky voice washing over him, making a beeline for his groin.

Her colorless face and tightly pinched lips belied her relaxed words and he was selfishly glad to know that he wasn't the only one having a hard time with their impromptu reunion.

"I'm glad to see that," he said, even though the truth was, he hadn't expected to come all this way to find her sitting on the edge of the hospital bed in designer clothes that probably cost more than he made in a week.

What an idiot he was for actually thinking she needed him.

At the same time, he wanted to drop to his knees to give thanks that she'd survived the head-on, that she wasn't wrapped head to toe in bandages, that there weren't doctors hovering over her, pumping blood into her, stitching up her organs while they tried to keep her alive.

The air in the room was strained and heavy. Ellen's eyes jumped between the two of them, back and forth several times, as if they were playing a tennis match.

Finally she offered, "I've got some phone calls to make for this week's lineup. I'll give you two some privacy."

Dianna nodded, her lips still pursed tightly, two pink spots of color emerging beneath her cheekbones.

"Sounds like a good plan."

"Call my cell when you want me to come back," Ellen told Dianna before she squeezed past him out the door.

Closing it behind her, Sam finally moved toward the bed.

Dianna's scent used to be fresh soap. The green Irish Spring bar. Now, she smelled expensive. Foreign. Out of his reach.

He didn't like it.

As much as he didn't like the inch of makeup she'd applied to her face with a spatula. She'd never needed anything to "fix" her beautiful, golden skin. Maybe all that makeup worked on TV, but it looked all wrong to Sam.

Those months they were together a decade ago, he'd thought he knew her. But when she left, he'd questioned everything. Seeing her now only confirmed those doubts. The old Dianna would have been simply glad to be alive after the car crash. The new one was clearly concerned with looking pretty.

Moving his gaze back to her face, he could see her mind racing behind her clear, apparently calm green eyes. She was trying to figure out how best to deal with him.

Hell, he was working out the same thing.

"What are you doing here, Sam?"

He didn't know how he'd expected her to react to his showing up unannounced, but given the sparkling jewels on her fingers and ears he'd have bet on cold and distant, that he was merely one of the many peons coming to worship at her feet.

He was surprised by the heat beneath her words, the unspoken accusation that he shouldn't have come—and that she didn't want him here.

Didn't she realize he hadn't had any other choice but to get on the next plane to Colorado? That hearing about her accident had sent him into a tailspin, into his own head-on collision with the past?

He'd never been one for telling lies. He wasn't going to start now.

"I needed to make sure you were okay."

He wasn't saying anything she couldn't have figured out for herself and he didn't feel as if he was giving away a deep dark secret. But when her eyes suddenly softened and she unclamped her jaw, he found himself adding, "Connor told me about your accident and I was worried about you. I couldn't sit at home without knowing how you were doing, without seeing you for myself. Considering how bad they said the crash was, you look good."

He desperately wanted to reach out to her, to touch her skin, to see if it was still silky soft.

"You don't just look good, Dianna. You look amazing. Simply amazing."

Dianna was stunned not only by his presence, but by everything he was saying.

She didn't know what to think. What to say. Where to look.

She wanted to stare at him, drink in his tanned skin, the sexy new lines on his face. She wanted to continue studying him until she figured out when and how he'd changed from the hot young firefighter she'd loved to this mature man, who looked rough and hard in all the right places and soft in none.

She forgot everything as she looked at him, her worries about April and the accident shrinking to a small glimmer in the back of her mind. All this time she'd convinced herself that she'd left her past behind her, but simply seeing Sam was pushing every last one of her painful emotions back up to the surface.

She was frightened by the attraction that still simmered between them. But most of all, she was alarmed by how much she loved seeing him, by how much it mattered to her that he came all the way to Colorado to check on her.

The last time she'd cared this much about Sam, he'd broken her heart.

Somehow, she needed to stop herself from falling all over again.

Thus far, she hadn't managed to play it cool, which was crazy. She was a master of cool. She'd been in a hundred uncomfortable situations on her TV set. She needed to draw on those experiences and pull herself together.

So although she was dying to know every last detail about the last ten years of Sam's life, she wouldn't allow herself to give in to her curiosity. Instead, she'd assuage it by asking about his brother. She'd be polite. Interested, of course, because she'd always liked Connor. But she'd pull back before the conversation had any chance of going too deep.

"You mentioned Connor. How is he?"

Sam's expression went from hot to cold so fast her head spun.

"None of us heard from you for ten years. You didn't leave a telephone number. Or an address. You didn't send Christmas cards to the station. You just disappeared."

The force of his words pushed her back against the pillows. She opened her mouth to defend herself, but no words came.

"I gave you what you wanted, Dianna. I let you be gone. So what do you care what happened to Connor?"

She was reeling from the anger—and hurt—behind

his words. But she couldn't ignore the red flag of danger that told her something had happened to Connor. Something bad.

"Something happened to him, didn't it?"

His lips tightened and the muscle in his jaw jumped. She held her breath, desperate now to find out what had happened to Connor, even though she already knew she wasn't going to like what she heard.

"He was burned. Last summer in a blowup in Desolation Wilderness."

"Oh God," she breathed, remembering the news reports from that wildfire. "Every time I heard about a bad fire in the Sierras, I thought about you," she said softly.

His face registered surprise and she mirrored it back at him. Suddenly it seemed important that he know just how difficult it had been—both then and now—to stop worrying about him and the rest of the men she'd known on the Tahoe Pines crew.

"Just because I left Lake Tahoe didn't mean I could pretend your job wasn't dangerous. I thought about everyone on the crew. About Connor. And I prayed that all of you would make it through unscathed."

When she stopped talking, she realized she'd broken her own vow to keep her distance. The beautiful man standing in front of her was too dangerous for such recklessness.

"We all came out of it fine," he said. "Everyone except Connor."

The thought of how much pain Connor must have been in sent a new wave of nausea through her.

"Where was he burned?"

"His hands and arms," Sam said in a cool, almost clinical voice. "His chest and the back of his head a bit."

She could only imagine how hard it must have been for Sam to watch his brother get hurt. To be so close and yet just far enough away that he couldn't save him, couldn't keep the fire from taking its spoils.

On the verge of saying this, she realized he was staring at her hands. Looking down, she realized she was cracking her knuckles and made herself pull her hands apart. The cracking was a sign of weakness. Dianna hated showing weakness to anyone.

Especially Sam.

"Tell me what happened, Sam. Please."

He was silent for a long while and she thought she understood why. Firefighters weren't big talkers, especially when one of them got hurt. Sam had explained it to her once, telling her that the most important thing was getting back out and doing their job, not stewing on what had gone wrong.

In truth, this trait had been one of the things about Sam that had driven her crazy: He'd always had her on a "need to know" basis. And as far as he'd been concerned, she simply didn't need to know the gory, scary details of his day-to-day, which meant she'd known next to nothing about his job and had to get her information from the newspaper like everyone else.

Sensing that more questions would only put him more on guard, she gently observed, "I just can't picture Connor getting hurt. He always seemed so invincible."

Sam finally sat down on the chair beside her bed, so close that the hair on her arms stood on edge, and goose bumps covered her skin.

Late at night, when she was exhausted and her defenses were down, she'd dreamed a thousand times about being with him again, but she never thought she would experience this closeness live and in person. She wanted to reach out and touch him to see if he was real or if he'd disappear like he always did in her dreams right before she pressed her lips against his.

"Logan, Connor, and I were working on clearing a patch of brush a quarter mile from the blaze."

He spoke quickly, as if he had to get the words out before it became too difficult to recount the event.

"Sparks must have jumped over us in the wind, and before we knew it, we were on top of the fire. Logan realized it first, even though Connor and I were closer to the fire. Logan should have made a break for it. He should have saved himself. Instead he came down the hill and saved our lives."

Dianna wasn't surprised by what Logan had done. Like the rest of the men on Sam's crew, Logan had been gorgeous and fearless, and yet he'd stood out to her. Not because she was attracted to him, but because she knew a kindred spirit when she met one. He hadn't needed to tell her that his life hadn't always been easy. She'd seen it in his eyes, in the set of his jaw, in the way he carried himself.

"I always liked Logan."

"He just got married."

Again, she was surprised by Sam's intensity. And the fact that there was no mistaking his meaning of, *"Back off, he's taken."*

Well, she wasn't going to rise to the bait.

"I'll make sure to send his new wife something pretty for the house." Getting back to Connor, she asked, "So the three of you ran up the mountain? And then what?"

His eyes clouded over and she wondered if he was back there in Desolation Wilderness with Logan and Connor, breathing in hot, black smoke.

"Death was right there, right behind us. We were almost out, when the breeze kicked up and the flames sucked Connor down."

She took a shaky breath. "It must have been horrible."

She knew the Forest Service sent in psychiatrists whenever there was an accident. She also knew that hotshots rarely talked to the suits, that they weren't willing to risk getting kicked off the crew later on because of a momentary weakness recorded in their official files.

"Have you talked about this with anyone?"

Sam shook his head once, firmly. The urge to take him in her arms and heal his bottled-up pain was so strong that she had her hand on his arm before she could corral her compulsion.

He stiffened and she immediately yanked her hand away. The skin on her palm and fingers felt like she'd grabbed on to a hot platter right out of the oven.

"I should have insisted on bringing up the rear," Sam finally said in a hard voice.

Clearly, guilt still weighed him down. Even though he'd almost died saving his brother, he obviously wished he could have done more.

"It should have been me getting burned. Not my little brother."

It was painful, this reminder of how much they both loved their siblings, an unbreakable bond that a part of her wished they didn't have. Still, she needed him to know that he wasn't to blame.

"He's alive, Sam. You pulled him out of the fire. It must have been so hard on you, having to go back out there and fight wildfires without Connor. You two have worked together for so long. And he's such an asset not only to you, but to the entire crew."

When he remained silent, she asked, "What's his prognosis? Will he fight fire again?"

"He's doing everything in his power to convince the Forest Service that he belongs back on the crew. He's gone through hell and back with skin grafts and physical therapy and never complained. Not once."

She wasn't surprised. The MacKenzie brothers had more than good genes in common. They were both strong.

Unbreakable.

"I'll bet he's still a swashbuckling ladies' man through it all, isn't he?" she said, forcing a smile.

But instead of smiling back, Sam turned the questions around on her.

"What about April? I've always wondered if you were able to pull her out of the foster system."

Regardless of how things had gone wrong between them, Dianna had never forgotten Sam's unwavering support during those first months when she was wading through paperwork and red tape.

"I got her, Sam."

Finally, he smiled back and she lost her breath.

She fiddled with the blanket as she gathered her composure, knowing it was only fair to tell him as much about April as he'd told her about Connor, even though it wasn't easy for her to talk about it.

"She's lived with me for the past six years."

He whistled softly. "It took you four years to get her back, huh?"

She'd never completely shaken off her frustration from those endless months of battling with the state.

"Every time I thought they were going to say yes, they found another reason to say no."

"But you got them to change their mind."

His clear admiration was surprising. She liked it far too much.

How could it still matter what he thought about her after all these years? After all her success?

"She must have been fourteen by the time she came

to live with you," he said, doing the math. "How was it, living with a teenager?"

It was tempting to let everything pour out, to pretend that the past ten years hadn't happened, that they were sitting together in his apartment talking at the end of a long day.

Thankfully, she still had some sense of self-preservation, a little voice in the back of her head warning her not to say too much or let him in any closer.

"It was hard at first," she said honestly. "I don't think adolescence is easy for anyone. It certainly wasn't for me. I'm sure she'll find her way eventually."

He raised an eyebrow as if to say he knew there was far more to the story than she was telling him, but fortunately, he let it go.

"I'm glad it worked out for you. For both of you."

Despite her warnings to herself, Dianna couldn't take her eyes off of his beautiful face. She wanted to stare at him for hours just to watch his expression change by degrees and admire the way his muscles flexed beneath his T-shirt.

Her feelings scared her. Really scared her.

All these years, she'd tried to convince herself that she'd fallen in love with a fantasy hero. That they were just kids fooling around. That the miscarriage had been a narrow escape.

She wanted to believe that there had been nothing real between them.

So then, why did it all feel so damn real?

Sam couldn't believe how much he wanted to stay with Dianna. She'd barely touched on April, but he also knew that she was right in keeping the details to herself. They were treading dangerous waters. Instead of keeping to the surface, they were diving down far deeper than they should.

She'd barely had to push him for details about the Desolation Wilderness incident and he'd crumbled. And yet talking to her about it felt unbearably right, as did her touch, when she'd reached out in empathy and placed her hand on his arm.

He couldn't believe how hard it had been to keep from reaching out and pulling her against him.

Hadn't he learned a damn thing ten years ago?

During their conversation, his brain had been working overtime to try to get used to her glossy veneer, to her perfectly white teeth and much blonder hair, to her perfectly manicured nails and soft, expensive-looking clothing. Interestingly, what helped most was watching her pop and crack her knuckles. He was thankful that at least one thing about her had stayed the same.

The bad habit stood out in sharp relief against the backdrop of her perfect, shiny beauty.

For the first time since he'd met her, he felt out of place, like the two of them didn't belong in the same room. Ten years ago, she'd been a poor, embarrassed girl with a drunk mother. She'd needed him to save her.

Hell, she'd needed him, period.

But this woman sitting in front of him wasn't the kind of person who needed saving.

He'd rushed all the way to Colorado thinking things were going to be similar to that first day they met at the trailer park. Her needing, him saving.

He couldn't have been more off the mark.

Of course he was happy for her success. What kind of asshole wouldn't be? But at the same time, he found himself wondering if this was why she left him; because she wanted to reach for a bigger, brighter life than being a fireman's wife.

She shifted uncomfortably in the bed and he didn't know if it was because of her accident—or his being in the room. Either way, he'd overstayed his welcome.

And yet, Sam couldn't make himself get out of the chair and say good-bye. He just wasn't ready to leave her. Not yet.

Not when looking at her and talking with her still did funny things to his insides, made him wish things had turned out differently for them.

There was only one solution to his problem, only one way to get his ass moving out the door. He needed to rewind back to that day when he'd walked in the front door of their tiny apartment, into the silence, the emptiness, and realized she was gone. And wasn't ever coming back.

For ten years, he'd been in the dark about why she'd

left him. He could deal with being dumped. People got out of relationships all the time.

What he couldn't stand was not knowing why.

It was finally time to find out.

"I'm going to head out in a minute," he told her, more than a little surprised by the answering flicker of disappointment in her eyes. "But before I do, I've got a question for you. It's something I've been wondering for a very long time."

For a split second, her eyes widened with alarm. Remorse for the pile of bones he was about to unearth hit him square in the chest. If she were injured at all, he wouldn't have gone here, he told himself, as if it was some kind of absolution.

She straightened her spine, moving away slightly from the pillows, and lifted her chin. "Go ahead."

*Shit*, Sam thought. He should have taken the high road. Instead, he'd started down a road with no exits.

And now he couldn't leave without hearing the truth.

"Why did you leave?"

Her mouth opened. Then closed. She shook her head, disbelief clouding her beautiful green eyes.

"You honestly don't know?"

He was at least as surprised by her response as she seemed to be by his question.

He bit back a quick retort, knowing he'd regret it. And then her cell phone rang and she seemed glad to turn away from him and pull it out of her bag.

She quickly flipped it open. "April?"

And then suddenly, Dianna's face lost all of its color and she kicked the blankets off of her legs to stand up too quickly.

Forgetting the need to keep his distance, Sam reached for her before she could fall and held her steady against his chest. He could feel her heart beating rapidly, and instinctively knew it had nothing to do with their close physical proximity.

Something was wrong.

"Where are you?" She held her breath as she listened to April's reply, then urged, "You need to tell me more than that. You need to tell me exactly where you are so that I can find you."

A few seconds later, Dianna pulled the phone away from her ear and began frantically pressing buttons before the phone dropped to the floor. When she looked up at him, he saw eyes as bleak as the ones that had stared back at him after her miscarriage.

"What's wrong?" he asked as carefully as he would a fire victim who'd just seen her house and all of her possessions go up in flames.

"My sister's in trouble. She needs my help."

# CHAPTER SIX

APRIL KELLEY hated how scared she was.

Her jaw was throbbing and there was tape around her mouth, hands, and ankles. Blinking hard to clear her foggy vision, when she looked up she realized she was sitting on the floor of a coat closet.

She'd never been a big fan of small, enclosed spaces, not after one of her foster families had made her sleep in a windowless room about the size of a closet for a couple of weeks when she was seven. The long hanging jackets brushing against the top of her head and shoulders made her feel even more claustrophobic, and she shivered, her teeth somehow managing to clank together behind the tape.

She wasn't asthmatic, but the various pediatricians she'd had over the years claimed she hovered right on the brink of the disease. Feeling her lungs start to seize up, she forced herself to take long, slow breaths in and out of her nose. Dianna had been really into meditation for a while and even though she'd thought it was really lame at the time, April was suddenly grateful for the knowledge.

When she'd gotten hold of her breathing and felt confident that she wasn't going to start freaking out again, she tried to work out what had happened.

After April woke up in an uncomfortable ball on one of the ICU waiting room chairs, one of the nurses told her that Dianna had been transferred to a regular room on the fourth floor. Relieved that her sister was doing so much better, she'd bummed a cigarette from one of the janitors to smoke before going up to see Dianna. She hadn't smoked since moving to the Farm three months earlier, but her nerves were shot and she couldn't think of a better way to check out for a few minutes.

She'd barely stepped outside and lit up when all of a sudden there was a hand over her mouth and nose and a gun in her side.

"Don't make a sound," the guy had whispered.

The hand on her face felt shockingly strong. Finely honed instincts from childhood told her that if she didn't obey his order he'd pull the trigger, which was why she let him push her away from the building and shove her into the passenger seat of his car.

April's experience as an ex–foster kid came to the fore as she sat quietly in the guy's passenger seat. The best thing to do in any new, scary situation, she knew, was to keep her mouth shut and wait to see the lay of the land before making any sudden moves.

As he drove, one hand on the steering wheel, the other holding the gun still trained on her, she tried to figure out why he'd grabbed her.

She'd heard stories about girls being nabbed off busy streets and sold to creepy rich guys in foreign countries, but she couldn't believe anyone would want her to be a sex slave. Not right now, anyway, with her jeans soaked and muddy from the thighs down and her hair practically in dreads for want of a good hot shower and some of that expensive conditioner Dianna always put in the bathroom.

Then again, maybe this guy—and any rich clients he might have—had strange tastes.

What else did she have to offer him but her body, she wondered helplessly. She wasn't rich, didn't have any jewelry on that he could steal and sell off. And then it hit her. Dianna had all of those things. Her sister wasn't a big shopper, but the money was definitely there. April couldn't believe the number she'd seen on her sister's latest contract when she'd been snooping around her home office last year.

"My sister's rich," she blurted, praying that money might be a good trade for sex with her. When he didn't reply, she added, "She's a big star. I swear I can get the money from her. And I know she won't want to tell the cops or anyone about this, not if it means getting her name in the papers."

Stopping at a light, the man turned to her, his gray eyes frighteningly cold. "I don't need your sister's money."

He pointed the gun square in the middle of her face. She imagined him pulling the trigger, blowing a hole right through.

Gulping hard, she scooted as far away from him as she could, pressing herself against the passenger door. Bile rose in her throat and she barely managed to swallow it down.

"Now shut up or I'll make you shut up."

He was pretty average sized, but his grip on her in the parking lot had been surprisingly strong. Considering she was about ten pounds underweight at the moment, April knew she'd be no match for him if he decided to pull over and force himself on her in the car.

Her stomach continued to churn. She wasn't a virgin, but the number of guys she'd slept with didn't matter anymore.

She knew she needed to stop being such a cowering baby and get the hell out of his car. But as she waited for her opportunity to escape, the minutes only ticked by faster and faster, bringing her another step closer to ending up his prisoner.

Each minute that clicked by on the digital clock on the dashboard felt like an hour and she prayed that something would happen, that they'd get in an accident or a cop would drive by and see the gun. Of course, none of those things happened.

But just when she thought she was permanently out of luck, the traffic picked up and the rain started falling harder. April shot the man a surreptitious glance. He was focusing more on driving than on keeping his gun trained on her.

This was her chance.

Quickly unlocking the door, she threw herself out of the moving car onto the street. Her kneecaps and elbows and shoulders all hurt like hell as she rolled on the blacktop, but she barely noticed as she got back on her feet and started running. She needed to go somewhere crowded.

He wouldn't try to grab her again if there were people around, would he?

Sighting a gas station across the street, she ran as fast as she could through the rain on the slippery four-lane road. People were filling up their tanks and didn't seem to take much notice of her as she slid to a stop in front of the mini-mart.

Pulling her phone out of her pocket, she called Dianna, not remembering until the last second that her sister was in the hospital and might not have access to her cell phone.

Amazingly, Dianna picked up and April's words all ran together. "Some guy grabbed me. I need help. I got away from him and I'm at a gas station."

April was frantically scanning the front of the building for any street numbers on it that she could give, when she felt the familiar pressure of a gun shoved into her ribs.

"Stop talking and give me the phone or I'll kill you right here, right now," he whispered.

She hesitated for a moment and he cocked his gun.

"Trust me, little girl, I don't have a damn thing to live for. I'll shoot you first, then I'll shoot myself. It'd be just as easy to do it here as it is somewhere else. But if you do what I say, you just might get to live."

April's hand shook as she handed him her phone and watched him shut it, then followed his instructions to get back in the car without making a sound or looking like he was forcing her.

"Who did you call?"

"I couldn't get through," she lied, but he had already flipped open her phone. DIANNA was at the top of her call list.

He slammed the gun into her jaw and she was stunned by the flash of blinding pain that ran through her.

"What did you tell her?"

"Nothing," she moaned around the blood in her mouth.

He hit her with the gun again, harder this time across the forehead, and the pain was so ferocious she barely heard him say, "You stupid bitch, you better not have ruined everything for me. Does she know where you are?"

She was in too much pain to lie and the "no" escaped her before she could pull it back. Even as she waited for his next blow, the sunlight seemed to dim. The last thing she heard was a muffled, "Fuck," before she passed out.

Hours later, finding herself bound and gagged in a closet, she couldn't help but wonder, *Why does bad shit always happen to me?*

Three months ago, she'd thought leaving San Francisco was the best thing for everyone. Especially after she'd overheard Dianna's public relations team tell her she'd better "rein April in before she does something to make headlines." She hadn't stayed to hear Dianna's response.

Sure, April knew she was a screwup that no one wanted, but it killed her to hear the words come out of someone's mouth.

Clearly, the whole sister-as-guardian thing was a nice gesture on Dianna's part, but it hadn't worked out. So when April's new boyfriend, Kevin, asked her to come with him to Colorado, she didn't even have to think about it, she just packed a bag and got on the bus.

The two-day ride gave her plenty of time to think. All her life, she'd been angry with Dianna for getting to stay with their mother while April had been sent off to live with strangers. At the same time, when Dianna finally pulled her out of the system, she hadn't known how to respond to Dianna's overwhelming affection, to the way she wanted to hang out all the time and do girl stuff like go to the mall and get makeovers.

Life as a foster kid either made you weak and scared of everything—or it gave you calluses. Everywhere. In the throes of teenage angst, the more her big sister tried to reach her, the more she'd pulled away. Rebellion was what April did and she did it well, but then even that got old. Predictable.

By the end of the bus ride to Vail, April had made the decision that she was ready to stop being Dianna Kelley's screwed-up little sister. She was ready for something new.

She was ready for a better life.

It was a two-day hike through the Rockies to the Farm and frankly, she was a little freaked out about living in an intentional community.

But, amazingly, she'd found herself fitting in with the band of misfits. And for the first time, she almost felt like she was part of a family.

Her brothers and sisters on the Farm accepted her for who she really was. They didn't try to change her clothes, her hair, or the music she liked. While Dianna had always coddled her, she was given real responsibilities on the Farm as a cook. She was surprised by how natural it felt to stand over a hot fire, to pound herbs together with a mortar and pestle, to knead bread until it was just the right consistency. Up in the Rockies, she felt more at peace than she ever had.

And then guilt started creeping up on her, slowly but surely, day after day, week after week. When she'd finally asked to use the Farm's lone phone line and checked her voice mail, she cringed listening to Dianna's anxious string of messages. It was time to set up a meeting to show her ubersuccessful big sister that she was finally doing something good, that she was finally on the right track with her life and was coming into her own.

With the only access road newly blocked by fallen trees, it was another two-day hike into town. It wasn't an easy journey, but April liked knowing that she had the skills to take care of herself, that she didn't need to rely on Kevin or anyone else to get where she needed to go. Besides, Kevin had split the Farm a few weeks after they'd arrived. He hadn't expected the workload to be so high or the drugs to be nonexistent. She hadn't been particularly sad to see him go.

Dianna had been waiting for her in the café on Vail's main street, and for a split second, April had been so happy to see her sister that she'd almost hugged her. Excitedly, she tried to tell Dianna about the Farm, about what a good experience it was. But before she could figure out how to best explain her new living situation, Dianna had started pushing all her buttons.

*"Tell me why you want to stay in Colorado,"* Dianna had asked. *"Why you won't come back and enroll in junior college? I'm willing to give you another chance to get back on your feet. We need a part-time research assistant on the show. I'm sure Ellen would take a chance on you."*

April was proud of her new skills and hoped Dianna would be too. *"I've already got a job."*

*"Doing what?"*

*"Cooking."*

It wasn't hard to see how shocked Dianna was. And that she wasn't the least bit impressed.

*"Cooking? You've never even wanted to watch the cooking channel with me. Tell me where the restaurant is, what it's called. I'll have a word with the chef. He'll understand that you need to come home with me."*

*"I'm not working in a restaurant,"* April explained. *"I'm cooking for everyone on the Farm."*

Before she could explain things more clearly, Dianna said, *"The Farm? What in God's name is the Farm?"* Her expression suddenly grew even more anxious than it already was. *"Oh God, April, you're not mixed up in some kind of cult, are you?"*

April had made a face, tried to tamp down the sudden rush of anger, tried to recover the sense of peace she'd felt for the past couple of months.

*"No, of course it's not a cult. A commune is totally different from a cult. We're an intentional community."*

*"No way,"* Dianna had said in a hard voice that April had never heard her use. Even when she'd done something bad, her sister had always been gentle with her. *"I'm not letting you live on a commune or a Farm or whatever you're calling it. I didn't work this hard to get us out of a trailer park so that you could turn around and live in mud huts with a bunch of hippies."* She grabbed April's arm. *"We're going to get your things and then we're going to leave."*

April yanked her arm out of Dianna's grasp. How could she have thought that Dianna would understand?

*"I already told you, Dianna. I'm staying here. In Colorado."*
April let her mouth twist into a satisfied smirk. *"On the commune."*

*"Jesus, April. You haven't always made the best choices, but I didn't think you were stupid."*

That was when April finally snapped. *"It must hurt to have a pole rammed so far up your perfect ass."*

She'd gotten the hell out of the café before Dianna saw her tears.

All she wanted was to be back at the Farm with her new friends, but it was raining way too hard, so she spent fifteen dollars to stay at the nearby youth hostel that she and Kevin had slept in their first night in Vail. Curling up on the hard bed, she tried to sleep, but a group of teenage girls was blaring the TV in the main room.

Suddenly, she heard someone say her sister's name and she sat up in bed, hitting her head on the top bunk. A sick premonition rushed over her as she ran out of the room in her underwear and heard the news report about Dianna's crash.

On the floor of the closet, her stomach churned with a sick mixture of guilt and remorse. Dianna wouldn't have been on that winding road in that storm if it hadn't been for her. And now, if she couldn't get out of here, she might never get the chance to say she was sorry.

Abruptly, her train of thought was broken by the sound of loud footsteps.

*Oh shit, he was back!*

The door opened, and before she could so much as

make a sound, he was coming at her with a needle. She tried to get away from him, tried to scream behind her muzzle, but there was nowhere to go, no way to escape.

The man watched the girl go limp and waited for the satisfaction of how easy it was to keep her hostage.

Instead, he felt numb. From top to bottom, inside and out. He barely even saw the girl, his mind clouded with visions of his brother lying cold and stiff beneath a white sheet.

"What do you want me to do with her?"

He turned to Mickey, a brawny but simple man he'd hired a handful of times when he felt that he was entering a potentially dangerous situation. Early on in the business, he'd learned that for the right amount of money, Mickey would do whatever needed to be done, no questions asked.

But he needed sleep in order to think straight. He'd simply keep the girl locked up until he fleshed out his plan.

"Just watch her. Make sure she stays put."

Mickey stepped closer, looked in the closet. He smiled, revealing a lack of good dentistry. "She's pretty."

"Don't touch her." The man's round face fell with disappointment and he amended, "Not yet."

He didn't want Mickey to be too rough with the girl before Dianna was here to witness it. He almost smiled at the image of the rich, blond TV star bitch being forced to watch the brute sodomize her sister.

Fortunately, he thought as he went to get some sleep, it wouldn't be long before both he and Mickey got exactly what they wanted. Mickey could have the girl.

And he'd have his revenge.

# CHAPTER SEVEN

DIANNA HEARD someone say, "Take deep, slow breaths," and realized Sam was counseling her in a gentle voice as she stood in the comforting circle of his arms.

It was the very last place she'd ever expected to find herself.

"You need to sit down."

She wanted to race straight out of the hospital room to search for April, but he was right. She'd be no good to April until she calmed down and came up with a clear-headed plan.

Sam helped her back onto the bed and covered her legs with a blanket, then got her a cup of water and made her drink it.

Her mouth was dry despite the water. "I'm scared, Sam."

In her early years at the TV station, she'd taken night classes in elocution, learning to keep her voice even and moderated. She barely recognized this squeaking anxious woman talking to Sam as herself.

"Where is she? What did she say?"

"Some guy grabbed her, but she got away and was calling from a gas station."

"Did she tell you which one?"

Her hands began to shake. She might have created an amazing career and bank account for herself during the past ten years, but even as a broke eighteen-year-old overwhelmed by the crowded city streets of San Francisco, she'd never been this frightened. This freaked out.

"The line went dead before she gave me any other details. Oh God, who could have grabbed her? And what if he's hurting her right now?"

"You can't let yourself think like that. I promise you, we're going to find her."

Relief flooded through her, even though he was only trying to make her feel better.

"I'm going to need you to tell me everything you can about April, past and present, so that I can help you figure this out."

Dianna was afraid that every additional second that ticked by could have terrible consequences for her sister. But at the same time she knew she had to think through the situation as calmly as possible. Thank God Sam was here to help her.

With everyone else, she'd always felt that she'd had to

gloss over her problems with April. For so long, she'd been afraid of the press picking up the story and running with it and she hadn't wanted to give away any potentially damaging information. Not to her various boyfriends over the years. Not even to her close girl-friends.

But Sam was different, wasn't he? After all, he could have sold her story a long time ago, told everyone about her trailer park roots, about her drunk mother, but he hadn't. It was safe to come clean with him.

"April and I have problems. She hates all of my rules. She says I'm too strict. I'm pretty sure she moved to Colorado to get away from me." Her tongue felt like dry leather inside her mouth and she took another sip of water before continuing. "I saw her last night at a café in Vail for the first time in a couple of months, but I was too hard on her and she stormed out."

Sam didn't look surprised by anything she was saying.

Did he really know her that well? Did he still know her better than anyone else ever had—or ever would?

"What did she want when you saw her at the coffee shop? Money?"

"No. But I gave her some anyway." She pressed her palms to her eyes. "She wants me to treat her like an adult, but how can I when all I ever see when I look at her is a four-year-old girl crying for me to save her?"

"Don't blame yourself for doing whatever you need to do to take care of her," he said softly. "She's not the only one who was put through the wringer by your mother. You were, too."

She pulled her hands away from her eyes, amazed all over again that Sam was sitting in front of her. And that he was helping her through another of the most difficult moments of her life.

He'd been there when she and her mother had almost gotten stuck in their trailer during the wildfire. He'd been there when she needed help with April's case. And he was here now.

At least for the next few minutes, she wasn't alone.

"How do you always manage to be here right when I need you?" she asked in a whisper.

His eyes darkened and her breath went as she waited for him to respond.

"What did you and April argue about?" he asked instead of answering her loaded question.

Disappointment flooded her. He obviously didn't want to get any closer to her than he had to.

He was right to keep his distance. She knew she should be doing the same thing, and yet his smackdown still hurt. Like crazy.

Fortunately, it was also a good reminder that he hadn't *always* been there for her. Like after she lost the baby, for instance, when he'd all but disappeared from her life.

In any case, what was she doing focusing on anything but April?

"She's living on a commune," she said in answer to his

question about her argument with April. "I wanted her to come back to San Francisco with me and she refused."

If Sam was shocked about April living in a commune, he didn't show it. "Did she tell you where the commune is located?"

Fortunately, April had thrown a few details at her before storming out of the café. "No, but she did tell me that it's very controlled. That they don't let just anyone up there and visitors need to have special permission. She said there aren't any roads and they don't like trespassers. She seemed to think the isolation was a good thing."

April had seemed utterly enraptured by her new home, almost as if she'd been brainwashed into believing that living like a wild animal was a good thing.

"She told me they get to live on their own terms. And that it's really exclusive and an honor to be allowed to live there. I just know that place has something to do with what's happened to her."

Sam held up his hands as if to try to slow her down.

"I know you're worried about your sister, but from everything you've told me she isn't exactly Little Miss Perfect, is she? Could this phone call be just another bump in the road for her? A prank to see how high she can make you jump?"

She couldn't stop herself from going to April's defense. "She's had a hard life. She's still figuring things out."

"You had it rough, too. But you always knew what you wanted. Always kept yourself on track and found a way to achieve your goals."

Sorrow came at her. Did he even realize that she'd gone completely off track ten years ago? Didn't he realize that apart from her sister and mother, he was the only person whose love she really wanted? And that losing him was a big enough failure to trump all of her later successes?

"You're absolutely positive that April isn't just messing with you? Trying to get your attention. Trying to get you to prove your love."

"No."

She shook her head hard and immediately felt dizzy. Sam was at her side in an instant, his hands on her shoulders, pushing her back into the pillows.

"You need to take it easy."

But they both knew she couldn't. Not when her baby sister needed her.

He was sitting so close that she could breathe in the fresh scent of his bath soap, reminiscent of dry pine needles in a warm and sunny forest. It would be so easy to fall into his arms, to press her lips against the pulse beating strong and steady on his neck.

Despite her intense longing, she still couldn't forget how badly he'd hurt her. Those painful memories gave her enough self-control to shift away from him on the bed.

"April wouldn't do something that horrible to me,"

she told him again, knowing that even though April wasn't the easiest person to love, she wasn't evil.

"That may be the case," Sam replied, "but I'm not going to let you go rushing off to find her. You need to continue resting and getting better."

Why was she so shocked by the fact that he'd already made up his mind about what was best for her? He might not look exactly like the twenty-year-old boy she'd loved, but he sure acted the same.

On the verge of telling him to mind his own business, she realized she'd forgotten a very important detail.

"She was here. At the hospital, to visit me. But I was sedated and didn't see her. The nurses said she fell asleep in the waiting room."

Not wanting to wait another second to file a missing person report with the police, she reached for her phone, but before she could finish dialing 911, Sam reached out and took it from her.

"There's no point in calling the police."

She glared at him. "Give me back my phone."

Ignoring her demand, he laid out his reasons in a nauseatingly calm voice. "It hasn't been twenty-four hours and she doesn't exactly have the world's best track record."

Her rising indignation swiftly plummeted when she realized he was making sense.

All she'd ever wanted was a real family. Once upon a time, she'd actually thought it was possible to have that big happy family, to be Sam's wife, to watch their children play together. Seeing Sam again only made the gaping hole in her heart feel bigger.

For the past ten years, she'd been just fine, but in only one hour he'd clouded her brain and heart and body with foolish desires and dreams. She couldn't think straight around him. And she was going to need every last one of her mental resources to find April and bring her home again.

She had to be strong and send him away.

"Thanks for coming to see me, Sam. But I don't want to take up any more of your time. You've been a great help, but I can take it from here."

Like hell he was leaving her to head off on some wild-goose chase after her flighty sister. A woman like Dianna wouldn't last a minute in the Colorado Rockies.

The trees and rivers and mountains looked beautiful, but looks were deceiving. You couldn't make your way through miles of rough terrain if you were worried about breaking a nail or messing up your hair. Not if you wanted to come out of it alive.

Sam moved away from the bed and walked over to the window to get a grip on his frustration—and his lust. Being this close to Dianna was driving him insane. He could barely control himself around her. He felt like an animal about to bust out of its cage.

No question, it was long past time to leave. He'd

simply come to the hospital to make sure she was all right. Instead, he'd walked into an episode of *Without a Trace*.

On top of everything else, Dianna had no business leaving the hospital yet. Even though she'd miraculously escaped injury in the car crash, she had to be exhausted by the entire ordeal.

At the same time, he understood exactly why she was so frantic. He'd be going just as crazy if he thought Connor was in trouble. Hell, he'd barely kept his shit together when his brother had ended up in the burn ward the previous summer.

When he'd first walked into Dianna's room, she'd looked so strong, utterly impenetrable despite her harrowing accident. Now, he could see all of the cracks in her glossy veneer, everything from knuckle-cracking to the way she bit her lower lip when she was nervous.

Viewing her as a shiny celebrity had been so much easier than seeing her as a vulnerable woman who desperately needed his help and protection.

Yet again, just like that afternoon so many years ago when she'd told him she was pregnant, he was left with only one choice.

"I'm going to help you find her."

Dianna looked at him in obvious confusion. "Why would you want to help me?"

Her question was a painful reminder of how he'd failed her ten years ago. He hadn't been there when she'd miscarried. He hadn't protected her or the baby well enough, and he'd never be able to make it up to her completely, but perhaps if he could be here for her now, he'd find a small measure of peace down the road.

Drawing a parallel to his relationship with his brother, he said, "If anyone ever threatened Connor, I'd do whatever it took to hunt that person down and make him pay. I know you feel the same way about April."

She looked wary about working together and, truthfully, he didn't know if he could make it through even one night in close quarters without ripping her clothes off. His balls were going to be bright blue by the time they found her sister.

"No," Dianna insisted, but he could tell she was wavering when she added, "This isn't your problem. I'll figure it out."

He had one last shot to convince her. One last shot to keep her safe.

"Look, I've got the wilderness skills you need to get through the Rockies in one piece. If you want to find April fast, you're going to need me around."

Grasping at straws, she said, "I can hire someone."

He crossed his arms over his chest. "Do you really think you'll be able to convince a stranger to head out on a wild-goose chase at a moment's notice?" Even with all of her money, he was one hundred percent sure she couldn't buy that kind of help.

"Fine," she finally agreed, "You can help me."

Okay, so he'd won this first battle with Dianna. Now he needed to win one with himself by getting one very important thing straight: Regardless of how he used to feel about her, from here on out he needed to treat her like a stranger in need, like any one of the thousands of people he'd helped as a hotshot. The key to success was to approach their mission methodically, rather than emotionally.

But even as he vowed to resist her, he was hit with the buzz of knowing their reunion didn't have to end yet. It was impossible to push away the powerful anticipation of being with her again.

"We need to find the commune."

It took him far longer than it should have to tune in to what she'd just said. So much for staying grounded and treating her like a random fire victim. He'd have to work a hell of a lot harder than this if he was going to keep himself from veering off the tracks.

"I agree," he said. "The commune is the last place she was living and I think it's our best shot at finding clues as to where she went and who she's with."

Dianna scooted halfway off the bed. "I'll pack up my things so we can get going right away."

Sam shot toward her and put his hands on her shoulders, immediately getting aroused by her nearness, her scent.

"Stay right there."

Jesus, he thought as he took his hands away, if he'd gotten that hard with her sweater as a barrier between his hand and her skin, what would happen to his self-control if he accidentally touched a bare patch?

"I've got a friend on the Rocky Mountain hotshot

crew who knows these mountains like the back of his hand," he said, working like hell to get back on task. "It's possible he'll know the locations of any communes in the more remote areas like the one April described to you."

The unabashed hope in Dianna's eyes nearly did him in. Those weeks after her miscarriage, he'd wanted so desperately for her to look at him like that.

She never had.

Already heading to the door, he said, "I want you to rest while I go call my friend Will."

He stepped outside before her green eyes saw too much. Before she could guess how much he still cared.

# CHAPTER EIGHT

AS SOON as Sam closed the door, Dianna lay back against the pillows and closed her eyes. The room was spinning and she felt nauseous.

Knowing her sister was in trouble made her heart race and her skin feel clammy all over. But she wouldn't be able to help April if she lost it. She had to keep it together, had to remember that her sister was a tough little cookie with more street smarts in her pinkie than Dianna had in her whole body.

And then, simmering beneath everything else, there was Sam.

He was the strongest man she knew, just as comfortable climbing a sheer rock face and jumping out of an airplane as he was putting out a raging wildfire.

On top of that, he was breathtakingly beautiful . . . and utterly dangerous.

When he'd read her the riot act about cutting him and everyone else in Lake Tahoe out of her life, she'd wanted to come back at him with all the ways he'd hurt her, wanted to hold a mirror and show him that he'd deserted her first, wanted to remind him that instead of being there for her after her miscarriage, he'd signed up to fight every goddamned wildfire in the western hemisphere.

And yet, she couldn't deny that, right now, he was the very best person to help her find April.

But despite her immense gratitude for his help, Dianna was incredibly wary of working as a team. She'd been in charge of her life for ten years, calling the shots on her own TV show for four. Now, she was about to put herself in a position where she knew nothing, where she had to rely on someone else—a man, no less—for everything.

No. Not for everything. Just to help her find April and bring her home. That was it. Nothing more.

At the end of this journey, she'd shake Sam's hand and thank him sincerely for his help. They would never again be friends—how could they be?—but she would be forever grateful for his willingness to forget about their past and help her find her sister.

As long as he stayed on his side and she stayed on hers, everything would be fine, she thought as exhaustion hit her and she fell into an uneasy sleep on top of the covers.

She woke at the creaking sound of the door opening and looked up to see Sam stepping back inside her room. One look at his tanned skin, his broad shoulders, his flexing biceps as he moved toward her was all it took for her to know she was full-on lying to herself about keeping her distance: She was powerless against Sam's charms.

How long could she possibly hold out?

"I spoke to Will," he said. "Evidently there is one main commune around here that is commonly referred to as the Farm by its residents. Given its proximity to Vail, he's pretty sure it's the same one April's been living in."

When he didn't say anything else, didn't tell her if it was a "good" or "bad" commune, her heart rate sped up. Just like always, he was afraid she couldn't handle the truth and was keeping the full details from her.

No way. She was a big girl now. Whether or not she could handle the truth was beside the point. She had to not only handle it, she had to face it head-on. For April.

"There's more you're not telling me, isn't there?"

A muscle jumped in his jaw. "Will's heard rumors."

"What kind of rumors?"

"The Feds have been trying to shut it down for years, sure that they're hiding something. Evidently, the Farm looks clean from the outside, like nothing more than a group of green advocates wanting to live off the land."

"Maybe it is clean," she found herself saying out of desperation, even though she was suddenly sure that her fears for April's safety were completely justified. "Maybe they aren't doing anything worse than growing medical marijuana. Maybe they're all just looking for a simpler life?"

"Maybe. But word is the owner of the Farm hasn't been off the mountain in more than a decade. He's built his own little world up there. Doesn't need any part of civilization. Makes you wonder why. Especially since most communes aren't growing pot anymore." His expression was as serious as she'd ever seen it. "Methamphetamine is king, Dianna, and the drug makes people crazy, obliterates their brain cells. Don't forget what happened in Jonestown," he said, referencing shootings, poisonings, and mass suicides at the intentional community in Guyana led by California cult leader Jim Jones in the '80s.

*Oh no,* she thought, no longer able to wallow in denial, *what have you gotten yourself into, April?*

"There is a primitive dirt road that heads toward the commune, but it's totally impassable right now due to some trees that went down during late spring storms."

With every word he said, she could feel herself sinking deeper and deeper into despair. "But we've got to get there, Sam."

"My friend will drive us as far up the road as he can get."

His eyes moved from her face to her arms, then her

legs. He was clearly trying to assess her in some way. But how?

"I've spent a lot of time in these mountains, both as a hotshot and for pleasure. Everything within a fifty-mile radius of Vail is rugged mountains," he informed her. "Fast-running rivers, steep rock faces, vertical hikes over boulders. It looks like the fastest way to the commune will be by river and then up through the mountains on foot."

For the first time, Dianna wished she was less well versed in designers, and more in bagging high peaks. The only research she'd done on mountaineering had been when the star of *Man vs. Wild* had been a guest on her show, but even then she'd known that her viewers had been more interested in his smoldering looks and sexy British accent than his outdoor skills.

She figured she could easily handle camping and rafting. Water and dirt weren't her problems.

Heights, however, were.

*April. Think of April.*

She didn't have time for the butterflies in her stomach. She hadn't gotten to where she was by allowing herself to be weak or to ever give in to her fears. She wouldn't start now, when it mattered most.

"I can handle it, Sam. I work out at the gym with a trainer and I've taken some self-defense classes for a segment we did a couple of months ago, even though I haven't spent much time outdoors. Not since—" She made herself finish her sentence. "Not since I moved to San Francisco."

He looked into her eyes for several uncomfortable moments. "I can find your sister alone, Dianna."

Wasn't he the one who'd told her that he admired her for never running from a challenge? Regardless of the possible danger, she wasn't going to back down. No matter how hard the going got.

"No way," she said as evenly as she could, given how fast her heart was racing and how irritated she continued to be with his heavy-handedness. "I'm not going to sit here and wait for you to bring her back."

"It's not going to be easy," he warned her again.

"Nothing ever is."

His mouth tightened. Clearly, he wasn't happy with her choice. Well, too bad.

Moving back toward the door, he said, "We've got to be prepared with tents. Whitewater equipment. Climbing ropes. I'm going to head out into town to pick up some gear before the stores close for the night. I want you to stay put while I'm gone."

She didn't have time to respond to his latest order before he was gone, knowing she had no other choice but to rely on his judgment and decisions for the time being. But as soon as she got her bearings back, she was going to let him know that she was subservient to no man.

Her head was still throbbing, so she downed a couple of Tylenol before packing up the clothes and toiletries she wouldn't need in the Rockies to send home with

Ellen. It didn't take a wilderness pro to see that pretty much everything in her suitcase except her underwear would be useless on their trek to the commune.

Throwing her lingerie into a pile on top of the bed, she called her friend to quickly explain the situation. Ellen rushed into her room from the cafeteria a few minutes later.

"Are you crazy? You can't go into the wilderness to find April!"

But Dianna's mind was made up. "I'll be safe with Sam," she told her friend, even though, in truth, the exact opposite was true.

Although she knew with absolute certainty that he would keep her safe from the elements, she also knew that it would be nearly impossible to keep clear of the dangerous temptation he presented. Especially when his touch made her skin tingle and her brain forget why locking lips with him had been—and still would be—such a terrible idea.

"I promise to check in with you as soon as I can." To forestall any further discussion, she said, "Thanks for taking my bag back home with you."

"I really don't like the sound of this," Ellen said again.

Dianna silently agreed as she gave her friend one last hug good-bye. The entire situation was a powder keg ready to blow up at any second.

Sam came back to the hospital with two large backpacks full of gear. He'd had to push past the same wall of reporters on his way in and he was more irritated by them than he had any right to be. They were simply doing their job, even if he hated the way they were all trying to get a piece of Dianna.

She'd been all his once. Now she was a public commodity. And he was as much a stranger to her as any one of the reporters outside.

To make matters worse, he couldn't get away from the look on her face when he'd asked her why she'd left.

*"You honestly don't know?"*

Damn it, no, he didn't. But now that she was tied up in knots over April's disappearance, there was no way he could push her on it.

He never should have asked her for an explanation in the first place. Not when it only gave away exactly how much he'd once cared about her. Not when neither of them needed another reminder of how hot their passion had been and that they'd had a bond that went beyond the physical.

She was moving restlessly around the room when he walked back in. He got a full twenty seconds to appreciate her curves before she noticed him.

"Oh, you're back!" she exclaimed, her hand moving over her heart. Her cheeks were flushed and she looked kissable. Utterly irresistible.

Wanting to keep something in front of the raging

hard-on he was sporting, he dumped the contents of the backpacks on the bed.

"Climbing gear, sleeping bags, life jackets, lightweight shirts, pants, socks, waterproof boots."

"I didn't realize we'd need so much stuff."

Still trying to push lust away, he went into teach-a-rookie-the-ropes mode.

"As far as I'm concerned, hightailing it through the Rockies is going to be no different than going in to fight a wildfire. I make sure my guys respect the power of the flames before they head out to beat the crap out of them. I want to make sure you have a healthy respect for nature's power, too."

Her eyes grew big as she took in the amount of equipment. He hadn't meant to overwhelm her, hadn't meant to make it all sound so frightening. But before he could take a step back and gently explain what everything was, he saw the pile of sexy lingerie sitting in the middle of the bed.

A cold sweat broke out across his forehead. Even at eighteen, when Dianna hadn't been the least bit into fashion, he'd been amazed by how sexy her undergarments were. All that lace and silk had driven him crazy.

Just thinking of Dianna wearing the red panties made his blood run hot enough to start a fire. Way too close to the edge already, Sam simply couldn't stop from wondering what she was wearing right that very second beneath her sweater and jeans.

How the hell could he keep it all business, all the time

when all he wanted to do was pull Dianna into his arms and taste her sweetness? He shoved a life vest back into the backpack so hard that the shiny fabric nearly popped beneath the force of his fingers.

"Will's going to meet us in back of the hospital at five thirty a.m. tomorrow." His voice was husky with repressed need so he cleared his throat before continuing. "Do you feel well enough to check out right now?"

"I'm fine."

"Good," he said, even though he wasn't sure he believed her.

If he saw anything that made him question her health—dizziness, slurred speech, grimacing—he'd go after April on his own.

He hoisted both packs onto his shoulders. "I saw a motel next door—figured we'd try there first."

As if he'd be able to sleep with her only a wall away. Maybe they could get rooms on opposite sides of the building. Maybe then he wouldn't feel like a chunk of metal being drawn against his will to her sexy-as-hell magnet.

"I scoped out a back exit so we can avoid reporters. I'm assuming you don't want them to know about April, right?"

She shook her head and sighed. "I can't believe I forgot about the press. Do you really think we can get out of here without them noticing?"

"Here," he said, slipping one of the backpacks on her shoulders.

She stumbled beneath the weight for a split second before finding her balance. He pulled out one of the hats he'd bought and shoved it on her head.

"They won't think to take a second look at a hiker."

He didn't want her to know the truth, that anyone who looked closely would be able to see her poise and grace beneath the backpack and goofy-looking hat.

She gave him a weak smile. "If it works, I'll have to try this disguise again."

Jesus, he actually felt like his heart skipped a beat as he looked at her smiling at him.

A few minutes later, after they'd seamlessly made their getaway and were heading into the motel's lobby, she said, "I'd better wait outside until you have the key."

He nodded, knowing if anyone at the motel got wind of their high-profile guest, it wouldn't be long before they put in a call to the reporters.

A TV was on as he headed to the front desk, a clip of Dianna interviewing a pop star playing. Momentarily mesmerized, Sam stopped and watched it.

He couldn't help but be impressed by how good she was at her job. She made talking to a twenty-year-old with whom she had nothing in common look effortless. He'd hung out with enough kids that age to know how difficult it could be to find any common ground whatsoever.

Pulling out a credit card, he got them each a room, knowing it wasn't exactly what they'd prefer, but deciding to take what they could get at this point.

He didn't beat around the bush when he emerged from the lobby. "They only had one room left."

Her eyes widened in alarm. "You've got to be kidding me."

"I want you to stay here, just in case there are more reporters roaming around town. Don't worry, I'll find another place to sleep."

"No, that doesn't make sense." She took a deep breath. "I can handle sharing a room if you can."

Well, shit, he couldn't exactly admit that he couldn't control himself around her, could he?

"No problem," he lied, even though he couldn't think of a much bigger problem at present.

He hadn't come here looking for trouble. But he seemed to have found it at every turn.

The motel room was extremely basic with only a bed, a dresser, a TV, and a small sofa. It struck him that Dianna looked like a mouse caught in a small cage, looking for anywhere to escape.

Clearly, he wasn't the only one having a hard time with their little reunion. He got more satisfaction from that than he should have.

His stomach growled and when hers quickly followed suit he said, "I'm going to call for a pizza."

"No thanks. I'm not hungry."

He frowned. She'd always been up for a meal, any time of day or night. It had been one of the things he liked about her, that she was a pretty girl who ate like a normal person, rather than starving herself to fit into a pair of jeans. Had that changed, too?

"Guess you've got to stick to salad to fit into all those fancy clothes, huh?"

Her mouth tightened. "I'm not on a diet. I'm just not in a very hungry mood right now."

Shit, he was acting like an insensitive jerk again. It was just that being with her again pushed all of his buttons. Buttons he hadn't even realized were there until today.

In lieu of an apology he said, "I know you may not feel like eating right now, not after what you've just found out, but you're not going to do April any good if you're starving."

Shrugging as if she didn't care either way, she said, "You're right. Order pizza."

He said, "Everything on it," at the same time she did and their eyes locked together in an electric moment of remembered awareness.

All the signs of arousal were there—the way her skin flushed, the rapid pulse in her neck, the speeding up of her inhalations. He could have her horizontal and naked on the bed in sixty seconds.

It took every bit of self-control he possessed to force himself to turn away, pick up the phone, and order the pizza.

After hanging up, he paused to wipe all the desire off his face. When he turned around to face her, she was standing in the same place, her eyes still on him.

"Thank you for helping me," she said in a soft voice. "I know things are kind of weird and—"

He held up a hand. She was about to take them straight into the danger zone. He couldn't let her do it.

There was only one way to diffuse the bomb of their relentless attraction: clear ground rules.

"Let's concentrate on finding your sister and bringing her home safely. And because we're going to need to work together and trust each other, I've decided that the best thing we can do is keep the past in the past."

# CHAPTER NINE

DIANNA REELED in disbelief. Had he really just issued her an order? *Here's how we're gonna do it, babe. No questions. No answers. Just suck it up and get with the program.*

But after she'd had a few seconds to digest it, she realized it was less what he said than how he said it that really got to her.

She hated his cold, emotionless voice.

"On the contrary," she finally replied in a steely voice that not only matched, but raised the frigidity another level. "I don't think there's any point in having a big white elephant in the room with us the whole time."

In her experience managing a sometimes-conflicted

staff for a live TV show that couldn't afford any screw-ups, she never allowed grudges to linger between team members. Between her and Sam, however, she might have been tempted to take the high road and let sleeping dogs lie.

That is, if he hadn't acted like such a bull in her china shop.

Crossing her arms over her chest, she said, "Because we're stuck together in this motel room for tonight, I think we should lay everything out on the table and be done with it already."

Maybe, she suddenly thought, if she got her grievances off her chest, she'd be able to get him out of her system once and for all.

Before she could think better of what she was doing, she continued with, "In the hospital you asked me why I left. Well, I'm ready to tell you my reasons, Sam. Because frankly, I'm sick and tired of carrying them around with me all the time."

"Forget I asked," he said. "It doesn't matter. We should be focusing on April right now."

No way, she wasn't letting him backpedal to try to shut her down.

"Of course I'm upset about April," she said as calmly as she could. "Of course I'm freaking out about what could be happening to her, but if we don't find some common ground, we're going to have a very hard time working as a team."

But he was still shaking his head, his expression completely closed. "I don't want to fight with you, Dianna."

"Don't you see, Sam?" she asked, exasperation breaking through again. "That's part of the problem. You never wanted to fight. You never wanted to have any kind of conflict between us. I know your parents had a shitty relationship, I know they never stopped fighting, but that doesn't mean people can't disagree with each other sometimes."

"Stop right now, Dianna," he said, each word a warning, "and we can still do this. We can still go forward and find April."

But the train she was on was moving too fast for her to just hop off. Even though she was heading straight for a brick wall.

"You haven't changed a bit, have you?" she said, any pretense of calm now blown to smithereens. "You always thought you knew what was best for both of us."

"I wouldn't make accusations you can't back up," he said in a hard voice.

She took a step closer, too swept up in her fury to remember to keep her distance from all of his mouthwateringly hard heat.

"Oh, you want backup? Let's see, how about the first time we had sex and you didn't bother to tell me that the condom broke? Or what about when you'd come back from a fire where people had lost their homes, or even their lives, and I'd ask, 'How are you?' all you'd ever say was, 'I'm okay.' And when I pushed you on it, when I said there was no way anyone could be okay with the things you'd seen, you wouldn't tell me a damn thing about how you were feeling. All I wanted was to be a part of your life, Sam. For you to let me in. But you refused to give me anything, to open up at all."

Somewhere in the back of her mind she knew that there was no way Sam—or anyone else, for that matter—could possibly respond to her laundry list of grievances. And yet, when he didn't even try to defend himself, she couldn't stop herself from taking it a step further.

"Honestly, I could have forgiven you for all of that. In fact, I *did* forgive you. Until you went and broke my heart completely."

His jaw jumped and the sinews on his crossed forearms were taut.

"No need to keep me in suspense any longer, Dianna. I'm a big boy. I can take the blame, so feel free to dish it out."

Oh God, she hadn't felt this close to breaking down, to completely falling apart in years. Not since that night she'd left Lake Tahoe.

"After I miscarried, I knew I'd spent too long crying, too long feeling sorry for myself," she admitted. "So one night I got out of bed, took a shower, actually put on clothes instead of my nightgown."

She closed her eyes and the details came back to her, one after the other as if it had all happened a week ago, instead of a decade ago. She remembered taking the time to shave her legs and blow-dry her hair, even putting on makeup when she noticed how pale she was, how much weight she'd lost. She was planning to go for a walk or to the grocery store. Something, anything, to get out of the apartment and try to start living again.

"You'd been gone on that Reno fire for three weeks and I missed you so much. None of my friends from school understood how hard it was to lose a baby and I knew my mother would probably be too drunk to even know what I was telling her. Or maybe she'd tell me I was lucky to have narrowly escaped becoming a mother."

She opened her eyes and forced herself to look at him, even though she didn't know what she'd see on his face.

"I was so lonely, Sam. All I wanted was for you to come back home and hold me. So when I saw on the news that the fire you'd been fighting was out, I was so happy. I couldn't wait to see you and tell you I was ready to make a fresh start."

At the time, she'd thought there'd be other babies, a whole crew of boys with his naughty grin, girls with his dark, silky hair. How stupid she'd been. How pathetically hopeful. Pitifully naive.

"But you weren't at the station, and when I asked

Bev where you were, she was beyond embarrassed to have to tell me that you'd gotten back from the fire hours ago."

She'd hated knowing how sorry the hotshot station administrator had felt for her. Even though Dianna knew there were no secrets on a hotshot crew, it didn't make it any easier for everyone to know your business. Especially when her business had been falling apart.

"It wasn't hard to find you guys. You were at—"

"The Bar & Grill," he said, finishing her sentence in a gruff voice.

She nodded. "I walked into the bar and it was like another world in there. Laughter. Pool sticks hitting balls. Pinball machines beeping." Her voice cracked. "That was when I saw you, sitting at the bar. I could see you smiling, flirting with the bartender."

"I wasn't flirting, Dianna."

She felt her mouth open in amazement. Was he kidding? Did he think she had amnesia? He hadn't been home for weeks. And when he was free to come home, he'd chosen to stay away.

"Maybe you weren't," she forced herself to concede, "but I couldn't remember the last time you'd smiled at me like that or leaned in close to me and laughed at something I'd said."

She angrily wiped away with her knuckles the sudden tears that were blurring her vision.

"You were the first man I ever trusted. When you said 'I love you,' I didn't think you were saying it just to get me into bed."

"Goddammit, Dianna, you know that's not why I said it."

But she wasn't done yet, wasn't ready to listen to any of his excuses. "You said you weren't marrying me because I was pregnant. You promised you'd be there for me forever. You'd convinced me that I was important to you. That's what made it hurt even more."

All her life she'd vowed not to let her hopes and dreams get wrapped up in a man. From that moment forward, after leaving the bar, throwing her clothes into the backseat of her car, and driving away from their apartment for the very last time, she hadn't ever again made the mistake of trusting another man with her heart.

"You let me down, Sam." She held his gaze. "That's why I left."


A knock sounded at the door and it took Sam several seconds to figure out where it was coming from when all he could hear were Dianna's words spinning around and around inside his head.

The sound came again, accompanied by a voice this time.

"Pizza delivery. Do I have the right room?"

Feeling as if he were sleepwalking, he made his way to the door, gave the kid some money, and took the pizza.

Dropping the steaming box on the scratched-up dresser, he knew he needed to get a grip before he turned around and blasted back at her. But even though some of the things she'd said made sense, even though it didn't take a genius to see that he hadn't exactly behaved like a hero when he was a clueless twenty-year-old kid, he wasn't ready to concede a damn thing.

Not when she thought he'd only wanted to marry her because she was pregnant.

Not when she'd accused him of "doing the right thing," instead of truly loving her.

If she couldn't see that he loved her with everything he had back then, he sure as hell wasn't going to waste his time convincing her now.

"Do you have any idea what it was like to come home to an empty apartment?"

He'd never been able to erase the picture of her thin gold engagement ring lying on the Formica kitchen counter.

She didn't say anything, just clasped her hands tightly in front of her chest like a shield over her heart.

"You didn't even leave me a note. You just packed up your things and left. It was like being kicked straight in the gut."

He'd never believed in love. Not after watching his parents tear each other to shreds his whole life. But he'd believed in her. Until she'd betrayed him by walking out of his life without a word.

"You let me down too, Dianna. So I guess that means we're even."

The words were barely out of his mouth when he noticed her shoulders rounding as if the fight had gone out of her. In the dim light of the lone lamp by the bed, her eyes looked haunted, with dark circles beneath them.

She sat down on the edge of the bed, her eyelids at half-mast, and he felt like the world's biggest bastard for temporarily forgetting what she'd been through in the past twenty-four hours.

First the crash. Then her sister's Mayday call. Now him railing at her for something that happened long enough ago that he should have been over it already.

"You're tired," he said, abruptly changing the subject.

It would be better for both of them if he got out of the small motel room. No question that he needed to walk away, regroup.

"Eat some pizza and get some sleep. You're going to need the food and rest for our adventure tomorrow. I'll be back in a bit."

She didn't say anything as he walked out of the room, didn't call his name or ask him to stay. Why the hell would she, he asked himself as he made the short walk down the street to the closest bar.

The grizzly bartender slid him a pint of Guinness and he chugged half before he set the glass back down. Midway through his second pint, after her claims had time to settle, he suddenly found that he couldn't refute them. All these years he'd been so busy blaming her for leaving. But now he saw that he'd taken the easy way out. He hadn't wanted to take a frank look in the mirror and ask himself what he'd done wrong or how he'd fucked things up.

In that instant, he realized why he'd lost it after she left: Way down deep in his subconscious, he'd known that he'd driven her away.

Staring bleakly at the dried condensation rings on the bar top, he realized that although he'd defined his entire life by saving people, in the end, he was helpless with the people he cared for the most. Dianna and her miscarriage. Connor and his burns.

He hadn't meant to leave her to cope all by herself. Those first couple weeks after the miscarriage, he'd tried to be there for her, but it was so hard to know what to say, to know what not to say. Most of all, he didn't want to talk about anything that would make her cry any more than she already was. When she finally told him to go back to work, it was such a relief to stop feeling like the clumsy giant tiptoeing around the apartment that he'd grabbed the chance with both hands.

Stupid kid that he was, he'd thought that maybe after both of them had some space to come to grips with what had happened, things would return to how they were before the baby. He'd wanted everything to go back to normal, for the hardest choice to be what kind of pizza to order. At twenty, it had just been easier to go fight fires. To tell himself he was needed on the mountain.

Leaving his unfinished beer on the counter, he headed for the door.

He'd bailed on Dianna once. He wouldn't bail on her again, even though sticking around was by far the hardest thing to do.

# CHAPTER TEN

DIANNA TOSSED and turned in the hard, lumpy motel bed. Not only was she terribly worried about April, but she felt horrible about the way she'd behaved with Sam.

After he'd left the motel, she'd barely had the strength left to strip out of her clothes and crawl beneath the covers. She didn't remember anything after that, not until two a.m., when she woke up. She was disoriented at first, having slept in two strange beds during the past twenty-four hours.

But quickly, she realized she wasn't alone.

Sam was only a couple of feet away, which meant she'd never be able to get back to sleep, not when she could hear him shift on the sofa and breathe in his delicious scent.

He aroused her senses like no other man ever had.

As anxious as she was about April, it was still hell on her system being so close to him, knowing that if she wanted to, she could crawl out of bed and wrap her arms around his neck, curl up on his lap, and bury her face against his chest.

And that was just the problem: She wanted to. Badly. Even when they'd been fighting only hours before, he was still the one she wanted to run to for comfort.

And for pleasure.

She'd never been able to resist him, not for one single second. She'd moved to San Francisco because if she'd stayed in Lake Tahoe, she would have inevitably returned to him, despite how empty, how broken their relationship had become.

Again and again while he breathed evenly beside her, Dianna considered waking him up and apologizing for the things she'd said after leaving the hospital. It wasn't that she didn't mean them, but lying awake in the dark with nothing to do but think, she realized she could have approached the confrontation differently. She hated knowing she hadn't given him so much as an inch of space to respond to her grievances.

She'd been on the attack. Intent on full-on, outright damage.

And yet, amazingly, he'd come back to their room. After the way she'd ripped him to shreds, he hadn't left her to search for April alone. Or taken off altogether.

If she hadn't been able to push him away last night, then was there a chance that nothing she said or did was going to make him run? Did the fact that he was sleeping in the cramped sofa mean he'd changed?

Propping herself up in bed with the pillows, she watched him sleep soundly, his inhalations seemingly peaceful and even. All hotshots were trained to catch rest wherever they could, and it suddenly occurred to her that she didn't know if he'd come straight from a fire to the hospital or even how long it had been since he'd been to bed.

Quite possibly, she realized as her stomach twisted into a tight knot, he hadn't been alone in that bed.

He didn't wear a ring, but that didn't mean he wasn't dating someone. It didn't mean he wasn't getting ready to pop the question to some small, cute brunette who worshipped his every move and made him feel like a million bucks.

She hated to think of anyone else touching him. Kissing him.

Sam was a magical lover, paying special attention to every inch of a woman's body, the curves and peaks, the hollows and sensitive spots. He was a woman's ultimate dream come to life. Six foot two, tanned and hard all over, with blue eyes that grew lighter or darker with the sun or clouds, with the time of day, with what he was feeling. Women wanted big, strong hands like his on their bodies, wanted to run their fingers through his dark, silky hair.

Her breath came faster as she remembered their lovemaking in full detail, warmth creeping up her body, between her legs, to the tips of her breasts.

It would be so easy to fall back into bed with him. Way too easy. But they would both only end up getting hurt again.

And yet, even as she remembered how difficult it had been to get over him, she was touched by his willingness to help her now. She hadn't even had to ask him for help. He'd simply offered it. Even though finding April was potentially dangerous, he hadn't backed off, hadn't rescinded his offer.

She didn't know what to think about Sam sticking with her. Was it simply that he was a hero through and through? Or had he stepped in because *she* needed him?

These questions ran on repeat through her brain again and again until sleep finally started to settle around her like a blanket.

It was pitch-black outside the thin motel curtains when he woke her up. "Will's waiting for us. We'll leave in fifteen minutes."

She rolled off the bed, took her small medicine bag into the bathroom, brushed her teeth, and applied the tiniest bit of makeup. Sam had always taken his good looks for granted, whereas she'd had to uncover hers and cultivate her appearance so that people would treat her in a way that came naturally to the gorgeous firefighter.

She'd sensed his disapproval at her transformation

when he'd walked into her hospital room and saw her in cashmere with diamond studs in her ears. She wasn't going to apologize to him for who she'd become. She'd built a good life for herself and April through plenty of hard work. No one had handed anything to her on a silver platter.

Nonetheless, she enjoyed the rare chance to wear minimal makeup. Although she hadn't let anyone in public see her without her game face on for a decade, she much preferred bare skin. It was how she'd grown up and she felt younger, softer somehow.

Ten minutes later she emerged dressed in her new clothes, a lightweight long-sleeve shirt, khaki cargo pants, and shiny brown leather boots that squeaked a little as she walked. The only purchases she'd left in the plastic bag were the sports bra and cotton panties. She'd never been a cotton girl and she was wearing her regular silk and lace undergarments.

Sam's eyes widened when he saw her, and she pushed back her shoulders and lifted her chin. She'd thought the outfit was pretty cute, but she'd been wearing different versions of the same thing for so long, it felt strange to put on something completely different. Almost as if she'd shed a layer of skin and stepped into a new, unfamiliar one.

"Everything fit okay?"

She would have expected him to have forgotten what size she wore by now, but he'd remembered exactly, all the way down to her size nine boots. A rogue butterfly flew loose in her belly at the thought of their intimate past, and the realization that he hadn't forgotten about her any more than she had him.

"Perfectly," she said, and then, "I haven't thanked you yet for buying everything for me. Thank you."

She was usually the queen of thank-you cards, of hostess gifts. But Sam made her flustered. Awkward.

"I want you to know I'm going to pay you back for everything."

Dianna wasn't comfortable with letting a man buy her things. For the past ten years, she'd always paid her own way—and oftentimes her dates' as well.

"I don't think I have enough cash in my purse, but—"

He grabbed their packs and headed to the door in the middle of her sentence.

"I can cover it," he said, his voice suddenly hard.

Well, that was about as clear as it got. She assumed he was still angry from the night before and she knew she needed to apologize for her mudslinging right away. But he was already halfway across the parking lot and she had to jog to catch up with him.

"Sam, I—" she began when she got her breath back, but when she looked up, his hotshot friend was waiting for them outside the back entrance of the hospital, leaning against the bumper of his truck. There was no way she could explain things in front of his friend, Will.

She wasn't at all surprised by the local firefighter's tall, rugged good looks. Hotshots were a shockingly good-looking bunch who attracted women like bees to nectar. Dianna knew firsthand how difficult—scratch that, impossible—it was to resist a wildland firefighter.

"Nice to meet you, Dianna. Sam tells me you're looking for your sister?"

"Her name's April. And I'm afraid she doesn't have a clue what she's mixed up with."

Will handed a map to Sam as they got into the truck. He held the front seat passenger door open for her and her stupid heart actually went pitter-patter at his chivalry.

"I've highlighted the route I think you should take to the commune," Will said. "Any questions?"

Sam studied the map in the extended cab as they exited the hospital's parking lot. Dianna pulled her hat down tighter over her hair and averted her face as they passed a TV news van.

"Looks pretty clear," Sam told his friend.

"There's no cell coverage anywhere in the area," Will said, looking concerned. "So don't get hurt, okay? Could take a little while to find you if you do."

Dianna shivered at his warning. She'd lived in the city for so long she'd forgotten that there were places cell phones couldn't reach, that you couldn't always call for help the minute you needed it.

They quickly left town and started climbing into the mountains, the pavement turning to gravel, then dirt. Will switched into four-wheel drive as the road became increasingly primitive and rutted. The three of them remained silent as they drove between tall pines and towering redwoods. Thirty minutes later, he stopped the truck in front of a huge tree trunk that was lying across the road.

"I'm afraid this is as far as I can take you."

With Will's engine off, she could hear birds singing, the river gurgling, even the way the breeze was turning the leaves into mild-mannered wind chimes.

Out here, amid mountains and streams, was Sam's world. This was where he belonged, whereas she was utterly out of her element.

Maybe he'd been right and she should have let him go alone?

She squashed the thought as quickly as it came. It was only fear speaking. She'd been afraid before and she'd survived. Thrived, in fact. She'd do any and everything she had to do to find her sister and bring her home.

After saying his good-byes, Will was clearly reluctant to leave them, and as he slowly turned the truck around and headed down the road, Dianna also wished he would stay a little longer.

Anything to avoid being alone again with Sam.

Her mouth went dry as he held out her loaded backpack. Turning her back to him, she slipped her arms through the straps and braced herself for the heavy weight. But instead of pulling her off balance, it was surprisingly light.

She'd seen how much gear there was to carry the

night before, and as he strapped on his own pack, she saw that he was loaded down with most of her things.

"You don't have to take everything for me," she said. "I want to do my fair share."

He barely looked at her. "I'm used to the weight. You're not."

Case clearly closed. No discussion. No room for debate. She knew his word was law out here. The question was, would she ever get used to taking orders from a man? From Sam?

Seconds later, he was disappearing into the woods and she had no other choice but to hurry and catch up with him.

The day wasn't going well so far, Sam thought as he led them down the trail to the river's edge.

He'd woken up with the best of intentions, planning to smooth over the rough edges they'd pulled up the night before. But then she'd gone and insisted that she would pay him back for the hiking gear and his pride had gotten twisted up all over again.

He'd never been intimidated by anyone's money before. He still wasn't. But he couldn't ignore the dichotomy between her salary and his. His parents hadn't been happy about his career choice. They'd wanted him to be a doctor, a lawyer, or an engineer. But he'd never been comfortable with walls around him. Becoming a hotshot had been a perfect fit.

And then, when she'd met Will, it had seriously grated watching her charm the pants off his friend. The eighteen-year-old Dianna he'd known had never been particularly comfortable with male attention. She'd hidden her curves behind baggy shirts and pants. But now, instead of deflecting a guy's admiration, or simply ignoring it, she seemed to bask in its glow.

He'd wanted to think it was all an act, a performance she'd honed over the years to get high ratings, but the truth was, she'd always been charismatic, simply lacking in confidence.

Worse still, his instincts were screaming at him to get Dianna out of here. Away from the mountains, from the river and the trails, from the quick-changing weather, from the bears and cougars lurking in the bushes.

The problem wasn't that she was a woman. He was all for women firefighters. They were easily as tough as the men on the crew, often tougher. Hell, women made it through the agonies of childbirth, then usually went and did it again.

But he couldn't stand the thought of seeing Dianna hurt. Regardless of what had gone down between them, Sam wanted to know that she was safe and sound, back in a TV studio, her only concern how pretty she looked.

He'd spent plenty of time in the Rockies, both fighting wildfires and vacationing during his off-seasons. Fact was, Dianna wasn't trained for swimming through level-five white water back to an overturned raft. When Sam was ten years old, he'd cut his teeth on the class-five rapids on the American River in California. He'd been thrown out of the raft a dozen times that day and had knocked his head into enough rocks to have a healthy respect for the immense power of white water.

In a few minutes he was going to take a complete novice on similar waters in a lightweight inflatable raft that was prone to overturning in heavy water.

Was he out of his fucking mind?

She didn't have the skills to scale a rock face or hike deer trails through thick brambles and dead brush that would rip up her skin. And she'd never been big on heights, he remembered that much.

Shit, who was he kidding? He remembered all of it. Every last thing about her. From the way her nose scrunched up when she laughed to the little sounds she used to make before she exploded beneath him in bed.

Fuck. He couldn't go there. Not with her a few feet behind him, close enough that he could stop, turn, and kiss her before she knew what hit her.

A handful of minutes later, they were standing on the banks of the river. Staring at the swiftly moving water, Dianna didn't look scared, exactly, more concerned. But even in the khaki cargos and hiking boots, she was still a pampered princess who didn't belong within a hundred miles of a fast-moving river or rocky footpath.

Needing to look away from her incredible beauty, he pulled the two-person raft out of his pack and began the hard work of inflating it.

Abruptly, she said, "Last night, when you said we needed to work together to find April, you were right."

Wanting to avoid another blowup, he didn't look up from the raft. "I'm good if you are."

Hoping like hell that she'd take him at his word, he was surprised when she knelt down beside him and put a hand on his arm. Unable to keep from turning his head in her direction, her green eyes sucked him in before he could put up an invisible barricade.

"I owe you an apology for the way I behaved last night. I'm ashamed of my behavior."

Jesus, she sure knew how to turn a guy speechless. Sure, her presentation had sucked in the motel, but even he couldn't deny that she'd spoken the truth.

When he didn't say anything right away, she continued with, "I had some time to think last night after you left. Time to take a hard look at myself in the mirror. Frankly, I'm not proud of what I saw."

She paused, licked her lips nervously. "Those first couple of weeks after the miscarriage, you were great. I didn't give you any credit for that last night and I'm sorry I didn't. It's just that I was so racked with guilt after losing the baby I think it was easier to blame you than to have to look at myself."

Guilt? He wasn't following. "What did you possibly have to feel guilty about?"

"I'd been so scared about having a baby. I felt so unprepared. After the crash I couldn't get away from the voice in my head that told me that I'd caused our baby's death, that I made it happen through sheer force of will."

Her revelation blew him away. "Jesus, Dianna. You weren't responsible for the miscarriage. You were hit by a car. It's crazy to think anything else."

But even as he negated her statement, it occurred to him that he'd felt the same responsibility for not protecting her better. If they'd known how similar their thoughts and reactions were back then, was there a chance they could have held it together as a couple and moved forward?

She laughed but there was no joy in it. "Crazy. That's exactly how I felt. And it was almost a relief when you finally mentioned going back to work. That way I could grieve alone, without having to keep up any kind of appearances for you." Her green eyes were full of remorse. "The truth is that I pushed you away, Sam. You didn't leave on your own."

Totally disarmed, he found that he wanted her to know that she wasn't the only one who'd screwed up the night before and said all the wrong things.

"I owe you an apology, too, Dianna."

"You don't have to, Sam. I'm the one who behaved badly."

"I shouldn't have left you alone in the motel room last night, knowing how upset you were about April."

She made a motion to wave away his concern, but he wasn't nearly done.

"And I had some time to think, too. You're right. I did let you down."

He had hid out in the wildfires. Fighting fire should have been more dangerous than staying home, but strangely, it had been the far safer route.

"I'm not proud of the way I behaved. I'd like to say it was because I was a confused twenty-year-old, or that I was trying to cause you less pain by not talking about the miscarriage, but that's no excuse. I want you to know, if I had it to do over, I hope I would make different choices. Better choices."

She moved toward him, coming close enough that he could pick up the soft, floral scent the breeze blew off her hair.

"You were trying to protect me," she said slowly. "I can't believe I needed you to spell it out. Especially when shielding people from pain is what you do, is what you've always done, whether it's keeping your brother out of your parents' cross fire or saving strangers' lives as a hotshot."

She was gravity and he was falling. But just because they were starting to break down some of the walls between them, he couldn't make the mistake of falling back in love with her. Not when it had fucked him over so royally the first time around.

"It's good we've talked this through," he finally said, "but I think we should get out on the raft and concentrate on the river."

She quickly nodded, her relief evident that their discussion was over. "How far will we go by water?"

He smoothed the map down over a large rock. "We're here," he said, pointing to a spot on the map, "and we need to head here. We'll be on the river for about ten miles."

"And then we'll hike the rest of the way?"

"That's the plan." He left out the rock-climbing part of the equation for the time being.

She looked up into the mountains. "Fun."

That little bit of sarcasm in the face of a difficult task was so much like the girl he'd known that as he headed back over to the raft and got to work inflating it, it took everything he had to keep his focus on finding April, rather than all the reasons there were to fall back in love with her beautiful sister.

# CHAPTER ELEVEN

SAM HANDED her a life jacket and helmet, donned his, then picked up the front of the raft and pulled it onto the bank of the river. Dianna's mouth was dry and she had the beginnings of a headache, so she drank some water from a bottle clipped to the waistband of her pants.

Living in Lake Tahoe she'd watched enough tourists suffer from altitude sickness to know the signs. She could feel her heart working harder just standing still, so she drank more water before carefully stepping into the raft. The last thing she needed was to be laid low by a migraine or nausea. After a decade of living at sea level, Dianna knew the risks of being at 8,000 feet again.

When she was a kid and needed to escape—if her mother was on a bender or a really gross guy had moved in to the trailer and they were doing it all the time—

Dianna would go out to the woods, hike to a mountain lake, swim in the frigid water, and pretend she was someone else, usually a normal girl with perfect parents and brothers and sisters she could play with.

Now that she was about to paddle down a dangerous river on a quest to rescue her kidnapped sister, those childhood dreams felt like they belonged to someone else.

"Getting your balance is the hardest thing," Sam said as he eased them into the water with his paddle. "Once you figure that out, you'll be fine."

His matter-of-fact tone was soothing, almost as if what he was really saying was, *"Don't worry. Everything's going to be all right."*

After torturing herself all night over what a bitch she'd been, it was a huge relief to know that he wasn't holding a grudge against her. Even better, she felt as if they'd made some headway.

Was it too much to hope that they'd cleared away the worst of the tension that had been crackling between them? All she wanted was some breathing room to push forward together to find April.

At the same time, as she watched the muscles of his arms and legs flex next to her on the raft and rivulets of water ran down his chiseled jaw, she had to face facts: Yes, they'd overcome their anger, but the sexual tension hadn't disappeared.

If anything, the new understanding she had for what he'd done only made her want him more, damn it.

Turning her focus back to the river, working hard to stay upright on the edge of the raft, her thighs immediately started to burn from the strain, and her shoulders and neck stiffened until they were rigid.

She wished she'd gotten more sleep the night before, but her dreams had been so dark and intense, it had almost been a relief when Sam woke her up. She'd had similar dreams in the first few weeks after losing the baby where she felt as if she were trying to reach the light at the end of the tunnel against the force of the quicksand pulling her deeper.

Sam's warm voice broke into her thoughts. "Try to keep your limbs loose and your grip on the paddle relaxed."

He was a good teacher, knew exactly how to tell her she was doing it all wrong without getting her back up. How could she have forgotten that about him, that he was so strong and yet so gentle at the same time? Instead of making her feel like a fish out of water, rather than highlighting the fact that she was the queen of TV instead of outdoor wonder girl, he saw how hard she was trying and was being incredibly supportive.

So even though her brain was telling her not to loosen her grip on the paddle or she'd die, she followed his directions to relax and quickly found that he was right on the money. As soon as she stopped trying to control the water, she expended a great deal less energy.

"You've got it," he said encouragingly.

His patience meant a great deal to her. Not only did

she want to prove to herself that she had what it took to ride the rapids, but foolishly she wanted to impress Sam, too.

Unfortunately, just as she was starting to feel at ease, the water turned white and frothy. They bumped and banged over the water and it splashed into her face again and again, quickly soaking her from head to toe.

She guessed she looked like a drowned rat, with freezing cold water streaming off her nose and chin. And it bothered her, even though only Sam could see her—and he'd seen her look much worse.

"Our first drop is coming, about a hundred yards ahead. You ready for it?"

"You bet," she fibbed, wondering what the heck a "drop" was, but knowing that saying no wasn't an option.

The water started churning faster, harder, and it took every ounce of her concentration just to stay seated on the raft.

"You're doing good, Dianna. Keep paddling, just like that."

And then, suddenly, they hit a wall of white water and she felt like they were in an elevator whose lines had been cut, falling down, then hitting bottom so hard, she choked on her own saliva and nearly bit her tongue.

Dianna did everything she could to stay on the raft, but the water was tougher than she was, and the next thing she knew she was flipping over the edge of the raft. Holding her breath, she tried not to panic as she bobbed up toward the surface, the strong rapids continuing to push her downstream, over the rocks that were scratching up her legs and arms something fierce.

When she was finally able to come up for air, she saw Sam leaning over the edge of the raft, reaching for her hands.

"You okay?" he asked, his expression clearly concerned as he gripped her upper arms with both hands and pulled her into the middle of the raft.

Concentrating on getting back into the raft, she kept her gaze averted so he couldn't see how clumsy and stupid she felt.

Trying to make light of the situation, she said, "You didn't say anything about a drop being a waterfall." Her upper arms tingled from where he'd wrapped his big hands around them.

"I didn't think you knowing that's what a drop actually meant would help any," he said, his light words softening all the places she'd been trying to keep cold and hard.

"Besides," he continued, "it's always good to get your first flip of the day over right off the bat. Makes it easier to stay on board for the really big ones."

*There were bigger drops ahead?*

She pushed the hair dangling in her eyes back up under her helmet. No amount of hair spray could save her now. If her staff could see her now they'd die.

But ultimately, she knew her looks didn't matter. Neither did the fact that Sam was an even bigger puzzle than he had been ten years ago. All that mattered was finding April and bringing her home.

The sun rose higher in the sky as they paddled down-river, worries about April closing in on her again, heavy and bleak like her dreams from the night before.

Where was she? Was anyone hurting her? And would her baby sister even be okay when they finally found her?

It struck her, yet again, how lost she'd be without Sam's support. And it scared her to know how much she was depending on him.

Just like she had so many years before.

Sam wasn't sure he liked what was happening. It was too easy to admire how well Dianna was doing on the river, especially given that she was instinctively better at raft-ing than most of the guys he went rafting with during his off months.

And it was too damn difficult not to notice how beautiful she was.

Even with a life jacket covering her curves and a hel-met over her plastered-down hair, he was mesmerized by the slight bounce of her breasts, and her tongue com-ing out to lick a drop of water off her lips.

Forcing his gaze back up to her face, it was unsettling to read a whole host of worries in her expression.

At first, her face had been a picture of concentration and he'd been glad that the river was giving her a reason to think about something other than April for at least a few minutes. But now, it wasn't hard to guess that she was running through worst-case scenarios.

He sympathized. If they were looking for Connor, he would have been a wreck, too. But doing search and rescue had taught him that once you gave up hope, you were screwed. He couldn't allow fear to paralyze her, especially not when paddling through the white water should be taking every ounce of her attention.

It was time for a break and some food. Maybe even a pep talk, if he could figure out how to pull that off when he was still wading through a thick, unending bog of desire and deteriorating self-control.

He steered them over to a small beach in the curve of the cliffs.

"Why are we stopping?" Dianna asked.

"Food. We're quickly burning through our reserves and we need to keep our energy high."

She opened her mouth, probably to argue with him, and he cut her off at the pass with, "And you need to give your body a rest. Rafting is hard enough, but doing it after an accident like yours is borderline crazy."

He'd noticed that she was favoring her left shoulder. Paddling was tough work. Just one day after her crash she had to be stiff and sore all over.

Given their wet clothes and the brisk breeze whipping down the shady river, Sam decided to pull out a camp stove and some bags of dehydrated food to help warm them up before they got back on, and likely flipped back into, the ice-cold river.

"When did you learn to cook?" she asked him as he put their meal together.

"I wish I had," he lamented. "I promise you, this is going to taste terrible."

It was good to see a small smile on her face as she teased him, "I don't know. A part of me can see you throwing knives around in a kitchen. It'd be kind of hot, actually."

Her cheeks flamed as she realized what she'd said. For Sam, instead of the blood rushing to his face, it went straight to his groin.

He gripped the metal spoon he was stirring so hard it nearly snapped in two. "It's windy out and I don't want you to end up with hypothermia. Go change into dry clothes."

His gruff tone did nothing to hide his desire.

*So much for giving her a pep talk.* More like he was going to throw her down on the sand and take her like an animal if he didn't get a grip.

Dianna moved away quickly, clearly more than happy to get away from him. A few minutes later, after changing behind a couple of trees and laying her wet pants and shirt out over some flat rocks on the sand, he handed her a steaming stainless steel bowl.

"It's rice and chicken."

She looked at the gray clumps in the bowl. "Really?"

"That's what it says on the packet."

She took a bite and grimaced. "Um, wow. I'm not sure it's legal for them to make a claim like rice and chicken."

He bit back laughter. After the fancy white-tablecloth lunches she was probably used to, he was impressed when she continued spooning the nasty mess into her mouth.

"Most people get about halfway through camp food and turn green."

After swallowing another gritty, lumpy bite, she softly said, "I'll eat whatever I have to eat if it means finding April."

Just as he'd suspected, her fears for April were consuming her. Okay, then, he'd try another tack.

"You're doing good on the river. Really good."

"How can you say that when I almost got us both killed back there?"

"The river almost killed us. Big difference."

Their eyes met and he felt like he'd stepped on a downed electric line. His fingers ached to wrap themselves around her curves. His lips burned with the need to taste her mouth. And he was huge and throbbing beneath his zipper.

Trying one last time to keep her mind off of April—while hopefully staying on safer ground—he said, "Tell me about your job. Do you like it?"

At her bemused expression, he suddenly felt like he was thirteen and trying to talk to a pretty girl for the first time. But he couldn't tell her that he was trying to divert her attention from her worries. He'd never succeed if she knew his goal.

"Sure," she said. "It's great."

Clearly, she was the one used to asking questions, rather than answering them. Trying to draw her out, he asked, "How'd you get started?"

Looking even more confused, she said, "Seriously, you want to know?"

He shrugged, tried to act like it was perfectly natural for him to be asking her these questions. Truthfully, now that he'd started down this road, he wanted to know her reasons for picking TV.

"A lot can change in ten years," he replied.

Everything except how much he wanted her . . . and how fucking pointless those feelings were given the way things had turned out the first time around.

"I really want to know."

Specifically, was she dating—or sleeping with—anyone, even though it was none of his damn business.

"Okay," she said slowly. "I got a job working behind the scenes on another show that Ellen was producing and eventually they offered me my own show."

She made it sound so simple, but he guessed she'd worked her butt off to get where she was. People didn't come by the kind of rocks she had in her ears and those soft fancy sweaters she'd been wearing in the hospital without putting in the sweat equity.

Besides, he'd always known how smart she was. She'd

been the only one who hadn't seemed totally convinced, probably because her crap mother hadn't done a single thing to encourage her daughter in eighteen years.

He wasn't going to let her act like her accomplishments were no big deal. They were.

"Seems like it's a good fit for you," he said. "You know, talking to people, asking them questions. You were always curious about things."

"You're right. My show is a good fit. I really do love it." She shifted on the sand. "Actually, April is part of the reason I chose TV. I felt like I needed a really high-profile job for the state to entrust me with her care."

She paused, made a circle in the sand with her finger, and he sensed she was about to say something more.

"And I guess after feeling like I didn't have a voice for so long, living with my mother in the trailer park, I wanted to feel like I was somebody, if that makes any sense."

"It makes perfect sense," he found himself saying. "I feel the same way about my job. Knowing I'm making a difference in people's lives. It's a good thing."

She bit her lip and he wondered why she suddenly looked so unsure of herself.

"You do such amazing things every day, Sam. What I do isn't nearly as important."

Hating to hear her belittle herself, he said, "You don't need to put out fires to make a difference."

But hadn't he done the same thing she was doing

now, immediately assuming that she had to be looking down on him and his salary?

How much of the blue-collar, white-collar dichotomy was in his own head? Was it simply that he was threatened by her going and changing on him?

After trying to tell himself that her new glossy look was nothing but a fake mask, he could finally admit that the changes she'd made weren't necessarily bad.

Besides, how could he fault her for pulling herself out of the trailer park and making something of herself?

"What about you?" she said, shifting on the sand to get a better look at him.

Oh shit, he'd accidentally opened up a can of worms by asking her about her job. Hoping to head her off at the pass, he said, "My life's pretty much the same as it always was."

Except for the blip after she left and he nearly lost everything.

Undeterred by his terse answer, she said, "Do you still live in the same part of town?"

Hell no, he couldn't stand to drive through the same neighborhoods where they'd often go walking late at night when there was a full moon.

"I'm closer to the beach."

Leaning forward with her elbows on her knees, she was one hundred percent focused on him. "What about the guitar? Are you still playing?"

Only a handful of people knew he played. How could he have forgotten that Dianna was one of them? Or that the only songs he'd ever written had been three-chord love songs dedicated to her?

He shrugged. "I haven't played in a long time."

He had no intention of admitting that he hadn't touched his guitar since the day she left. How could he, when every note he played reminded him of her?

Clearly getting frustrated with his reticence, she asked, "You must be one of the more established guys on the Tahoe Pines crew, right?"

"I am. As you can imagine," he said, dropping his guard for a moment, "I'm not opposed to kicking the rookies' asses around the block when they need it."

She grinned at him. "Who else do I know on the current crew?"

"Only me and Logan."

Shit, how could she have forgotten his brother?

"And Connor, of course."

Talking about his brother felt like venturing back into a minefield, so he quickly said, "In the off-season I've been helping lead some adventure tours for a friend's company."

"Ah, so that's why you know how to do all of this." She gestured to their gear and the river. "Any chance you'd consider doing a segment on your friend's company for my show sometime? It's just the sort of thing my viewers love."

Oh shit, he couldn't let himself think about the future. About seeing her again.

Or, worse, not seeing her again.

"It's getting late. We should get back on the river."

Hurt flashed on her face before she wiped it away.

"I'll clean our plates," she said, grabbing everything and heading toward the water.

The thin fabric of her pants outlined the swell of her hips, her taut thigh muscles. When she knelt down on the sand to wash out the tin cups they'd eaten out of, even though he knew he shouldn't be watching her, he couldn't tear his eyes away.

From the first moment he'd met her, he'd desired her. Intensely. If anything, the years between that first meeting and the present had only made his yearning grow stronger.

The water had washed off her makeup, and without the fancy clothes and hairdo, she looked more and more like the eighteen-year-old girl he'd fallen in love with.

Finished shaking out the cups, she turned away from the river and caught him staring. Her eyes opened wide, her nipples peaked with awareness. Sam knew it would be the easiest thing in the world to lower her onto the sand and release their pent-up cravings for each other's bodies.

Hell, no. He couldn't go there again.

He quickly packed up the food and stove and they got back on the river, an uneasy silence hovering between them again. Damn it, was there anything they could talk about that wasn't a minefield?

Guiding the raft around a tight curve after several

tense minutes of easy rafting, he suddenly squinted into the distance, unable to believe what he saw.

They were coming up on a strainer.

Formed by trees on the banks, with piles of large rocks in between, a strainer was incredibly technical and dangerous. Water could flow through it, but a boat couldn't.

Especially not one moving this fast.

If he'd been in the raft by himself, or with Connor, they'd have had a better chance to get through the strainer without too many broken bones or a concussion. But with a total novice beside him, Sam had to think fast.

"Get ready to jump out."

Dianna whipped her head around to face him. "Are you kidding?"

As they moved closer to the strainer, he barely had time to say, "We're going to jump together," before he wrapped his arms around her waist and pulled her onto his lap.

She was stiff in his arms and he knew he had to make a move before she tried to pull away.

"Take a breath and hold it," he said, and then they were falling over the swirling, rushing water.

Using his body to cushion her from the fall, he felt her start to panic a moment too late. She slipped out of his grasp and her head went under.

The raft flew over the water into the wall of tree limbs and rocks, and he knew that if he didn't get to her soon, she'd smash into it as well. Swimming hard across the current, he jammed his knee into a rock and barely flinched.

*Where the hell is she?*

He couldn't see her head or hair above the white water and a thousand agonizing images flashed through his brain.

Finally, Dianna's head rose out of the white foam. Ignoring the burning in his arms and legs and lungs, Sam heaved himself through the water and reached for her. He had almost grabbed her shirt, almost grabbed her arms, when she sank beneath the surface of the water.

# CHAPTER TWELVE

---

DIANNA RELAXED into the wonderful dream.

She was floating and felt warm all over. And then suddenly there were big hands pulling and shoving at her and she was fighting them, trying to get back to that sleepy place. But the hands were stronger and they dragged her up through thick, wet foam.

Cold air slapped against her cheeks and she started coughing and choking.

*Oh God,* she finally realized, *I was drowning.*

Sam had saved her life.

He cradled her against his chest on the riverbank, and as she gasped in air, trying to refill her empty lungs with oxygen, he removed her helmet and gently ran his fingers lightly over the goose egg on her forehead.

"You hit your head pretty hard on a rock," he said, his

voice warm and soothing as its low tones swam through her. "It's probably going to bruise."

As she got her bearings back in Sam's arms and the initial shock of being thrown out of the raft receded, it suddenly hit her that there could be far bigger problems ahead than healing from a bruise.

"Did we lose the raft?"

"Fortunately, no. It's up ahead, jammed between a couple of tree trunks. It'll stay there until we get it out."

Relief flooded her that all was not lost and she knew she needed to push past the throbbing in her head and sit up. But even though remaining this close to her biggest temptation was a very bad idea, she couldn't bring herself to move out of his arms.

For the first time in a very long time she felt safe.

Comforted.

With gentle fingers, he massaged her sore shoulder muscles, grown tight from endless paddling.

Did he know that his touch made her heart race?

That even without touching an erogenous zone, she was getting hopelessly aroused?

"I shouldn't have let you leave the hospital so soon after your accident." His voice was husky. "Jesus, Dianna. How the hell did you manage to walk away from the crash?"

His question echoed the same one swimming around in her head since waking up in the hospital with only a smattering of cuts and scrapes: Why had she been saved?

And now, after being spared for the second time in a matter of days, instead of dying when anyone else would have, she couldn't hide from the fact that she'd been given a second, and now a third, chance to get things right.

But what was she supposed to change this time around?

The big change couldn't have something to do with Sam, could it? Especially now that they'd cleared the air after their motel room blowout and could actually talk without biting each other's heads off.

The dangerous bend of her thoughts sent her stumbling out of Sam's arms to her feet.

She needed some space, some breathing room, needed to get away from his dangerous pull over her so that she could behave rationally, rather than reacting to a base physical urge.

Sam was at her side in a heartbeat, one hand on her elbow, the other on the small of her back. "Easy now."

"I'm okay," she told him.

It was a lie. She wasn't okay, and not just because of her fall.

Being close to him like this, feeling his bare hands on her skin, made her burn up inside, with a fever that only he could quench.

She swayed into him and his words were barely

louder than a whisper. "God help me, Dianna, I still want you. More than ever. More than I should."

Her tongue came out to uncertainly lick her lower lip, and then, suddenly, his hands were in her hair and his mouth was on hers, almost hard enough to hurt.

And yet his rough kiss was exactly what she needed.

Exactly what she craved.

He slid his hands over the wet fabric covering her collarbone, then over her shoulders and down the length of her spine to the small of her back. Grabbing her hips, he pulled her in tight against him.

She was standing on just enough of a rise that the hollow between her thighs fit perfectly around his erection.

"I want you, too," she whispered against his lips when they pulled apart an inch. "So much I can't stand it."

He backed her up against a smooth rock face, and as he ran kisses down her neck, from her earlobe to the hollow of her shoulder, she shuddered in his arms. His hands found the gap between her shirt and pants, and as he brushed his fingers over her belly, she moaned softly.

And then he kissed her mouth again and she slid her tongue against his. His fingers went higher and higher, and when he finally found the edge of her bra, she heard herself begging, "Please touch me."

Slipping his fingers under the thin fabric, he curved his palm over her breast, her nipple hard against his hand.

She cried out and he covered her sound of pleasure with his mouth as he gently squeezed her tingling flesh. With painstaking slowness, he slid her shirt up over her skin, his lips nipping at hers, drawing out a low moan from her throat. And then he was pulling his mouth away and going to his knees and she could feel his warm breath on the exposed skin of her stomach. He pressed his lips to her belly once, twice, and then he was moving up the center of her rib cage, finally sucking one hard nipple into his mouth, then the other, cupping both breasts with his hands, rubbing his lightly stubbled chin against her skin.

Another moan escaped her, this time around his name, and then he was undoing the button at the top of her pants and sliding down the zipper, pulling the fabric down her hips to pool at her ankles.

He stopped laving her breasts with his tongue and lifted his head to watch her face as he slipped a finger into her panties. She pushed her pelvis into his hand, more aroused than she could ever remember being.

Knowing he wanted her as badly as she wanted him made her even wetter, even more aroused.

Circling the spot she so desperately wanted him to touch, he finally made contact—oh yes, right *there!*— and she gasped as exquisite sensations moved through her, from her core outward. Again and again his fingers slid between her slick folds. Up, then down, they moved between her labia, bumping over the hard nub of her arousal. His mouth found her next, his warm breath and soft lips covering her mound, his tongue probing, tasting as she cried out with pleasure.

She'd never felt so ripe, so ready to explode. She'd waited ten long years to feel this good again, and now that she was here with Sam, and his hands and mouth were on her, she wanted to make the incredible sensations last forever.

But she was so ready, too ready, and she couldn't stop herself from grasping the back of his head and pushing her pelvis into his tongue and teeth. And then his fingers joined his mouth, stretching her open.

Even this wet, it had been so long since she'd been with a man that his touch felt brand-new and she panted, "Oh God, Sam," against his shoulder as he kept the rhythm of his fingers and tongue steady.

"You feel so good," she groaned as she closed her eyes and tilted her head back, sucking in a hard breath in the same moment that her inner muscles clamped down hard on his fingers.

Her entire body shuddered into a powerful orgasm and Dianna felt like she had bypassed death and gone straight to heaven.

In the past decade, she hadn't forgotten how potent Sam's touch was. Forgetting something so wonderful would have been impossible.

But this all-encompassing pleasure was a shock to her system, nonetheless.

If she could, she'd stay like this forever, but they were

far from done, and she wanted to tear his pants off and take him deep inside.

She sank to her knees in front of him and cupped his face in her hands as she leaned in to kiss him. Their tongues mated, a salty-sweet dance that was unbearably exciting. Dying to relearn his beautiful body, the hard planes of muscle and the deep indentations in between, she ran her hands over his damp shirt, awed by his broad shoulders, his hard chest, his impressive abdominal muscles.

"Dianna," he said, the low rumble of his voice making her want him more than ever. "I've never had a problem controlling myself. Only with you."

It was the same for her and all she wanted was to give him the same pleasure he'd given her. But even as she ripped at the buttons on his shirt, she knew loving him was as much for herself as it was for him.

At last, the buttons came undone and she stilled as she took in his magnificent bare chest. Tanned, with only the lightest sprinkling of hair between his pectoral muscles.

"You're so beautiful," she murmured. "I've dreamed of this a hundred times. Tell me this isn't a dream."

"It couldn't be more real," he said before threading his fingers through her hair and kissing her.

She was blown away by the passion and desire that radiated from his mouth and hands and body. Second by second he was sweeping her farther and farther downriver, heading straight for a waterfall, and even though she knew there was no way to be prepared for the drop, she didn't care.

All that mattered was the way she felt right here, right now, in Sam's arms.

When the kiss finally ended, she lay her cheek on his chest and closed her eyes to listen to the rapid drumbeat of his heart. His arms were wonderfully strong around her as he held her close and it was only the insistent throbbing between her thighs that made her shift away from his heat so that she could kiss his chest.

He groaned with pleasure when she found his nipple with her tongue. It had always driven him crazy when she circled it, then flicked it lightly. His excitement fed hers and she fumbled for the waistband of his jeans. The edge of her palm brushed against his erection and even with two layers of fabric between his shaft and her hand, her need was so intense that she couldn't stop herself from palming the long, thick length through his clothes.

He twitched once, then twice against her palm, and she was reaching for his zipper to set him loose, when his hand came over hers and squeezed.

Wait. Something was wrong. Something had changed.

It took longer than it should have for her brain to send out the alert that this wasn't a warm, loving touch; it was a warning.

"We can't do this, Dianna."

Alarm shot through her, fast and furious, embarrassment close on its heels. With fumbling hands, she pushed away from him and fixed her pants, her bra, her shirt.

Despite his previous warnings about staying away from their past, despite her own strong misgivings, he'd seemed to want her as much as she wanted him. And on the heels of her thoughts about second chances, she'd jumped at the chance to be intimate with him.

Why hadn't she stopped herself? Wasn't she older? Wiser?

Shouldn't she have known better than to dance this close to the scalding flames?

But just as she was trying to close the lid on her feelings for Sam, forever this time, she heard it again, a voice in her head saying, *You fought for your sister. You fought for your career. Maybe this time you should fight for Sam.*

A combination of feeling sorry for her and being scared shitless by almost losing her in the river had made him act stupidly. He'd been so glad she was alive, he'd given in to the urge to see if she tasted as good now as she always had.

Only to find out that she was so much sweeter than any of his memories.

Touching her, kissing her, hearing her cry out in ecstasy had taken Sam straight to the edge, even though his clothes were still on and he'd only gotten to third base. But then, when she turned the tables and started kissing him, it had been nearly impossible for him to stop, to take a frickin' breath and remember why making love to Dianna was a terrible idea.

From deep in his subconscious, Connor's voice rose up and nailed him. *"She's bad for you, man. And you were royally fucked-up after she left. I don't want to see you like that again."*

Jesus, how could he have forgotten? At this rate, he'd end up with far more than he'd bargained for when he'd agreed to help find her sister. Much more than some incredibly hot sex against a rock.

He'd end up back in love with her.

And then when she left him to go back to her glossy, celebrity-soaked world, he'd be staring straight into a black hole again.

Getting kicked in the heart once in a lifetime was enough for him, thanks.

The sick feeling in the pit of his gut grew as she scrambled away from him. He forced himself to stand up and take a step away from her, even though he was desperate to make her come again.

"I screwed up, Dianna." Each repentant word was harder to spit out than the last. "I lost control and acted stupid."

A heavy silence hung between them as she stared at him with unblinking green eyes, not saying anything.

"Fortunately, we're almost to the end of the river," he said, hoping that getting back on task would permanently halt this twisted game they were playing. "If all goes well, we might be able to get to the commune by tonight."

Hurt and confusion flashed across her face at his emotionless, businesslike words. He was back to playing asshole again. Making her come and then shutting down the second her orgasm was over.

Unfortunately, he couldn't see any other way to proceed.

Needing to break out of her sexual force field, he turned around and strode into the water to retrieve the raft. Minutes later, he was disconcerted to note that her eyes remained glued to him as he dragged it through the cold water and up onto the shore.

"Maybe it wasn't a mistake, Sam."

She paused, licked her lips, giving him just enough time to run through everything that had happened against the rock, all the places he'd kissed and touched.

"Maybe what happened was inevitable. Maybe you and I are inevitable."

Desire tightened around him with each word. He never should have kissed her. Never should have told her that he couldn't stop himself from wanting her.

"No," he said, acting instinctively to stop the pull. "You and I were over ten years ago. We're here to find April. That's it."

He watched her flinch at his hard words, but instead of telling him he was a jerk like any other woman would have, she took a step closer.

"I wanted it just as much as you did," she said, refusing to back down, to take no for an answer. "After everything we talked about last night and this morning, I think we agree that we're different people now. We both lived through the miscarriage. We lived through the breakup. I know why you acted the way you did. And you know why I acted the way I did."

Another step closer.

"I've never cared about another man, Sam. Only you."

So close that he could reach out and pull her into a kiss.

"Tell me you love someone else—tell me you've loved anyone else like you loved me—and I'll drop it."

He knew the lie he needed to tell to shut her down forever, but standing on the banks of the Colorado River with her sweet scent lingering on his fingers, he just couldn't do it.

"There isn't anybody else," he admitted. "There's never been anyone else."

Her eyes flashed hope, and he forced himself to say, "But whether we've loved other people doesn't matter, Dianna. This is still a bad idea."

He watched as she pulled back her shoulders, straightened her spine, and tilted her chin, gearing up for a battle.

"You say we were over ten years ago, but you touch me like we're just getting started," she challenged. "Give me one good reason we shouldn't try again."

Fuck. Thus far he'd been able to keep his period of self-destruction buried. But she'd never drop the notion of getting back together, of trying again, if he didn't lay everything on the line.

"When you left—"

Shit, sacrificing his pride was harder than he'd thought it would be.

"I fought every goddamned fire this side of the Mississippi, but I just couldn't get over you."

She took another step closer, coming only inches away. "I couldn't get over you either, Sam."

He held up a hand to halt her forward momentum. "You asked for a reason and I'm giving you one. You went to San Francisco and grabbed a better life with both hands. I almost threw mine away."

Confusion furrowed her brows. "What are you talking about? You're still a hotshot. Still living in Tahoe surrounded by your friends, your crew, and your brother."

"I almost lost it all, Dianna. I jumped straight into a black hole, wanted it to swallow me up."

Shaking her head as if nothing he was saying made sense, she said, "I don't get it. What do you mean, black hole?"

He ran his hands through his hair, hating every second of soul baring. He would have happily given up a limb instead.

"After you left, I reverted to the same place I was in during high school. But worse. More drinking. More all-nighters. Waking up and not knowing where I was. Skipping out on the rest of the crew. Not showing up for fires and working half-assed and hungover when I managed to get up the mountain."

Understanding suddenly flooded her eyes. "I'm so sorry," she said, "sorry about everything." Her eyes clouded with regret. "When I look back now, I can see what a scared, confused eighteen-year-old kid I was," she admitted softly. "If I'd known what was going to happen, what leaving would do to both of us, I never would have . . ." She let the rest of her sentence fall away, saying instead, "You can't beat yourself up for one bad choice, Sam."

"It wasn't one bad choice, it was a hundred bad choices. If it weren't for Connor . . ."

He didn't bother to finish his sentence. He'd saved her once, but she'd left him anyway. Maybe she'd only needed him to get away from her mother and out of the trailer park. Maybe not.

Either way, odds were, as soon as they found April, this rush of adrenaline—a rush that felt like desire and love—would dissipate.

And she'd walk away from him again.

"Look, I get why you're thinking about second chances. You've survived two big accidents. But you were right when you said that we've changed. We're in two different worlds now."

Her eyes were flashing and he knew he was hurting

her again with his harsh words, but it was better to sever the thin thread that remained between them now, rather than the mess of trying to untangle themselves later.

Climbing back into the raft, he said, "You ready to get going again? We don't want to waste any more time."

# CHAPTER THIRTEEN

IT WAS only Dianna's years of learning to keep calm in front of the camera no matter what her guest was doing or saying that enabled her to steadily hold Sam's gaze after he'd ripped her to shreds.

But on the inside, she was in pieces. Just as she'd been the day she'd left Lake Tahoe.

He was the only man who'd ever made her break her vow to depend only on herself. She couldn't let herself do it again.

Take their conversation during lunch, for example. He'd gotten her to talk freely about April, about her career, but then when it was his turn to share, he'd clammed up and held her at arm's length.

It hurt like hell to watch him be so guarded, to know that he didn't want to trust her with what was in his heart. Yes, she now saw that she'd betrayed his trust all those years ago by leaving. But she'd been young and scared and stupid. Was her behavior as an eighteen-year-old really enough of an excuse for him to keep pushing her away?

She didn't trust herself to speak as she climbed on to her side of the raft. They paddled for another thirty minutes in silence without any other disasters, but the small comfort zone they'd found during their lunch on the riverbank had been blown to smithereens by the sexual encounter and then their very unsatisfactory post-makeout discussion.

A short while later, Sam steered them back over to the edge of the river.

"This is as far as we go by water."

She got off the raft, and as it deflated, he methodically laid out an overwhelming array of rock-climbing gear. Looking up at the quartz slab, which had to be several stories high, she was newly shaken.

How could she possibly climb a rock face with no experience . . . and a borderline fear of heights?

He held a harness out, clearly expecting her to step into it. But although she knew Sam was a man of few words, it didn't seem the least bit fair that he should unilaterally decide to shut down their dialogue.

Taking a deep breath, she tried to shore up her insides for the roller coaster her words were about to launch.

"You might be done talking about what happened with us, Sam, but I'm not. You got to ask your big question; now it's my turn."

He was an impenetrable wall before her, his eyes shuttered, the lines of his body stiff and unyielding. There was no satisfaction in knowing that Sam was cornered, with no place to run.

"Go ahead."

Working to project a serene confidence she certainly didn't feel, she said, "If you cared so much about me that you fell apart when I left, then why didn't you come after me?"

She held her breath as she waited for his response, her heart kicking up so fast she could have been sprinting, rather than standing still.

"I did come after you," he finally admitted. "A couple of weeks after you left Lake Tahoe."

Oh God, all this time she'd assumed that he'd been happy to see her go. Was there more to the story? Had she been wrong all these years?

Sam watched confusion, even doubt, run across Dianna's beautiful face.

"But I never saw you," she protested, before admitting, "I didn't exactly make myself easy to find, did I?"

"I found you," he said, his words harder than they should be.

Her hands moved to her chest, almost as if she felt the need to shield her heart from him.

"Then why didn't you tell me you were there?"

He dropped the harness to the sand and moved away from her, remembering that unseasonably warm day in foggy San Francisco. He'd parked outside the return address on the letter from Dianna that he'd found in a pile of her mother's unopened mail in the trailer. Donna hadn't seemed to know—or care—that her daughter had broken up with her fiancée and skipped town, and Sam couldn't help but wonder if Dianna was running away from more than just him.

He'd been about to get out of his truck when he saw her, walking out of the apartment building. Her hair was blonder, softer somehow. Her clothes were different. Fit her better than anything he'd ever seen her wear. Even her green eyes seemed brighter.

"You were already different," he explained.

And then she'd waved at a skinny guy on a bike who came over to say hi and her smile was bigger than Sam could remember seeing. At least since the miscarriage.

"It wasn't hard to figure out that you already had a new job. New friends. And it looked to me like your new world fit you so well, so much better than being some kid from a trailer park ever did." He let out a long breath. "Do you have any idea how hard it was to walk away? To accept that you were finally in your right place?"

Dropping her hand from her chest, she reached out to him. "If I'd known you were there, then maybe I—"

"Maybe you would have what? Married me anyway and had a bunch of babies?" He scowled. "I don't think so."

"How can you say that?"

"You're the one who wanted to postpone the wedding. Not me."

Clearly stung by his accusation, she said, "It sure seemed to me that you were perfectly happy to postpone the wedding, too. I'll never forget that day I told you I'd taken the pregnancy test. You looked like I was holding a gun to your head, saying, 'Marry me or else.' All my life I'd told myself I wasn't going to repeat my mother's mistakes, but then there I was having some guy propose to me because he had to. Getting a marriage proposal should have been one of the best days of my life. Instead it was one of the worst. Because I knew how compelled you were to do the right thing. And I knew it would break us eventually." She paused, shut her eyes tight for a moment before opening them again. "I just didn't think it would happen so soon."

After ten years of shoving his feelings as far down as they could go, Sam could barely believe all of this anger and frustration—and love—actually belonged to him.

But more than that, he couldn't believe the things Dianna was saying. It was time to set her straight.

"You and I both know it wasn't like that."

To his amazement, she laughed in his face. Actually laughed. "You honestly expect me to believe that you were looking for a wife and kid at twenty? That you weren't wanting to go to bars, play the field, live your life like any normal young firefighter?"

What the fuck did she expect him to say to that? Of course that's how he'd felt.

"Are you saying that's what you wanted?" he asked, turning the question around to her. "That instead of wearing my engagement ring, you wanted to play the field and mess around with other guys?"

She shook her head, then buried her face in her hands. He couldn't believe how much he wanted to pull her into his arms. Even though they were standing on opposite poles.

"No," she finally said, when she lifted her head. "I was in love with you, Sam. I didn't want anyone else." Her beautiful lips turned down at the corners. "But that didn't mean I was ready for a baby. And neither were you."

There was no point in lying. They were way beyond trying to keep anything from each other.

"You're right, I wasn't ready." He hoped he could find the words to make her understand. "But that didn't mean that when it happened I didn't get excited about it."

A lone tear streaked down her face and he had to bunch his hands into fists to keep from wiping the wetness away from her smooth skin.

"I felt exactly the same way," she admitted in a shaky voice. "I couldn't believe how much I was falling in love with this little person growing inside of me. Because even though I knew we weren't ready, I still hoped we could figure things out." Her eyes closed and she whispered, "Instead, a piece of me—of both of us—died that day. And I didn't just lose the baby, I lost you, too."

His self-control disappeared and he couldn't stop himself from gathering her into his arms.

He wasn't angry anymore. How could he be?

"I'm sorry, Dianna," he said softly against her hair.

A short while later, she said, "I am, too," and when she moved out of his embrace, letting her go was one of the hardest things he'd ever had to do.

Dianna was relieved that they had found this place of mutual understanding. They'd been too young, too naive to have acted out of malice. They'd been confused kids, plain and simple.

There was no way of knowing where she and Sam would go from here, or if they would ever be willing to risk their hearts to each other again, but something told her that whatever choice they ended up making, it would be the right one.

For both of them.

"Thank you for being so honest with me," she said.

His answering smile took her breath away. "You're

welcome." He nodded toward the rock. "How about you and me scale that wall?"

She forced a nod, hoping she looked braver than she felt.

"Let's get this on you," Sam said, picking up her gear again, and she made herself step into the leg holes of the harness that she assumed was supposed to hold her in the air. Sam's hands came around her waist, snapping the waist belt shut.

"You're going to be fine," he said softly.

If there was any possible way she could avoid climbing up a wall into thin air, she would stop the madness right here, right now. But with a rock wall standing between her and finding April, she had no choice but to climb it.

He leaned in even closer, his mouth brushing against her earlobe. "I'm going to be right behind you. I won't let anything happen to you."

The memory of another time he'd said those words to her—right after they made love for the first time—smashed into her. She lost her balance and had to reach out for the rock to steady herself and refocus.

"If you start to fall, here's what you do."

She watched him twist the ropes around his arms and waist as if her life depended on it. It did.

"You're going to lead the climb. I'll bring up the rear."

For the umpteenth time, she tried to project a confidence she definitely didn't feel. That first year she hosted *West Coast Update*, she'd done the very same thing. No one had known that her knees were knocking together beneath her dress. And Sam didn't need to know that she was practically having a coronary just gazing up at the rock face.

Yet again, he was an excellent, extremely patient teacher, as he directed her on how to screw the metal bolts into the rock face, then how to clip her carabiners into them.

The first few feet weren't so bad, and she was able to tell herself that if she fell, she'd possibly break something, but she'd walk away pretty much unscathed. Still, with each new hand- and foothold, her breathing grew increasingly labored. Sam told her where to put her hands and feet and she did exactly what he said.

Until she made the mistake of looking down.

Her stomach roiled and she froze in place. Minutes felt like hours as she clung to the rock. All of the weight was on the tips of her toes, and her muscles started spasming.

"Dianna? Talk to me."

"I can't get my legs to stop shaking," she admitted through dry lips.

Sam moved closer to her on the rock and unclipped her backpack so that he could transfer it to his own shoulders.

"Lean into me for a second."

She didn't hesitate to take him up on the offer.

"Everyone gets sewing machine leg on their first climb."

The fact that he was talking to her as if they were sitting in a coffee shop rather than clinging to cold rock a hundred feet in the air helped snap her out of her panic. She needed to follow his lead, keep the conversation going, pretend she was shooting a live show.

"There's a name for what my legs are doing?"

"You bet. It's perfectly normal."

He didn't offer to help her down off the rock and she appreciated how well he knew her. Even though she was scared spitless, she couldn't turn away from helping April.

"I want you to trust me, Dianna. Tell me why you're afraid of heights."

She was so surprised by what he was asking that for a moment, she forgot she was hanging on to the edge of a cliff with her fingertips.

"I just am."

He laughed softly, the mellow sound running through her veins like a sedative. "Nice try. Now what's the real reason?"

God, she didn't know. She'd just always stayed away from ladders and rooftops. But before she could say this to Sam, a picture flashed through her mind and she gasped.

"What is it?" he asked, holding her steady with his body.

Her breath came fast again. "I think I saw a man fall when I was a little girl."

"Who was it?"

She closed her eyes, tried to place his face. "I don't know."

But something told her he was important, especially when she thought about the way her mother had behaved later, crying and raging at Dianna.

"I think it was one of my mother's boyfriends."

In a soothing tone, Sam said, "The man fell, Dianna. Not you. It wasn't your fault. You were just a little girl who saw too much."

Amazingly, her heartbeat began to slow. Was he right? Could she have developed a phobia because of what she'd seen happen to someone else?

"Do you want to talk about it some more?"

Her heart swelled, knowing that he was no longer angry at her, that at the very least they could get through this as friends helping each other.

"No, I think I'm okay now."

"Good. Then let's try doing this a different way. We're going to climb up together."

God love him, he made it sound so easy.

"How?"

"Like this, with you cradled against my body. I'm going to strap your harness through mine. Every move you make, I'll make with you."

Again, instead of making her feel like an idiot for diving into deeper water than she could possibly swim in, he was putting his own life on the line. Then again, hadn't he jumped into this rescue mission without a thought for himself from the very beginning?

"I can't let you do that, Sam. I could kill us both."

The low rumble of his laughter blew across her ear-lobe again. "Don't worry, babe, I won't let you do that."

Of all the insane places to be hot for a guy, this one took the cake, stuck on the side of a rock, wrapped up in ropes. It struck her, then, that he'd done the impossible. He'd eased her fear enough for crazy desire to come rushing back in.

Slowly, inch by inch, they climbed up together. She couldn't see the ground around his large body, which was a very good thing given what had happened the previous time she'd looked down. She focused all of her energy on the peak, and although rock climbing ranked as one of the most difficult things she'd ever done, before she knew it, she was actually making it up the side of a mountain.

"We've got it under control," Sam said.

Safe in the curve of his large body, Dianna almost believed him.

The muscles in her arms and legs and stomach ached as she hugged the wall. Even the rest periods where they held on to a small ledge so that she could catch her breath were hard work. And then, after what seemed like an eternity, but was probably only twenty minutes or so, she was gripping the edge of the rock and pulling herself up to the top of the cliff.

Standing at the peak brought an unexpected smile to her face. She couldn't believe how powerful she felt after facing down one of her biggest fears. Her first climb safely behind her, she was able to see what a huge adrenaline rush it had been. It was a new sensation, totally different from the rush of taping a live show for millions of viewers.

She'd assumed she'd be a complete wreck after climbing up the rock, but the reverse was true. She felt invincible, ready for any challenge that came her way, which was good because the challenges were lined up before her, one after the other.

Why, she suddenly wondered, had she been afraid of heights for so long?

And what else was she afraid of that she shouldn't be?

They donned their heavy packs, and when they hit the hiking trail Sam said, "You set the pace. If my coordinates are right, we should be there in about thirty minutes."

She led the way up the narrow deer trail, moving steadily, and she was actually grateful for the hard physical labor, for anything to focus on besides her worries about her sister, which only increased as they hiked closer to the commune.

Constantly looking at her watch, the minutes ticked down. Twenty-five, then twenty, then fifteen as they traversed a steep switchback, until suddenly, Sam grabbed her arm.

"We're here."

She looked around and saw nothing but tree stumps and bushes, but she knew the GPS on Sam's watch was accurate. He motioned for her to give him her pack and when she did he slid both of their bags into the bushes.

"Are you ready to do this?"

Dianna's heart jumped into her throat, but she said, "I'm ready."

# CHAPTER FOURTEEN

"I'M GOING to take the lead now," he told her quietly. "If anything looks dangerous, if it looks like we're in any kind of danger, I want you to get the hell out of here."

She shook her head. "You shouldn't even be here. April's my sister, not yours. And no matter how dangerous the commune is, I'm not leaving without you."

His expression was harder than the granite they'd just climbed. "I can take care of myself and I *will* find your sister. But I won't let you risk your life. And I won't let you get hurt. Promise me you'll go for help if something happens or we aren't setting one foot onto the commune."

"Okay," she finally said, accepting that Sam couldn't shed his protective instincts. He needed to hear her say it. "I promise I'll go for help."

Slowly, they moved through thicker and thicker brush until they reached a chain-link fence. She wasn't sure what she'd do if they came upon someone with a gun. The only ones she'd ever seen were the ones who moved in with her mother's boyfriends and, fortunately, moved out when they left. No one had warned her not to touch them as a kid; she'd just known.

"Who are you?"

The high-pitched voice startled her, and she jumped against Sam. He put his hands on her shoulders and she was thankful for his reassuring strength.

A short, plump girl with dreadlocks and bad skin stood in the bushes. "This is private property. Go away."

Dianna was surprised by the hard words out of the baby voice. But she was relieved to see that, as far as she could tell, the girl didn't have any weapons on her. Based on what Will and Sam had both said about the suspected drug-related activities on the commune, Dianna had almost expected armed guards.

"I'm looking for April Kelley. I'm her sister."

The girl's eyes widened before she shifted into a sneer. "You must be the rich celebrity, huh?"

Dianna was taken aback by the stranger's vitriol and it took her a few extra seconds to find the words, "Is she here?"

She held her breath as she waited for the girl to reply, never having been able to let go of that small shred of hope that her sister would be alive and well on the commune when they arrived.

The girl looked at her like she was extremely slow. "Of course not. She went to see you."

The crushing blow came too quick for Dianna to deflect it. Fortunately, Sam was right behind her with an arm around her waist.

Picking up the questioning, he asked, "Has anyone heard from her since she left?"

The girl shook her head. "When she didn't show up for chores this morning we figured she'd decided to head back to San Francisco without telling anyone."

"No," Dianna said, finding her voice again. "That's not what happened. She called me yesterday. She's in trouble."

Dianna didn't know what she'd expected. A little panic on the girl's part might have been nice. Instead she just shrugged.

"I'm sure she's fine."

Something told Dianna that this girl didn't care for April much. She wanted to know why—and if it could have something to do with her sister's disappearance.

But before she could give her the third degree, Sam said, "Could you show us where she's been living so we can see if she left any clues as to where she went?"

The girl looked wary. "We don't normally allow strangers onto the Farm."

"I'm not a stranger. I'm her sister."

Narrowed eyes scanned her, top to bottom. "Whatever. I guess, since you're her sister and all. Although I'm sure Peter will kick you out soon enough." But rather than lead them inside the gates, she turned to Sam. "Who are you?"

"Friend of the family. You lead the way."

It was a barely masked command that the girl couldn't help but obey.

As she motioned for them to follow her through the brambles, Sam whispered, "Let's see what we can learn from April's friends before we jump to any conclusions. They probably know more than they think they do."

She wasn't sure she believed anything he was saying, but it didn't stop Dianna from sending up a silent thank-you that he was here with her. She'd need to siphon off his strength until she could relocate her own.

They stepped beyond the fence and the thick vegetation and Dianna was surprised to find that the commune was extremely clean and orderly. Neat rows of fruit trees and plots lush with vegetables grew to the west of the low-roofed barns. There was even a white house with a porch at the top of the meadow, which looked down on the land below.

Even more surprising, there was a faded baby stroller at the entrance of one of the many huts that cropped up along the edges of the meadow where the tall trees began again. She heard laughter and saw children playing with a cute little puppy who was lying on its back while they rubbed its belly.

Had April been telling her the truth when she'd said it wasn't a bad place?

"This is the Farm," the girl said, waving her arms across the rolling open hills.

It was an incredibly beautiful valley, surrounded by high mountains on all sides. A low, distinctly nonhuman sound bellowed at them and she jumped in alarm. Sam motioned to his left and she realized they were standing beside a sheep's pen. Pigs and goats were in separately fenced sections, and even though she had no livestock experience whatsoever, the animals' pens looked pretty darn tidy.

And yet, a chill passed through Dianna that had nothing to do with the light breeze rustling the leaves on the tall aspen trees. She'd grown up in a dark and scary place, and although her eyes couldn't find anything scary about the bucolic scene before them, the fact that her sister was missing kept the same dark presence hovering over it all.

Crossing between vegetable patches, they followed the girl over to a small shack, no bigger than a ten-by-ten garden shed.

"This is where she lived?" Dianna asked, instantly aghast at the lack of heat, running water, kitchen, or toilet.

"We live as simply as we possibly can. April really embraced it."

Was that true? Would April have embraced a surrogate "family" even though she'd pushed her own flesh and blood away?

The shed was clean and simple and yet, almost as

soon as she stepped into the building, Dianna found that she couldn't spend another second inside April's primitive room.

Ever since moving out of her mother's trailer for good, she'd never done well in small spaces and absolutely hated feeling trapped, which was why she'd bought a condo with floor-to-ceiling windows, and every room had a spectacular view of the Golden Gate Bridge. It made her feel like she could escape at a moment's notice, gave her the illusion of not being held down, of not being trapped.

In so many ways, even though it was much cleaner, this little cabin felt like the trailer she'd grown up in. She'd sworn she and April would never live like this again.

How could her sister have made this choice? Especially given all of the opportunities that Dianna had worked her butt off to provide?

If only she and April had been able to see eye to eye. Then maybe none of this would have happened.

She pushed past Sam to get back outside and he gave her a look that seemed to say, *"Everything is going to be okay."*

But she wasn't sure that it would be, especially not when she saw three men—two so huge they looked like giants flanking the third—waiting for her outside April's shed.

Sam heard Dianna cautiously call his name.

Damn it, he chastised himself as he walked back outside and saw that Dianna was standing in front of three men. What had he been thinking to take his eyes off her for even a second?

Moving quickly to her side, he slid his hand through hers. *Touch her and die* was the message he wanted to come across loud and clear to their new friends.

"And who are you?" the regular-sized man said to him.

"Sam MacKenzie," he replied, not bothering to hold out his hand in greeting.

"My name is Peter Cohen."

The man didn't bother to introduce his two large friends, whom Sam quickly deduced were the palace guards, which seemed to mean that Peter was the man in charge.

"As I just said to your friend, Dianna, welcome to my Farm."

Sam knew he and Dianna weren't the slightest bit welcome. They were intruders. But he'd come here to find April. He wasn't going to let some smarmy cult leader get in his way.

Cutting any further bullshit off at the pass, he said, "April's disappeared. Do you know where she's gone?"

Peter's expression didn't change, save for a shifting of his dark eyes, which were too intelligent for Sam's liking. Sam felt like he'd known men like this before, men who had volunteered to be hotshots for a summer, not to save trees and houses and lives, but simply for the chance to be called a hero.

Sam was going to watch Peter Cohen very carefully. If there was any chance that he had staged April's kidnapping for his own profit—or to try to get at Dianna, who was both famous and rich—Sam was going to stop the motherfucker before he could make it to the next square on the board.

Without answering Sam's question, Peter commanded, "Come with me."

They followed Peter and his guards past the rows of crops, across an open field where children played, and up a set of stairs to the attractive white house that overlooked the commune's many acres.

Moving silently, a woman in Peter's house filled three cups with something hot and set the cups before them before backing silently out of the room.

Sam had no intention of drinking whatever it was and he sent a silent signal to Dianna that she shouldn't either.

"Before I tell you what I know about April, I want to know more about both of you." He turned to Dianna. "April said you have a TV show and that you are quite famous. Does anyone know you are here and how did you find us?"

Considering how upset she'd been inside April's shack, she barely blinked an eye as she said, "April told me enough about the Farm for us to locate it on a map."

Sam's respect for her—already in full measure after

the way she'd come back from a near-drowning to transcend her fear of heights, all in the same day—grew yet again. She'd deftly sidestepped Peter's first question without giving away Will's part in getting them to the commune.

Seeming satisfied with her response, the man turned to Sam. "And who are you?"

"I already told you my name," Sam said.

Peter raised an eyebrow. "We are very careful with regard to who we allow on the Farm. Are you a cop?"

Sam sized up the commune's leader. Broad-shouldered with cropped hair, he didn't look weak. And then, there was a question of bodyguards. What the hell were they hovering around for?

Clearly impatient for answers, Dianna leaned forward and pinned the man with her intelligent gaze.

"Sam is a firefighter, not a cop. And now that you've got your answers, I want to find out what you know about my sister's disappearance. Anything about where she might be, her last moves, if she'd ever left the commune before and with whom?"

Clearly surprised by her pointed questions, Peter looked concerned for the first time.

"I'm very sorry to hear that she's missing. Honestly, I doubt anyone here knows what happened to her. She's been a constant resident for the past three months. She came with a boyfriend named Kevin, but when he moved on a few weeks later, she remained behind. I believe she hiked down into Vail to see you a few days ago, is that not correct?"

A flash of pain moved across Dianna's face, so quickly Sam almost missed it.

"Yes, my sister and I met in Vail. Was April hanging around any strangers? Did she have any enemies that you know of?"

Peter shook his head. "As far as I know, she didn't have any enemies. But I will admit to being concerned about her in the beginning. She wasn't particularly good in group situations at first. I think getting her involved with the other women who cook helped turn her around." He licked his lips. "She makes the most marvelous herb bread."

Sam watched as Dianna struggled with her frustration at Peter's answers. "I can't believe my sister would be a part of something like this," she said, gesturing to the grounds below the house.

Peter cocked his head to the side. "Like what?"

Dianna leveled a hard stare at the man. "You tell me. What the hell are all of you doing hidden up here with no roads and no contact with the outside world?"

For the first time Sam saw the take-no-prisoners-reporter side of Dianna and it impressed the hell out of him.

Strangely, though, Peter didn't seem the least bit upset by the gauntlet she'd thrown down.

"We find that people often have misconceptions about an intentional community such as ours. We don't have a group religion. We support ourselves by making furniture and other handmade products, along with animal by-products such as honey and cheese. The people who live here do so because they love it. Your sister, I believe, was growing comfortable in our community."

Dianna sat back in her seat, clearly digesting Peter's words.

"Do you swear to me that my sister wasn't mixed up in anything illegal?"

Peter nodded. "As far as I know, she was simply here trying to find herself." He bowed his head and took a deep breath. "I can see how worried you are and I will allow you to ask her friends if they know anything more, although, I should warn you, not everyone here trusts outsiders." After a moment of silence, he added, "I'm also willing to let you set up camp here for the night. There is plenty of room in the meadow for the two of you."

Peter's offer sounded benevolent. Helpful, even. But to Sam's suspicious ears it reeked of wanting to keep an eye on them.

Unfortunately, the sun had already set behind the trees. Even if they chose to leave the commune, they couldn't get far in the dark. Besides, Dianna looked as exhausted as he'd ever seen her.

At Dianna's questioning glance, he said, "Fine. We'll stay."

"I wish I could help you more," Peter said as he walked them to the door.

Almost across the threshold, Dianna paused. "Do you have a phone?"

"Just one, here in the house."

"Could I use it?"

"Follow me."

The phone was in a small room by the back door. "Take your time," he said. "You can let yourself out the back."

Dianna put her hand on Peter's arm before she left the room. "I have one more request," she said in a smooth voice that belied her distress. "I'd like to give the Farm's telephone number to my producer. Just in case April calls, she'll know where to find me."

For a moment, Sam thought the man was going to refuse her request and he was preparing himself to "convince" him when Peter gave her the number.

Dianna picked up the old-fashioned receiver and dialed. "Ellen? It's Dianna. Is there any word from April?"

Sam watched as her face fell, just as it had when they'd talked to the girl outside the commune's gates and learned that April was, indeed, still missing. Quickly giving her friend the commune's telephone number, she disconnected, then dialed another number and typed in what looked like a voice mail access code.

Standing off to the side, Sam felt superfluous yet again. Sure, she'd needed him on the river and the rock. But she'd barely needed him since. Of course he was proud of her for being so strong, for asking the hard questions. And yet, it only confirmed that he had no real place in her life.

But when she hung up the phone and looked at him with tears in her eyes, saying "She hasn't left any messages on either of my phones," he finally realized another reason he was here: to pull Dianna into his arms and hold her when all hope seemed lost.

# CHAPTER FIFTEEN

GOING SHACK to shack, they talked with men, women, even teenagers. But no one knew where April was. Apart from the girl who'd stopped them at the chain-link fence earlier that day, the commune's residents seemed truly sad to hear that April was missing.

"I wish there was something I could do to help," said their final interviewee, an attractive woman in her early thirties with a drooling young baby on her lap. "April was always so good with Christy. I swear, sometimes it seemed like she was the only one who could get her to stop crying."

April was good with babies? Dianna couldn't help but wonder if they were talking about the same person.

"I don't think I've ever seen my sister interact with a

child before," Dianna told the woman, who smiled, revealing slightly crooked front teeth.

"Honestly, I think she was scared stiff the first time I dropped Christy into her lap." Chuckling, she added, "But I'm sure you know what a quick learner she is."

But Dianna didn't know that at all. Again, she had to wonder if April really had been growing and changing in a positive way on the commune. Sure, the primitive living situations pushed all of Dianna's buttons, but could it possibly be that roughing it in the woods was better for her sister than living in Dianna's penthouse condo in San Francisco?

Just then, the baby started crying and reaching for Dianna.

The woman laughed again. "She must think you're April. You two really do look a lot alike in so many ways." Pressing her lips to the baby's forehead, the mother cooed, "She's not April, baby girl," but it only made the baby cry harder.

The baby's wails tugged at Dianna's heartstrings and she held out her hands.

"Here. Let me try anyway."

A moment later, she was cradling the chubby infant in her arms, amazed when the baby's tears were immediately replaced with a gummy grin. Enthralled by her soft skin, her big brown eyes, and tiny little fingers, Dianna looked up to compliment the mother on her gorgeous child when she caught Sam's unblinking gaze.

It wasn't hard to figure out what he was thinking:

This could have been them ten years ago, had everything gone differently.

Sensing her distress, the baby started crying again and her mother picked her up out of Dianna's arms. "I know how exhausted you must be from your journey here today. Again, if there's anything I can do to help, please let me know."

Dianna compulsively cracked her knuckles as they headed out across the meadow to the spot in a circle of tall aspens where Peter had instructed them to set up their tent. Sam grabbed her hands and separated them for her.

"I'm sorry we didn't find out more from her friends," he said softly, still holding on to her fingers.

During the past couple of hours, she'd managed to hold it together, even though it seemed that they were even further from finding April than they'd been in the hospital. She'd desperately hoped that coming to the commune would provide them with answers, or at least clues. Instead, it had been a total bust.

The only thing she knew for sure was that she wouldn't be able to keep it together if he kept being so sympathetic.

She needed to get away from him.

"I need some privacy," she said as she pulled her hands out of his grasp. "Please."

Then she was tearing through the trees, stumbling over roots and rocks, her tears quickly morphing into sobs.

Sam understood why she wanted to be alone. They were similar that way, neither of them wanting to look weak in front of an audience. Instead, they both held everything they were feeling inside. When he realized she was sitting on a rock with her head on her knees, curled up into a ball, crying her eyes out, a pride of cougars couldn't have held him back.

Her head shot up when she heard his footsteps crunch through the dry leaves. She brushed the back of her hands across her eyes.

"Go away."

He knew why she was lashing out at him, knew that she was terribly worried, but he also knew she needed a loving friend more than she needed space. So he ignored her request and moved beside her on the rock. She was shivering and he didn't hesitate to put his arms around her.

"Why are you here?" she asked through chattering teeth, holding herself stiff in his arms.

"Because you need me," he said simply. "I know you're upset about April. I'm worried too, but we won't give up until we find her."

Her voice was muffled against his chest as she said, "All I've ever wanted was a happy family."

She began crying again, and he pulled her tighter, rhythmically stroking her back with his hands.

"I know you do, sweetheart," he said, the endearment feeling perfectly natural. Totally right.

If he were being totally honest with himself, wasn't a family all he'd ever wanted? Wasn't family what he'd tried to create with his crew? With his brother? Wasn't that why losing the baby and then Dianna had been such a crushing blow? Just when a real family had finally been within reach, he'd lost it all.

Silently, they held on to each other and it felt so good to be close to Dianna again that Sam almost forgot who was comforting whom.

A short while later, she lifted her cheek off his chest.

"Talking to April's friends makes me feel like I've really blown it with her all these years. Maybe I have been too controlling, too overprotective. Maybe I haven't listened to her enough."

He wiped away the wetness on her cheeks. "I doubt that's true. Sounds like you did everything you could for her."

"No, I really screwed up with her. She had another reason to leave, but I was too embarrassed to tell you about it in the hospital." She took a deep breath. "Right around Christmas, I had the really stupid idea of trying to get my mother and sister back together."

He raised an eyebrow. "It didn't go well, I take it?"

"You don't know how much of an understatement that is," she said on a hollow laugh. "It went terrible. Beyond terrible. April didn't want anything to do with Donna. Donna didn't want anything to do with April.

And both of them were pissed at me for shoving them together."

She took a shaky breath. "I don't think my sister said ten words to me between that meeting and leaving for Colorado. And she was right to be angry. I had some stupid reconciliation fantasy in my mind that had absolutely nothing to do with reality."

She was trying to put a brave face on it, but Sam could see how deeply hurt she was by what had happened.

"Have you talked with your mother since then?"

"No way. Honestly, I haven't seen her much over the years anyway. Seeing how horrible she was to April pretty much closed that door for me forever."

Wanting to let her know that she wasn't alone, he confessed, "I haven't heard from my father since last year."

She met his eyes for the first time since he'd joined her on the rock.

"Why? What happened?"

He fought the urge to make light of the situation, to stuff it back down and pretend it didn't matter.

"My parents came to see Connor in the hospital last summer, right after he was burned. He was the only thing that mattered. The only thing they should have been focused on."

"Oh no, Sam, they didn't start fighting, did they?"

"Like goddamned cats and dogs, right there in his room. They've been ripping each other to shreds for thirty years and they couldn't put the brakes on it for fifteen minutes? All I could think was that even though he was heavily doped up on morphine, what if he could hear them? What if their petty grievances were seeping into his subconscious and holding him back from healing because he didn't want to deal with their bullshit anymore?"

Now she was the sympathetic one, saying, "What did you do?"

He scowled. "I dragged their asses out of the hospital. And told them not to set another foot inside his room if they couldn't be civil."

"You did a good thing," she said softly. "Protecting Connor."

"My mother came by to see me a couple weeks later. She'd decided to file for divorce."

"Oh, Sam. After thirty years, they couldn't figure things out?"

"If you ask me, filing for divorce was the good choice." His mouth quirked up on one side and he could see that she was surprised by his half smile. "She should have divorced his ass years ago. But she thought it would be better for Connor and me if she stuck it out."

"So she was only trying to do what was best?"

"Yeah, she was. I don't know what the hell my father was thinking all those years, though. He mostly wasn't around and didn't say much when he was."

Suddenly, Sam looked up, and as his eyes connected with hers, he realized he'd just delved deeper into his mixed emotions about his parents' marriage than he ever had before—even in his own head.

Dianna's hand came up to his cheek, her fingers lightly brushing against the stubble on his chin.

"You're a good man, Sam. A good brother. And a good son."

He covered her hand with his and leaned close enough to taste her lips, which were warm and salty from her tears. She leaned into him and he licked them with slow strokes of his tongue, growing instantly hard when she moaned with pleasure.

Her tongue found his and their kiss deepened as one hand threaded through her hair, the other pulling her all the way onto his lap. Through her shirt and bra he could feel her nipples beading against the inside of his biceps, and his erection was cradled in her soft curves.

And then, suddenly, she was pushing out of his arms, her chest heaving as she tried to catch her breath.

"I'm sorry, Sam, it's not that I don't want to be with you." Her words rammed into each other like out-of-control train cars. "Obviously I do. More than anything. But—"

She put her hand over her mouth to stop the flow of words, and it took every ounce of control he possessed to play the nice guy and do the right thing.

"It's okay, Dianna," he managed to say despite the intense throbbing in his groin.

Her eyes pleaded with him to understand. "I heard what you said by the river, about not wanting to get involved with me again. And I respect that, Sam. I really do. So even though I want to be with you, right now I'm afraid I'm not in any frame of mind for sex without strings." Giving him a crooked smile, she added, "And I wouldn't want to go all psycho on you later."

Fuck. He'd dug this hole himself, hadn't he? What could he do but agree with her that not having sex was for the best? After all, it was his idea in the first place.

Willing his erection to disappear, he stood up and reached for her hands in as nonsexual a way as he could.

"How about we eat something and turn in for the night? It's been one hell of a long day, and things always look better in the morning."

"I just wish we knew what to do next," she said as they made their way back to their tent.

"Do people always tell you everything the first time you interview them?" he asked her, trying like hell to refocus on finding April rather than how much he wanted the woman beside him.

Looking thoughtful, she said, "No. Not usually. Sometimes I have to pull the information out of them." She shot him a sidelong glance. "Do you think that's going to happen here?"

"My gut tells me that something will turn up tomorrow."

"I hope you're right."

He made them another quick meal of lumpy chicken and rice stew, and as they ate in silence, then got ready for bed, Sam had to ask himself if his emphatic insistence on not giving their relationship another shot had actually been on target.

Had he put too much emphasis on who they were ten years ago and not enough on who they are now?

Because wasn't the real question less about whether he'd be screwed if she left him again one day than it was about whether she'd truly want to be with him now? Would she be willing to give up her fancy name brands and champagne lunches for a simple man in turnouts and a work shirt?

"You take the tent," he told her. "I'm used to sleeping outside."

Clearly too tired to argue, she climbed into the tent and zipped it shut. But Sam lay awake in his sleeping bag, staring up at the stars, one final question haunting him as the moon rose higher in the sky.

Was he willing to risk everything for the woman he'd never stopped loving?

# CHAPTER SIXTEEN

APRIL WOKE up with a start, her neck cracking as she lifted her head off her chest too quickly. Her shoulders ached and her legs and arms had gone numb beneath her bindings. Her mouth felt like it'd been stuffed with cotton, and she ran her tongue around the inside of her mouth trying to find any hidden pools of moisture, but it was a total waste of effort.

To make matters worse, she needed to pee. Bad enough that her bladder was going to burst if she didn't get to a bathroom soon. Her head was throbbing and she felt dizzy, too. Definitely not the best day she'd ever had.

Hoping someone was close enough to hear, she grunted loudly.

After what seemed like an eternity, a fat guy with

beady little eyes opened the door. "Shut up or I'll make you shut up."

His sour-milk breath made her recoil in disgust and she wondered where the guy who'd kidnapped her had gone. Still desperately needing a bathroom, she continued grunting and pleading with her eyes until he opened the door wider and ripped the duct tape from her mouth.

Tears sprang to her eyes. She couldn't believe how much that hurt!

"What the fuck is your problem?"

"I have to pee," she ground out in a hoarse voice. "And I'm dying of thirst. You don't want me to die of dehydration, do you?"

"Jesus, I'll get you some water and let you pee. Just shut up."

He pulled out a sharp pocket knife. "But no funny business or I'll have to use my knife to cut more than just the tape."

"I swear, I won't try anything."

And she wouldn't. Not yet, anyway, even though she definitely felt like her chances of escaping this guy were better than with her original captor.

A few seconds later, she was free, but when she tried to stand up, her numb legs were useless and she totally blew it, landing on her hands and knees on the floor.

The guy laughed and picked her up, getting in some major squeezing action on her boobs. April could feel the sharp prickling pains moving all through her arms and hands and fingers, toes and feet and calves as her blood started circulating again.

She bit her lip to keep from giving away her discomfort and balled her hands into fists to keep from clawing at the guy's touch, just clearheaded enough to realize that she should use the bathroom before she tried to escape again.

Looking around as he carried her, she realized they were in a big barn. There were no animals in it, only a smattering of hay on the packed dirt floor. Along one wall, dozens of boxes were stacked, almost up to the roof.

What was this place?

In the far corner, he kicked open a rickety door and plopped her down. Putting her hands on the wall, April's feet held her upright this time.

She peered into a dark, empty room. "Where's the bathroom?"

He pointed to a yellow bucket. "Right there."

Fine, she'd gone in grosser places. "Can I at least have a moment of privacy?"

He crossed his beefy arms across his chest. "No, I wanna watch."

She shrugged as she undid the top button on her jeans. "Okay, but I might have to do more than pee."

His face turned green. "Hurry the fuck up," he said, then kicked the door shut on her.

Squatting over the bucket, April quickly took care of business, then stood up and looked around the room for an escape route. Way up high, there was a small window. The glass was already shattered, which she supposed would help if she tried to break through it.

The question was, how would she get up to it?

Scanning the walls for something she could use as foot- and handholds, she heard a sound that reminded her of a hose turning on. Taking the chance to poke her head out through the door, she saw her overweight guard standing with his back to her, peeing like he'd been holding it as long as she had.

Adrenaline raced through her and she made the quick decision to bolt across the straw and out the main door. Several empty supersized beer cans lay on the ground, which explained why he was still emptying his bladder.

The sun was just starting to rise, and as she sprinted past several beaten-up trailers, it occurred to her that she'd been passed out since the previous afternoon.

Suddenly, she heard a loud roar. Oh shit, her guard must have finally realized she was gone.

Ridiculously thankful that Dianna had forced her to be on the track team in high school, April continued to run until she was surrounded by forest on all sides. She was tempted to follow a narrow deer trail, but she knew that would only make it easier for the guy to find her.

Not having time to second-guess her decision, she skidded down a hill. For the first hundred feet or so she was able to keep her footing, but as the mountain grew steeper, she was no match for the thick tree trunks and large rocks that kept slamming into her knees and legs.

She slowed down to navigate several large boulders, but just as she made it past the last one, her foot caught on a dead branch and she went flying down the steep hill, tumbling head over heels.

Curling up in a ball, she'd barely covered her head with her hands when she crashed into a rock.

A whimper of pain left her throat as she lay there, still in a ball, fighting back a heavy wave of nausea. Blackness threatened to take her and she knew she was just on the edge of passing out.

*No!* She couldn't give up now.

Slowly uncurling her limbs, she waited for a bolt of pain to tell her that something was broken. But when she realized she'd gotten lucky and everything was still in working order, she sat up and listened carefully for the sound of footsteps.

All she heard were birds chirping and water rushing.

Standing up, she carefully picked her way down the hill in her tennis shoes, holding on to tree trunks for support. Concentrating on each painful step, she finally got close enough to the river that she could see the water through the trees, clambering down the boulders until she got to the edge of a steep rock face.

After some quick calculations, she realized her only choice was to jump onto the sandy bank.

All the air knocked out of her chest as she landed. Lying there, trying to get her breath back, staring up at the sky, it was so tempting to just close her eyes and sleep.

*Damn it.* If only she weren't so tired. Or hungry. Or thirsty.

Scrunching up her eyes, she ground the balls of her hands into the sockets to wake herself up before rolling her stiff muscles into a sitting position. Getting up again, she waded into the water and followed the edge of the river downstream, hoping she'd see someone fishing or boating at some point.

After walking for what felt like hours beneath the bright sun and having no choice but to drink from the lake—giardia be damned—she finally heard the most beautiful sound in the world; little kids splashing and playing in the water while their mother yelled at them to be careful.

Moving closer, she saw the Colorado State Park signs along the river and a new burst of energy ran through her.

She'd actually made it.

She was safe!

Running out of the water, she jogged up an empty beach, then between RVs in their numbered spots, following the signs to the ranger station. Seeing a pay phone at the edge of a parking lot, she stopped and dialed the operator.

"I need to make a collect call," she said in a breathless voice, giving Dianna's cell phone number.

"I'm afraid the party you are trying to reach is unavailable."

Shit, Dianna's phone had gone to voice mail. Now what?

"Is there another number you would like to try?" the operator asked.

She could call the police, but her kidnapping was all so random that she was afraid they might not believe her. The only people besides Dianna who knew she was missing were her friends on the Farm. Figuring they had to be wondering where she was, she gave the operator the phone number for the Farm. It rang once, twice, three times, and she prayed that someone would pick up.

"Hello."

April was already talking when she realized Peter couldn't hear her because the operator was saying, "I have a collect call for you from—"

"April Kelley."

"Will you take it?" the operator asked.

Peter said he would and then April heard him say to someone, "Go get Dianna. Her sister's on the phone."

"My sister's there?" April asked, amazed that Dianna had not only found the commune, but had managed to get up there in one piece. Then again, why was she surprised? Dianna always succeeded, even when she attempted the impossible.

"She came looking for you last night," he replied, and then she heard him tell someone, "Yes, I'm talking with her right now."

"Oh my God, April," Dianna said, coming on the line. "Are you okay?"

Dianna's concern brought tears to her eyes. She felt like a little kid all over again, desperate for her big sister to come find her and take her away from her horrible life.

"I think so. I was abducted by some guy in the hospital parking lot and I managed to escape to a state park. The signs say Tigiwon on them." Sniffling, she admitted, "I was so scared. But I knew you'd try to find me."

"Thank God you're okay. I'm coming to get you."

Dianna sounded incredibly shaken up and April could hardly believe this was her ever-poised sister on the other end of the line.

"Go to the ranger station and wait for me. And April?"

April wiped away her own tears and cleared her throat. "Yes?"

"I love you."

Her tears started anew. "I love you, too."

She hung up the phone and was heading back out into the parking lot when she was struck with the bad feeling of being watched. But when she stopped and looked all around her, she didn't see or hear anything more suspicious than a group of children riding their bikes while their parents lounged on folding chairs and drank beer.

It looked like nothing more than a perfect summer afternoon, but as she quickly followed the arrow to the ranger's office, the hair on the back of her neck wouldn't stop standing straight up.

*Stop freaking out,* she told herself. *You did it. You escaped. You're safe.*

Dianna was coming, and this time, April was perfectly happy to let her sister take care of everything. At fourteen, she'd fought her sister with all her might, partly, she now realized, because fighting was all she knew. But right this second, she longed for comfort. For safety. For a warm bed and a glass of warm milk.

For so long, she'd raged against Dianna for treating her like a baby. Funny how a little coddling no longer seemed like such a bad thing.

# CHAPTER SEVENTEEN

"SHE'S SAFE," Dianna told Sam and Peter as she hung up the phone.

She couldn't remember ever feeling happier as Sam pulled her into his arms. It felt so good to hug him. Not in a state of fear, but, finally, with joy.

"I'm so glad she's okay," he said softly in her ear before releasing her.

She slid one hand down to lace her fingers through his, suddenly feeling like new beginnings might be possible for everyone.

"How far is the campground?"

Peter pulled a map out of a nearby bookshelf, opened it up. "It's somewhat complicated by the downed trees all over the area."

Dianna felt her chest tighten at the thought of not being able to get to April right away.

Sam leaned over the map. "I'm sure we'll have no problem following your directions." He didn't look at her, but she knew he was saying the calming words for her benefit.

Peter highlighted the various trails with a pen. "As the crow flies, it's approximately ten miles. The first chunk of miles will be the hardest." And then he smiled. "I do have some good news for you, though. I keep a dirt bike stashed on the last few miles of trail. After you hike to it, the bike should cut hours off your time."

She couldn't stop herself from throwing her arms around Peter this time, and even though he was stiff and uncomfortable, she didn't care. She was so happy that April was okay she saw no reason to contain her joy. Yes, she knew they'd still need to have April sit down with the police and describe the creep who'd grabbed her, but right now that felt like a small detail.

Hiking quickly across the Farm to their tent and gear, after Sam filled his pack with water, food, and first-aid supplies, they set off toward the campgrounds. Although April sounded fine on the phone, Dianna knew it was best to be prepared for the worst. Still, just thinking of having to use the first-aid kit really freaked her out.

"I would have packed the first-aid kit anyway," Sam told her, reading her mind like he had so many times before.

"I know," she said. "This situation with April could have been so much worse."

Sam reached for her hand and squeezed it. "Just like you've said, she's a tough kid. I'm not surprised she got herself to safety." He raised an eyebrow. "I'll bet you would have done the same thing in her situation. You two actually do sound quite a bit alike."

She bit her lip. Was he right? Were she and April really that similar? Dianna would have never used the word "tough" to describe herself, but maybe that was because she'd spent so long making sure everything looked perfect on the outside and rarely let anyone look at what she was hiding on the inside.

Sam's hand was warm and dry in hers and it felt strangely right to walk through the Farm and onto the trail beside him. Almost as if they were a couple.

"So—"

He paused and she wondered what he was having such a hard time saying.

"What's your schedule like? Do you get much time off?"

She hid her grin. It was so cute, watching him fish around for information without trying to look like he was fishing.

Trying to act like his question was no big deal—when the truth was that it was a *huge* deal that he clearly wanted to spend more time with her outside of their quest for April—she shrugged. "Working on TV is pretty similar to working fires. We're really, really busy for a few months, and then we get nice long breaks." She couldn't resist adding, "Plus, if there's a town I want to spend some time in, I can usually convince my producer to set a week's worth of shows there."

She left her obvious follow-up intent of, *"Like, say, Lake Tahoe,"* unspoken.

"Good to know," he said, before surprising her with, "By the way, your river rafting and hiking skills have far exceeded my expectations."

Dianna had to laugh at herself. She was glowing all over, unable to stop smiling at his praise. One would have thought she'd never heard a compliment before.

"Thank you, Sam, that means a lot to me. Although I suppose it helps that your expectations were pretty darn low to start with."

Instead of laughing with her, Sam shot her a very serious, almost chastened, glance. "Back in the hospital, in the motel room, I behaved like an ass. I made a lot of assumptions about you, your job, what you were capable of. I was wrong."

She shook her head. "No, you've been incredible, helping me like this. Especially after everything that went wrong before."

She was searching for the right words to try to solidify some future plans for the two of them when Sam suddenly let go of her hand and ducked into a small crevasse in the rocks.

"Good news, the dirt bike is right where Peter said it would be."

The hike over tree trunks and wide boulders had gone much more quickly than she expected. Entirely because of the company.

Sam pulled one of the helmets out of his pack, but instead of handing it to her, he plopped it on her head.

"Cute. Very cute."

She hadn't given much thought to her appearance since April's call, but now that everything was almost normal, it was nice to know she wasn't going to scare little children. And that Sam still seemed to think she looked okay.

"Climb on behind me," he said as he wheeled the miniature motorcycle out from its hiding place. Through the shield on the helmet she could see he was smiling as he said, "And hold on tight."

Oh yes, it would be her pleasure to wrap her arms around his waist and chest and tuck her hips against his muscular butt.

Sam revved the engine and then they were flying down the dirt trail. Her long hair was whipping out of the bottom of her helmet, dust from the trail soon covering her legs and boots.

She'd never felt so wonderfully alive!

Between the speed and Sam's closeness, she found herself laughing out loud. And best of all, she was getting to share this moment with Sam.

The beauty of the trees and mountains and blue sky above were so colorful, so lovely. She hadn't been able to appreciate any of it until now, and she prayed that once she and April were back in San Francisco, she'd get to share another incredible moment like this with Sam.

Being with him had always been her biggest thrill. A total rush.

It still was.

Sam heard her laugh and smiled. He never considered that he might find himself on a dirt bike with Dianna, speeding down a narrow trail in the Rockies. And yet, these had been the most exhilarating couple of days in recent memory. No wildfire could compare to Dianna. Not even the heat.

Seeing her look so happy this morning after April's call, it was impossible not to want to see her look that way again. The night before, he'd grappled with the question of giving things another shot. This morning, he couldn't remember his reasons why not.

She was beautiful. Smart. Loyal. And, despite everything he'd tried to convince himself she'd done during the past decade, incredibly loving.

He'd be a fool to let her slip out of his life again.

The bike was fast, and because Dianna didn't seem to mind the speed, he kicked it up another notch. Within the next quarter hour they were pulling into the campground's front gates. Heading for the ranger's headquarters, he put the brakes on and Dianna was off the bike and running up the stairs before he turned the engine off.

Seconds later, she came back down, her face pinched and tight. "She's not there."

Oh shit. April'd had plenty of time to get to the ranger's station. She should have been there.

And then, he heard Dianna gasp, her hand going over her mouth as all the color left her face, her finger pointing toward the sky.

A quarter mile to the left, in the direction of the river, a plume of fresh, black smoke was rising into the blue sky.

A building must have just been set on fire.

"Get on," he yelled, and once her arms were back around him, he sped down the paved one-way road that wound through the campsites, wanting to get as close as he could to the fire as quickly as possible before he went in on foot. A group of vacationing families stood huddled together in the parking lot watching the flames.

Again, Dianna jumped off and raced toward the cabin before the bike's tires had completely stopped spinning.

Leaping off the leather seat, the dirt bike dropping onto the dirt, Sam ran after her. She was fast, but he was faster. He grabbed her arms, not letting her take another step toward certain danger. She struggled hard, trying to pull away, and he had no choice but to imprison her against him, her back pressed hard against his front.

"What if April's inside? I have to save her!"

It was a big leap, but he understood why she'd gone

there. April's safety was all she could think about right now.

But if he couldn't get her to listen to reason, there'd be more than one casualty today.

"We don't know if she's inside. And it's not safe for you to go anywhere near that building," he said firmly in her ear to make sure she got it.

"But what if she is? I can't let her burn to death!"

There was no reason in her voice, only desperation. He understood, but it didn't mean he was willing to risk losing her.

The tall dry grass in front of the building was already engulfed in flames. Before he could even get near the cabin, he'd need to put out the grass fire. Still, he wouldn't let her go until she'd regained control.

"The only way I can get to the building is to light a backfire."

"No," she gasped. "Not more fire."

"When the two fires make contact, they'll burn each other out. It's the only way."

Finally, she seemed to understand, giving him an anguished "Okay."

He was still afraid that she'd make a run for it when he released his hold on her and pulled several flares out of his pocket. A couple spilled to the ground and Dianna picked them up. Looking at the trees, he studied the direction of the wind to make sure the flames weren't going to blow straight toward them, or toward the crowd of people who should have known better and evacuated the site already.

But he didn't have time to warn them of the dangers of loitering so close to a live fire. If Dianna's sister was inside, he had to save her.

If it wasn't already too late.

He'd been in the very same position with his brother Connor, had watched him suffer agonizing burns. Even though he'd done all he could to save him, he'd always wished he could have done more.

Would Dianna ever be able to forgive herself if April perished in the fire? And would she forgive him for not saving her?

He reached for her hand and she dug her nails into his knuckles as the fire ravaged the ground in between them and the cabin. And then, less than a minute later, a path cleared in the field into a mass of sizzling embers.

"I'm going to try and get in the cabin now, but I don't want you to follow me. It's not safe."

Sam could see that Dianna wanted to fight him on it, but he had to make sure she understood.

"I can't help whoever is in the cabin if I have to help you too."

"Just hurry," she said, quickly giving in. "Please."

Without his turnouts, the heat emanating from the ground was intense, but he'd been in far hotter forests. He ran toward the small building, all of his focus on finding a way to get inside, considering that the entire front half was already on fire.

Quickly jogging around the perimeter, he found no doors, no windows to enter from. He'd have to go in the front by diverting the fire from the door.

Grabbing a large branch off the ground, he climbed a nearby tree behind the building and launched himself onto the steaming roof. Moving quickly, he ripped off old roofing tiles, exposing the thin wood planks that covered the beams.

He worked fast with the stick, ramming it into the wood, busting a hole in the ceiling. Any second now, flames would find the new source of oxygen and shoot out the hole. If he wasn't careful, he'd be caught in them, but if he didn't make the hole big enough there wouldn't be enough oxygen to divert the flames from the rest of the structure.

A split second before fire rushed out of the hole he'd made in the roof, Sam jumped out of the way, launching himself the eight feet to the ground.

Like clockwork, the flames moved away from the door. Moving around the front, he kicked it in. The smoke was black and thick, but he'd spent ten years maneuvering through these kinds of conditions, and his eye was trained to look for limbs, to listen for coughing and look for bodies.

But the building was empty. Completely empty.

Sam heard the familiar crackle of a building about to implode and in the nick of time he got out of the building and ran like hell. The walls started falling in on themselves before he reached Dianna.

"Where is she?" Dianna screamed at him.

"She wasn't in there."

She fell to her knees, her face in her hands.

Sam had never felt so helpless in all his life as he squatted down to gather her in his arms.

The man watched Dianna Kelley from the parking lot, waiting for the perfect moment to make his move.

Her sister was already in the trunk of his car. When he got back to his compound, he'd punish the girl for the way she was thrashing around, for the noises she dared to make. Fortunately, with all of the commotion from the fire—children and women yelling and crying, sirens finally making their way into the campground from an oncoming Colorado Department of Forestry fire engine and police cars—no one could hear his prisoner struggle.

He'd been furious when Mickey woke him up out of his dark dreams with the news that April had escaped. But it had been fairly easy to guess where she'd end up. Tigiwon was as close as they got to civilization around here and straight down the hill from his lab.

After speeding down the single-lane road to the campground, he'd spotted her on a pay phone, probably giving Dianna instructions on where to find her. Moving silently, he'd followed the girl after she hung up the phone, keeping out of her range of sight until she made the mistake of believing she'd really gotten away.

As she took the narrow trail that led between the parking lot and the ranger's station, after first making sure they were alone, he'd jumped her, slamming his fist into her jaw once, then twice, until she crumpled to the ground.

Setting the cabin on fire had been pure genius. It was the perfect distraction so that he could not only take April to his car unnoticed, but given that he knew Dianna was on her way to collect her sister, it was the ideal opportunity to finally take his true prize captive as well.

If only that goddamned guy would leave her side for thirty seconds, maybe he could get close enough.

Moving away from his car, he headed toward the throng of people surrounding the fire engine. At the first available opportunity, he'd be ready to spring.

## CHAPTER EIGHTEEN

TWO HOURS later, after the cop cars and fire engines drove away, after the crowd of bystanders had grown bored and dispersed back to their campfires and card games, after she and Sam had circled the campground twice looking for clues and found absolutely nothing, Dianna was on the verge of giving up hope.

She'd never been able to forget the pain of being eleven years old and watching the state official drive away with April. Losing her own baby had been brutal and, of course, the breakup with Sam had been horrible. But sitting against a tree, her knees under her chin as she wrapped herself into a tight ball on the forest's dirt floor, knowing her sister was at the mercy of some anonymous creep . . . well, that was almost unbearable.

Sam had offered to deal with the police alone, but

although she'd felt so raw and her fears about her sister burning alive in that cabin were still jammed in every pore, every cell, every single breath she took, Dianna had felt that it was best if she spoke directly to the cops.

Not that it had mattered. Sure, the police had taken notes. They'd looked concerned. But they'd also made it perfectly clear that they didn't have the resources to jump on the case, not with a couple of recent murders in the area taking top priority.

"Why aren't they going to do more to find her?" she asked Sam. "It feels like they're hardly taking me seriously."

To Dianna, it seemed like the cops had been much more concerned about who had set the fire, asking Sam endless questions about how he'd been able to put it out without a water truck and fire gear.

Sitting beside her now, his arm around her shoulders a shock of warmth against her cold limbs, Sam pressed his lips against the top of her head.

"Nothing's changed from our original plan," he reminded her. "We're going to find April."

She longed to believe him, but she wasn't sure she could anymore. Her life had turned into a bad dream. A surreal nightmare. She desperately wanted to get the hell out of here and pretend that none of this was happening, that everything was exactly as it had been before she'd come to Colorado.

But she couldn't do any of those things. Because April

was still missing, even after they'd come so close to finding her.

"I'm not going to lie to you. I've been up against some pretty nasty wildfires, but I've never been in a situation like this before." He paused, brought her hands to his lips, and pressed a kiss against her knuckles. "I've never had you by my side, either. That's why I know we're going to find April and bring her home."

She wanted to listen to his words, rather than all of the voices in her head telling her that they were too late, that she was never going to see April again. But letting herself believe that everything was okay after April's phone call had been her biggest mistake.

Having hope ripped away had shattered her beyond repair and she felt broken inside.

"How can you have that kind of faith in me?" she whispered. "I'm failing her, Sam."

"You sure as hell aren't failing her. You're pushing yourself to the limits to help her. And trust me, April knows you well enough to know you're not going to give up. You're tenacious. And you love her. So even if she can't escape again, she's going to hold on and wait for you. She knows you're coming. She's always known it."

Dianna could hardly swallow past the lump in her throat. "I'm just so scared, Sam." God, she hated tears, hated feeling weak and completely out of control. "I hate that I don't know what to do next."

"Of course you're scared. She's your sister and you

love her. But you've got to see that this isn't much different from fighting to pull April out of the foster system."

"It is," she protested.

"Not really. You didn't know much about the people she was living with back then. But you knew she was unhappy, so you fought and fought and fought and fought for her. You won, Dianna. You won." He closed his eyes and bowed his head against her hands before looking back into her eyes. "You're going to win again. And I'm going to be with you every step of the way."

A flash of lightning crackled overhead and thick drops of rain began to fall.

She was still silently digesting his optimism, his faith that they'd find April despite this crushing blow, when he pulled her to her feet.

"I know you want to stay here in case she comes back, but we don't have our gear and I'm not going to risk you getting sick in the wind and the rain tonight." Before she could protest, he added, "And if she can get to a phone again, she'll know where you are. She'll call the Farm first."

She knew he was right, but even as she let him take her over to the dirt bike, she hated leaving the campground without having gotten one step closer to finding April, hated thinking that the person responsible for all of this pain could be standing in the forest watching them right now.

As they drove the dirt bike on the trail back to the Farm, Sam's heart went out to the incredible woman holding him tightly from behind. He thought he'd been through hell with Connor, but not only had he been able to immediately rescue his brother, he'd had the satisfaction of personally wiping out the fire responsible for melting Connor's skin. Whereas Dianna was moving forward with no clues, only more disasters, more misfortune.

There was none of the exhilaration of their ride in the other direction, none of the laughter. Even the blue skies were now gray, spitting cold rain at them as a final insult.

She shivered against him and all he wanted was to get her out of her wet clothes and settled in a warm, dry spot with some food and water. When they came to the first of the wide tree trunks in the middle of the trail, Sam made a spur-of-the-moment decision to try to carry the bike over the barrier.

Dianna's teeth were chattering as she got off the bike and Sam didn't have to think twice about hoisting the bike over to the other side of the trail. She'd easily scrambled over the tree trunks on the way to the campground, but now, between her fatigue and her despair, he knew she needed his help.

The fact that she let him assist her without protest worried him more than anything. He'd do anything to see the spark in her eyes return.

After what seemed like an eternity of grinding through mud and bumping painfully over endless rocks on the trail, then getting off and carrying the bike over to the other side, they pulled in through the Farm's gates. Sam parked the bike next to an ancient tractor.

Dianna's lips had a faint blue tinge to them, and he was so worried about her that he bent down, lifted her into his arms, and headed for Peter's house.

"I can walk on my own," she protested, but her voice sounded weak, wavery, utterly unlike her.

"I know, sweetheart," he told her. "Let me take care of you."

Again, it worried him that she didn't fight him on it. He needed to get her warm and dry as quickly as possible.

At least she noted, "Our tent is in the other direction."

"You need a hot shower," he explained, "and I figure Peter may be the only person here who's got one."

A short while later, after pretty much running across the meadow with Dianna in his arms, Sam pounded on Peter's door. The Farm's owner immediately ushered them inside the blessedly warm space looking concerned when he counted only two of them.

"You didn't find April."

"I'll explain everything soon enough," Sam said, cutting off any further discussion. "Right now, I need to get Dianna into some warm water."

Peter nodded. "Follow me."

Sam was surprised when Peter took them out a back door, down a short gravel walkway, and into a surprisingly nice little guest house, complete with a kitchen, bathroom, and fireplace in the living room.

"I'll have your bags, clean dry clothes, and food put out for you on the covered deck," Peter said before closing the door.

Tracking mud across the cement floor, Sam headed for the tiled bathroom. Still cradling her tightly against his chest with one arm, he turned on the shower with the other. Quickly, the water went from cold to hot and he carried her under the spray, both of them fully clothed.

The look on her face when she finally stopped shivering was breathtakingly beautiful. Telling himself that his job was done, he gently put her down on her feet.

"Are you feeling better now?"

A part of him hoped that she'd say no, that she'd beg him to stay.

Instead, she nodded, her big green eyes holding his captive.

"Thank you for everything, Sam."

Even though every cell in his body screamed at him to kiss her, he knew he couldn't. She'd been through enough already without having him paw at her while her every defense was down.

He forced himself to step away from the water, away from the way her clothes were plastered to her curves, outlining every delicious inch of her body.

"I'm going to grab our things and lay some dry clothes out for you on the bed."

God, it was going to kill him to stay out of this shower, especially when he knew she was about to peel off her clothes and let the water run over her bare skin. His cock pushed at the back of his zipper, desperate to come out and join the party. He made himself turn away before she saw how much he wanted her.

"Take all the time you need to get warm," he said, pausing at the doorway for one last look. "I don't want you getting sick."

Her cheeks were flushed and he told himself it was simply from the rush of going from cold rain to a warm shower, not that she was having similar thoughts of making love to him. Pulling from a nearly empty well of will, he stepped outside the bathroom and pulled the door shut.

Her sister was still missing, for fuck's sake. Finding April was the only thing he should have been thinking of.

But he couldn't erase the sensual image of Dianna standing in the shower, of how easy it would have been to strip off her clothes. In lieu of a cold shower, Sam walked out the front door, past the food and their backpacks, which Peter had already put on the deck.

Icy pellets of rain would have to do the trick.

With trembling fingers, Dianna undid the buttons on her shirt and dropped the soaked fabric to the tiled floor. She tried to take her pants off next, but when they got stuck at her shoes, she sat down and undid her laces.

The warm water flowing over her head, her shoulders, down her back, felt incredible. But not nearly as amazing as Sam's hands on her skin when he'd held her in the shower. The heat in his eyes had warmed her faster than the water and she'd been seconds from pressing herself against him and begging him to help her forget her worries by making love to her.

Pulling her shoes and muddy socks off, she sat on the tiled shower floor in her underwear and rewound to the moment Sam had run into the burning building at the campgrounds. He hadn't hesitated for a second, hadn't been the least bit concerned about his own safety. Instead, he'd been intent on making sure that she was all right, that she wasn't going to do anything stupid and hurt herself.

It was the first time she'd ever witnessed him in action. She'd never seen anything like it, not even in action films with actors playing the part of daredevil firefighters.

Sam had been a superhero come to life, running through flames, leaping onto the roof and smashing it in.

And he'd done it solely in the hope of saving her sister.

Watching him push through the front door of the cabin, her heart had been in her throat. She'd fought the desperate urge to run in after him, to somehow stop him from sacrificing himself for her.

Her heart squeezed as the unassailable truth smashed into her: She'd never stopped loving Sam. Never. And she would love him forever.

What she wouldn't give to share her love with him and have it returned.

Carefully standing back up, she unclasped her bra, her breasts feeling ripe and sensitive, as did the vee between her legs when she slipped her panties off. No question, the physical release of making love with Sam would be phenomenal. But that was only partially why she wanted to be with him.

Sam was her last tie to hope. To comfort. And faith.

More than anything, she wanted to be naked and warm in his arms, to pretend for a few precious moments that everything was all right.

Finding a bar of soap, she lathered up her hair and skin, realizing as the water washed the remaining dirt away how wonderful it was to be clean again. A simple pleasure, but a pleasure nonetheless.

Knowing Sam should have a turn in the shower before she used up all of the hot water, she switched off the tap and wrapped herself in a large brown towel. Everything on the Farm was surprisingly clean and she acknowledged that she'd been too hasty in condemning the commune in her conversation with April without coming to see it first. No wonder her sister had stormed out of the café.

Moving into the small bedroom, Dianna found dry clothes laid out on the bed. She quickly toweled off and got dressed, then went into the main room, where an array of food was laid out on a small table.

Obviously, Sam had brought everything inside, but where was he?

She was making her way to the front door when he opened it and walked back inside. Also in dry clothes, he looked surprisingly clean.

"Did you use Peter's shower?"

He ran one hand through his dark, still-wet hair, looking disconcertingly stern before one side of his mouth finally quirked up.

"Rain has its uses."

"You showered outside?" she asked, shivering just thinking about it.

When he nodded, she envisioned Sam standing naked in the rain and immediately heated up. He held his hands out, and she was so wrapped up in her fantasy of catching him bathing in the rain that it took her a little while to realize he was holding something warm and delicious.

"Peter just came by with this fresh-baked bread and I filled him in on everything."

She immediately sobered as the day's horror came back to her. Sitting down hard on one of the dining chairs by the door, her fear for April settled into the pit of her stomach like a rock.

"I don't know if I can eat anything."

Ignoring her, Sam put the bread down with the rest of the food, got a couple of plates and utensils from the small kitchenette, and began portioning out the food. Despite her heavy mood, her stomach rumbled.

Suddenly ravenous, she reached for a slice of bread just as Sam was handing it to her and their fingers collided. She shivered again at the touch of his skin.

His brows furrowed with renewed concern. "Cold?"

"No," she replied. Just the opposite. Despite everything, she was burning up with desire. "Just starved."

They ate in silence for several minutes until Sam said, "I'm glad you're eating after all. It's been a pretty rough couple of days. You need the energy."

"We both do," she agreed. "Going after April had been so much harder than I thought it would be. And, honestly, I thought it was going to be pretty damn hard."

He put down his glass and gave her a stern look. "That's why tonight is all about getting some rest."

Immediately going on the defensive, she said, "I'm not tired, Sam, and I want to get back out there looking for her."

But all he did was shake his head, just as she'd known he would.

"I checked with Peter. This storm isn't going to let up until morning. The sun's already on its way down and we're not going to make any headway in this rain. If anything, I'm afraid you'll get sick, and then we'll really be in trouble."

She pushed back from the table, feeling restless, hating knowing they were stuck for another night.

Also standing up, Sam said, "I know it's early, but I want you to go to bed, Dianna."

There was only one bed in the small house. "Where are you going to sleep?"

She held her breath as she waited for his answer.

He jerked his head toward the door. "I've got the tent set up on the front deck. I'll be right outside the door if you need me."

The rational part of her brain knew he was making sense. But logic wasn't enough anymore.

"Stay with me tonight, Sam."

His expression reminded her of the granite rocks in the river. He was trying to protect her, he'd always tried to protect her, but right now she needed him to give in, even if he thought she was making a mistake.

Moving closer, she put her hand on his arm. "I won't be able to sleep unless you're holding me. I need you, Sam. Please."

# CHAPTER NINETEEN

SAM'S NEED for Dianna was as close to an unstoppable force as he'd ever withstood. But it had been a hard day, and although she thought sex was what she wanted, he had to accept that it was just stress talking.

On top of everything else she was dealing with, he didn't want her to have to regret making love to him, too.

But how could he force his foot down on the brakes when he was mesmerized by her voice, by her beautifully expressive face, by the longing in her eyes as she moved closer?

"At first," she said softly, "when we were in the shower together, all I wanted was to try to forget. But now, all I want is to keep believing. For so long, I didn't believe that we were possible. I didn't have faith that you and I could ever find each other again." She reached a hand up to his face and ran her thumb across his lips. "But now I know that if you and I can forgive each other and make a new start, then anything is possible. Even finding April."

He threaded his fingers through her hair and then they were kissing, their tongues dancing together. Rekindled memories of the way they'd been collided with the sensation that he was loving her for the very first time.

Unable to go slow when he'd been wanting her for so damn long, he nipped and sucked at her sweet mouth, the sensitive bow at the center of her upper lip, the seductive plump flesh of the lower one.

Moving his hands down her back, to the curve of her hips, he pulled her closer, his raging hard-on throbbing and pulsing against her belly.

"It's been too long," he confessed against her lips. "I don't know if I can go slow."

He felt her smile again, heard her say, "I don't want slow. I just want you."

It was all the encouragement he needed to let the animal inside loose. Seconds later he was ripping off her shirt, yanking down her pants, while she mirrored his movements with her hands on his clothes. And then he was naked and her skin was bare beneath his fingers and he lost any last shred of gentleness, of patience.

Pulling her bra down, he pressed her breasts together with his palms and sucked her sweet flesh into his mouth. Moaning her pleasure, she arched her back and her nipples jutted against his tongue.

Stepping back to try to keep from losing it completely, he made the mistake of looking at her. With her head thrown back in ecstasy, skin flushed with arousal, she was a goddess, and instead of getting his game back, he dropped to his knees, yanking her panties down as he ran kisses along her flat belly. She opened her legs wider for him and it was all the invitation he needed to take her heat in his mouth.

Her hands grasped his rain-wet hair and his name reverberated off the walls. Using his shoulder to shift her legs even wider, he grasped her hips with his hands to hold her steady. He ran his tongue over her in long strokes, finally settling at the hard nub of her clitoris.

She tasted so good. She'd always been so responsive when he loved her like this, her body trembling in his hands.

Lightly swirling his tongue against her arousal, he shifted her weight so that he could hold her up with only one hand. Needing to be inside her even as he made her come with his tongue, he slipped one finger into her tight canal, her inner muscles grasping and pulling him deeper inside.

He could feel how close she was, knew that she was about to explode, so he slid another finger in to join the first, and as he bucked them in, then out, he flicked his tongue fast across her clit and took her all the way over the edge.

She was still gasping with pleasure when he pulled her down, holding her hips an inch from the tip of his hard shaft.

He forced himself to say, "I don't have any protection."

"I don't care," was her instant response, and then she was sliding down onto his hard shaft and taking him in, her expression one of utter satisfaction. Complete pleasure. Riding him hard, she moved up, then down on his cock, and even though a part of him wanted to slow down and savor every moment of their lovemaking, he was too far gone to do anything but call out her name and give in to one of the most powerful orgasms of his life.

Seconds turned into minutes as they held on to each other. Many times over the course of his hotshot career, Sam had run nearly vertical slopes, but he'd never had this much trouble catching his breath.

Dianna's long limbs still twined around him, he finally stood up, carrying her with him into the bedroom.

"I couldn't wait another second to have you, but now I'm going to take my time. I want to relearn every inch of your body, Dianna. Every beautiful inch."

Sam's intense words made her shiver as he climbed beneath the clean white sheets. She reached for him and he cupped her face with his large, wonderfully talented hands as he kissed her, one muscular thigh trapping her beneath him in the most delicious way.

She'd dreamed about kissing him again, so many times, more times than she would ever admit, but lying halfway across his hard muscles, pressing her lips against his, feeling the beginnings of a beard bristling across her skin, simply blew her mind.

Sensing that he was letting her lead, she pressed soft kisses along his lips, again and again as she relearned their contours, the extrasensitive spots, the places where they both used to get lost in pleasure. But her tongue was not nearly patient enough and it slipped into the corners of his mouth, then between his lips to run along his smooth teeth.

And then, suddenly, he stopped kissing her. Not knowing why, she followed his gaze to her upper arms. She'd been a little surprised herself in the shower to see that bruises covered both of them like a tattoo.

"You should have told me you were hurt."

Figuring she'd gotten these bruises during their white-water expedition, she said, "I'll heal," but she didn't want to focus on anything but the man sharing her bed. She ran her hands over his chest, his abdominal muscles.

"My God," she said reverently, "you're incredible."

His mouth moving into a smile, he teased, "You're acting like this is the first time you've seen me naked."

She pressed a series of kisses against the broad wall of his chest. "We were just kids back then. And you are definitely aging well." She looked up at him and licked her lips. "Really, really well."

"Not as well as you are," he said between kisses. "I didn't think making love to you could be better than before. But you've amazed me again, sweetheart."

Her nipples hardened against his chest and the vee between her legs grew even hotter at his words. He was right. They'd always been a good fit. Ten years after their first time, she couldn't imagine ever making love to another man.

Sam was it: the only man she wanted to share her bed with ever again.

But their bond was too new and she didn't want to say anything that would freak him out, so she simply put her lips back on his and pressed her breasts and hips up into his hard heat to tell him with her body.

His response was swift, one hand curling behind her head, the other moving down to cup her bottom. His thick erection pressed between her legs, effortlessly fueling her inner fire.

"You're mine," he whispered against her lips, before crushing them beneath his.

She felt the truth of his words deep in her bones, before giving herself up completely to pleasure.

No one kissed as good as Sam. No one knew right where to bite or how hard. No one else had ever found the exact spot to lick or the hidden places she liked to be stroked.

Only Sam.

She didn't know how long they kissed. A minute. An hour. All she knew was that she was drowning in desire, desperate for release, and that this time she didn't want to go without him.

He pulled away so that he could look at her, his gaze moving everywhere, taking in her slightly fuller hips, along with the bruises and scrapes that she'd weathered thus far in Colorado.

"So beautiful," he whispered. "You're so damn beautiful."

His declaration sent new blazes rippling through her, over her, as his hands cupped the undersides of her breasts, pushing them together, and then his tongue found her nipples again and she was moaning with pleasure.

Wanting to get closer, she arched her back as he cupped the damp vee between her legs with his palm. She gasped, involuntarily pushing her mound into his hand. The heel of his palm rocked against her and, again, she was so close, right on the edge of exploding.

Her limbs felt like melted butter and she wanted to spend hours tasting every inch of his body, but the truth was that she needed him too badly to take that kind of time or have that much patience. Not when she couldn't resist the urge to wrap her fingers around his shaft. He twitched several times in succession in her hand, so hard and big that she wondered for the hundredth time if she was dreaming.

No other lover had ever matched him in size or skill,

but, again, memories did nothing to live up to the reality of the man she now held in the palm of her hands. Moving her hand slowly up and down his hard length, he groaned—a sound that was half pain, half pleasure—and she smiled as she planted soft kisses against his shoulder, his chest, finally finding his nipple with her tongue.

She wasn't surprised when he removed her fingers and pushed her back into the bed. A spring in the bed pushed into a sore spot in her ribs and she winced.

Sam stilled. "I'm not being gentle enough."

"I'm fine," she insisted. "Better than fine. I've never felt so good in all my life."

To make sure he didn't try to play the hero again by pleasuring her and then walking away unsatisfied, she wrapped her legs tightly around him. She was so ready for him—had been dreaming of him for ten long years late at night when she was unable to control her subconscious self—that all it took was one thrust to send her reeling into another orgasm.

He drove her higher and higher, covering her scream of pleasure with a passionate kiss as her muscles squeezed him, pulling him back in with every plunge. Closing her eyes tight, she gloried in every last second of ecstasy.

When she finally came down off the incredibly high peak, she realized that he was still huge within her. Looking into his eyes, she whispered, "Sam," unable to keep everything she was feeling for him from wrapping around his name.

He didn't say a word, but she already knew what he was feeling from what she read in his eyes, on his face, in the way he touched her.

And then, he started moving again, slower this time, his hands moving from her hips, to her waist, then over her breasts, and she gasped as brand-new waves of pleasure ran through her, all the way to the tips of her toes.

She was burning up in his arms, goose bumps moving over her skin as he kissed her gently. As he rolled her nipples between his thumb and forefinger, a moan fell from her lips at the amazing sensations he continued to evoke in her. All the while, he slowly moved in, then out of her, holding off on his own completion so that she could be right there with him when he came.

She wrapped her legs even tighter around his waist and put her hands on his shoulders, pulling his head down. Their lips touched and they both careened over the edge, their hips bucking in perfect rhythm, their hands and mouths grasping at each other.

Later, as she lay against his chest, breathing hard while he stroked her hair and kissed her forehead, she no longer tried to hold back the truth of what was in her heart.

"I love you, Sam."

He couldn't believe she was giving him a chance to finally get things right, especially after he'd done so many things wrong. Not only had he screwed up by leaving her alone for so many weeks on end after the miscarriage, but when she fled to San Francisco, why hadn't he gotten down on his goddamned knees and begged her to come home?

He couldn't screw it up this time. She deserved the fairy tale this time. She deserved to be romanced.

She deserved to know without a doubt that she could count on him to be there for her. Forever.

Misunderstanding his silence, Dianna came up on one elbow and smiled at him.

"It's okay, Sam," she said softly. "I'm not in any rush. And I don't want to pressure you into anything. I just wanted to tell you what I'm feeling, that I've fallen in love with you all over again. And nothing you say or don't say is going to change my mind."

Her beautiful skin was flushed and rosy as she took his hand and placed it in the center of her chest. "Nothing is going to change what's in my heart."

Slowly stroking the pulse point in her neck with the tips of his fingers, he knew he'd never tire of looking at her, kissing her, laughing with her.

"What if I'm the one who's in a rush?" he asked in a husky voice.

Her eyes widened in surprise, and when her long limbs shifted against his, the sensual friction of their bodies amped up yet another level.

"I love you, too," he said. "I never stopped loving you, Dianna. I just tried to convince myself that I had."

"You were pretty convincing," she teased, but he hated to hear the lingering doubts behind her words.

"No, I was an idiot. And I only hope I can be the man you need me to be the second time around."

Her lips pressed gently to his. "You'll never run out of chances with me, Sam. I'm yours from here on out, whether you want me or not."

He grasped her perfectly shaped rear end and pulled her against him so that his growing hard-on was nestled between her soft thighs.

"You have no idea how much I want you. I've wanted you every single second, even when you were in that hospital bed telling me to get the hell out."

He brushed his fingers across her flat stomach and she sucked in a breath as he slowly trailed his fingertips over her midsection, the soft swell of her breasts, until goose bumps covered her skin. Wanting to touch every inch of her, he moved his hands to cup her breasts with his palms, then rubbed his thumbs across her tight nipples.

"Sam," she gasped, "it feels so good. You feel so good."

He brought his mouth down over one perfect, erect nipple and she arched into his mouth, trying to get even closer to him, and he marveled at how responsive she was to the slightest nip of his teeth on her sensitive flesh.

"How could I have possibly lived without you for so long?" he asked as he ran his mouth down her torso, aiming for the soft flesh on the undersides of her perfect breasts, her smooth stomach, then farther still, down to the shadowed vee between her thighs.

His fingers found her first, wet and slick, and then she was opening her legs for him and pushing her pelvic bone against his hand. Knowing what she wanted, he slid one finger inside her heat at the exact moment that he covered her mound with his mouth.

Loving her cries of pleasure, he slowly swirled the hard nub of her arousal with his tongue as he slid his finger in, then out, of her.

How could he have thought that he'd ever get enough of her? What an idiot he'd been.

And then, she was kicking off the sheets and sliding down his torso, her nipples branding his chest, and he was almost too deep in his fog of desire to realize that she had opened her legs and wrapped them around his waist.

Oh God, it felt so good when she took him inside, high and deep, again and again until he was losing control and they were driving into each other, making up for lost time with each thrust.

It was so easy to say "I love you" again, and then she was moaning his name and her inner muscles were pulling and squeezing his shaft as he roared with pleasure.

In the aftermath of their lovemaking, their stomachs full, their bodies sated, they held each other tight and slept.

The man's eyes hadn't left the girl all night long, partly to make sure she didn't escape, partly to make sure she didn't die on him before her sister arrived. He hadn't known his own strength until now, hadn't realized he could hit quite so hard.

Even though he'd barely slept in two days, he wasn't particularly tired. Not when rage still fueled him.

The previous evening, he'd left the campgrounds utterly furious. There hadn't been a single opening for him to grab Dianna. Not with the big fireman hovering around her like an annoying fly. But he had listened in from the sidelines when they spoke with the police, knew they were staying up at Peter Cohen's Farm. Twenty years ago, they'd had mutual friends, but Peter had ended up being more into peace than selling pot, disappearing up into the woods soon after to live with his green-loving friends, far away from the meth-soaked kids who made for good business.

He'd realized, then, that he had to come up with an alternative plan. And then he hit on it, the perfect bait, a clue to finding her sister that she couldn't resist following up on.

The girl had been limp, pale, and sweaty by the time he lifted her out of his trunk and dragged her back inside her closet. Perhaps he'd left her there for too long in the sun, with little oxygen, he thought dispassionately. At least she was still breathing.

He'd immediately paid Mickey off and told him not to return. The rest of his motley little drug-making staff was still on mini holiday as well, which left him alone with the girl. He could have easily made use of her unconscious body, but besides the fact that he'd never been into blondes, sex wasn't so much as a blip on his radar now. Revenge alone drove him.

He'd been sorely tempted to put his plan into motion that evening, but he could see that the major storm blowing through might complicate things. Knowing that the limp girl in the closet clearly wasn't going anywhere, not in her current condition anyway, and that the flash rains would die out by morning, he decided to bide his time, let his rage simmer a little longer.

At sunrise, he stepped outside and saw that it was, indeed, another beautiful day in the Rockies.

The perfect day for a murder. Two, in fact.

Five minutes after making a short phone call on an untraceable line, he grabbed his keys, laced up his hiking boots, and headed out the door.

Dianna Kelley—and her broad-shouldered boyfriend—were about to walk straight into his trap.

# CHAPTER TWENTY

SAM'S EYES opened as the first rays of light were finding their way in through the sheer curtains. Waking up with Dianna warm in his arms was as good as it got.

"Good morning," she said, rubbing against him like a frisky cat. He began kissing her, but just as his hands and mouth were getting carried away, loud knocking sounded at the front door.

Dianna yanked herself out of his arms, gasping in alarm.

"I'll go see who it is," he said, his instincts immediately telling him this wasn't another tray of food.

Something had happened.

Peter was standing on the porch looking uneasy. "The police called. They just received a tip about April."

"We'll be right out," he said, turning to find Dianna standing close behind him, still wrapped in the sheet.

He put his hands on her shoulders and when she looked up at him he read fear, hope, even her love for him on her face.

"Whatever we find out today, you're going to be all right."

She took a deep breath before giving a shaky nod. They quickly dressed, then crossed the narrow decking toward Peter's house, where he was waiting for them by the phone.

Dianna picked up the phone and identified herself, listening intently as the police gave her the information.

Her voice was strained as she said, "But every minute counts," then, "Later today?" and "When will that be, exactly?"

Hanging up, she said, "The police officers we met yesterday wanted to let me know that although they didn't learn anything from the witnesses they interviewed yesterday at the campground, they did just receive an anonymous tip from someone saying he'd seen April heading off on one of the trails yesterday."

As a wildland firefighter, Sam knew that although anonymous tips could be useful, they often weren't worth a damn. He suspected this was what the police had been explaining to her.

"Which trail?" Peter asked.

"Notch Mountain," she said, her expression almost angry. "The police said they're definitely going to follow up." She used her fingers as quotation marks. " 'When we can,' were his exact words."

Sparks shot from her green eyes. "When I pressed him on it, he said part of the problem is that it will take them a while to get someone up to such a remote location. But I'm not willing to wait for the police. I've got to go check out that trail myself. Because if someone thought they saw her . . ."

Sam knew Dianna was desperate to take action, and although he hadn't yet made up his mind about their next move, he pulled out the map Peter had given them the day before.

"Show us where the trail is."

Peter ran his finger along the paper. "It runs five miles from here to here."

Sam studied the map for a moment. "I don't see an access to that trail from this property."

"Actually," Peter said, "there is a private trail system that locals have used in these mountains for many years that leads straight to it."

Sam raised an eyebrow at the obvious implications of such a trail system.

Peter answered his unspoken question. "Personally, I've never witnessed anything illegal on the trail. I can't speak for anyone but myself, however."

Her hand on the doorknob, clearly antsy to get out

on the trail right away and search for April, Dianna said, "I'm going to finish getting dressed."

Instead of following her, Sam wrote Will's name, cell phone number, and Rocky Mountain station contact number down on a piece of paper for Peter.

"Honestly, I don't expect this anonymous tip to come to much of anything, but in the event that Dianna and I don't come back by tomorrow morning, I'd appreciate you giving my friend a call. He's a helicopter pilot with the local hotshot crew. If anything happens, he'll be able to find us before anyone else."

Peter's eyebrows raised. "You don't think this is a trap, do you? The police wouldn't steer you wrong, would they?"

"No, the cops definitely wouldn't mess with us, but then again, I doubt they're expecting to see us up there on the trail looking for April ourselves, either." Sam ran a hand through his hair, frustrated by the lack of good leads. "Problem is, Dianna isn't just some random person looking for her sister. She's a public figure and I can't discount the chance that someone has gone to all the trouble of kidnapping April as a way of getting to her."

He leveled a hard gaze at Peter. "At this point, I don't know that I should be trusting anyone we've met so far. Even you."

"Then why are you giving me this?" Peter asked, holding up Will's information.

"All I've got is what my gut tells me."

"Which is?"

"In a nutshell, you make a bad first impression, but I think you're all right. I also think this place you've got up here might have been shady at one point but isn't anymore."

Dianna was putting her hair up into a ponytail when he walked back in to the guest house.

"What should we bring with us?"

Sam took her backpack from her and put it down on the floor. "Slow down. We've got to be careful and think this through before running off after some anonymous tip."

"What is there to think through?" she countered, her soft mouth now hard and unyielding. "Someone saw April on that trail and we need to go see if she's still there."

"We don't know who we're dealing with or what their motives are. For all we know this story has leaked to the press and anyone could have called this tip in to the police." Wanting to make himself perfectly clear, he said, "What if some deranged fan of yours thinks this is the perfect way to finally meet you, way up in the Rockies with no one else around?"

Her cheeks flushed, her fists clenched, she said, "Can't you see that I can't even think about something like that right now? I'm not going to sit around when I finally have somewhere to look for my sister. I'm sick of taking time to think things through. Where has that gotten us so far? Nowhere! April's still missing. Anything could be happening to her right now. I'm going after her, Sam. I have to."

She dropped her hands to her side. "I'm sorry," she said in a hollow voice. "I shouldn't be yelling at you. You're only trying to help."

He put his arms around her. "You don't have to apologize to me for anything, sweetheart. You're right; we don't have any other choice but to get out there on that trail. Hopefully April has left us a clue."


For the past three days Dianna had faced constant physical tests and challenges she'd never planned to tackle. River rafting, rock climbing, and long, steep hikes on extremely narrow trails like this one, where one misstep sent loose rocks falling hundreds of feet.

With Sam's help, she'd partially faced her fear of heights before getting to the Farm, but it still killed her that she had to go slow, when all she wanted was to race up and down the trail to find April.

"I think we should take a breather," Sam said after they'd been creeping along the trail for the better part of two hours.

She shook her head. "I really want to get to the main trail the police said she was spotted on before we stop."

Stepping carefully, she continued to move forward,

making sure to keep one hand on the rock wall beside her at all times to feel more stable.

Thank God Sam was less than a foot behind her. She knew, without a doubt, that he'd be there to catch her if she started to fall.

She'd never been comfortable with how much she needed him. But this search for April had broken through what was left of her foolish pride. She'd had no choice but to accept his offer of help in the hospital. Three days later, her previous independence seemed less impressive and more lonesome.

She finally had something real to hold on to. She had Sam's love.

*He loved her.*

Just thinking the sweet words took her breath away.

Ten years after the first time they met, considering all the different ways their lives could have turned out, instead of having found love and creating families with new people, they'd rediscovered each other.

It was a second chance, after all.

And it was nothing short of a miracle.

Dianna wasn't blind to the fact that they still had a lot of decisions before them. Where to live, how to manage their very different careers. But she felt confident that they'd figure it all out. And that they'd truly transcended their past.

If only she felt as confident about finding April.

*Please,* she silently prayed, *I need to find April today, up here in these mountains.*

Her plea had barely floated up into the universe when she rounded a corner and stopped dead in her tracks.

The narrow path they'd been following had been swept away. The mudslide looked fresh, probably having occurred during the previous night's storm.

"The trail's gone, Sam," she said in a hollow voice. Unable to keep from spiraling off, she said, "What if other sections are washed out and the police can't get up here either?"

In lieu of answering, Sam unclipped his backpack and pulled out several rock-climbing bolts.

"I'm going to climb up and over to see how far it is until the trail picks back up." Before he went, he lifted her chin with one finger. "Don't you dare worry; this is just a minor bump in the road."

She forced a small smile, trying desperately to keep the faith.

After putting his pack back on, Sam got to work quickly screwing the bolts into the rock beside them, using them as hand- and footholds to climb up and over the rock. Too soon, he disappeared from view.

For three days, he'd only left her side once, when the cabin had been on fire at the campgrounds. After ten years of being alone, sixty seconds without him had her heart pounding, especially when her brain rewound to the conversation they'd had just before heading out here: *What if some deranged fan of yours thinks this is the perfect way to finally meet you, way up in the Rockies with no one else around?"*

She couldn't understand why anyone would want to go to that sort of trouble over her. But still, she found herself looking at the forest with wary eyes, until even the sound of the birds and the leaves rustling in the breeze fell on suspicious ears.

God, how she hated standing on the trail helplessly waiting for Sam to come back.

That's when it hit her—she didn't need to wait. She knew how to climb up the rock, and had left most—if not all—of her fear of heights behind her on that first rock face with Sam two days ago.

She was just reaching for the first set of bolts when she heard voices.

But who could Sam be talking to way up here on an unmarked trail in the middle of nowhere?

Her first thought was that the police had already come. But even from a distance what she was hearing didn't seem like a friendly conversation.

Oh God, she thought with increasing alarm, had Sam been right? Was the anonymous tip to the police a trap?

She knew what he would tell her; he'd insist on her turning around, going back to the Farm, calling the police, and waiting somewhere safe for his return. But there was no way she could leave him to fend for himself.

Sam had saved her so many times. Now it was her turn to save him.

Reaching for the bolts, she pulled herself up off the trail. Her heart immediately started racing, her palms began to sweat, and her legs trembled like crazy. But even though her body was still doubting she could do this, her heart knew differently.

Sam had taught her how not to be afraid.

Taking a slow, deep breath to calm herself, she put all of her focus on the goal of getting up and over the rock, refusing to leave even a smidge of room for fear to creep back in.

As she climbed, the grunts and curses from the other side of the trail grew louder, more intense. Moving as quickly as she could over the rock without slipping, she finally got high enough to see down over the other side to the trail.

Her breath caught as a stranger pointed a gun at Sam. But instead of backing off, Sam threw himself against the man, knocking him hard into the rock beside the trail. It occurred to her that something about the man's face was vaguely familiar, but she didn't have time to try to place it, not when she needed to find some way to stop Sam from being shot.

As she clamored across the rock faster than she would have ever thought she could, Sam looked up.

"Dianna, get the hell out of here!" he shouted, momentarily distracted by seeing her.

And then, as if in slow motion, the man gave an unholy roar and shoved Sam with all his might.

Her mouth opened and she thought she screamed as Sam's boots slipped on the slick trail and his heavy pack pulled him backward off the edge, sending him flying through the thin mountain air.

# CHAPTER TWENTY-ONE

SHOCK PARALYZED her, making her fingers slip off the cold metal bolts. She was sliding down the rock, but instead of hitting the trail and falling off the edge to her death, she was caught by the man who'd pushed Sam.

*No!*

Hands clamped down over her windpipe and she gasped for air. She needed to find a way to get away from this man and go get help for Sam.

*If he was still alive after his fall. If she could even find him.*

As she struggled to fight her way out of the man's strong grip, her mind, her heart, and her body were all revolting at the thought of Sam dying.

From the first moment she'd met him, he'd been larger than life. After all the risks he'd taken in his life as a hotshot, after all the fires he'd outrun, she refused to believe that Sam could die like this.

He had to be alive. She'd know if he were dead, wouldn't she?

Or was that just a lie she had to tell herself so that she could keep going without him? Especially when after ten years of stubbornly denying their love for each other, she'd known in her gut that they were on the verge of a new start.

Not a terrible ending.

The man's fingers clenched tighter around her neck and chills overtook her at the same time that her vision darkened.

"Don't pass out on me now, bitch," the man growled, removing his stranglehold on her neck just in time.

Taking in huge gulps of oxygen, when the fuzzy black dots finally cleared from her vision, she realized she was looking straight into the barrel of his gun.

"Big tough guy like that, you'd think he would have put up more of a fight. But I picked the perfect spot," the man bragged. "There's no way he could have survived the fall. Serves him right for being in my way. Always protecting you. Now that I've gotten rid of him, you're all mine."

A thick, murky fog came at her, swirling into her head, threatening to take her down. She'd fainted only once before when she'd worked too many hours under hot lights without a break and this was exactly how she'd felt before she dropped.

"Get up."

Everything was spinning as she rolled onto her hands and knees. Bile rose in her throat and somehow she held it down, instinctively knowing better than to show her fear.

Pulling herself to her feet against the rock face, she turned to look at him. His cold, glassy eyes, his twitching mouth, and his shaking, white-knuckled hands told her just how unhinged he really was.

She'd never seen anyone look so angry. So deadly.

"What do you want with me?" she finally managed to croak from out of her bruised throat.

"You killed my brother."

She stared at the stranger in disbelief. What was he talking about?

"I've never hurt anyone," she immediately protested. "You must have me confused with someone else."

He shook the gun at her, his finger poised on the trigger.

"Oh no, I know exactly who you are. Big, fancy TV star. Everyone wanted a piece of you at the hospital. But nobody gave a rat's ass about my brother."

He'd been at the hospital? Something sparked in the back of her mind, but the temporary lack of oxygen was still playing havoc with her synapses.

"Jacob is dead because of you. And now you're going to pay."

He practically spat the words at her and she recoiled at the force of his fury.

"I swear to you, I don't know anyone named Jacob."

But he wasn't interested in her claims. "Turn around and start walking," he said, shoving his gun into her ribs.

Temporarily out of options, she did as instructed. Was it at all possible that this guy was some whacked-out fan of hers who had gone off the deep end after his brother died? Had he somehow manufactured an imaginary scenario where she'd killed his brother and that's why he was calling her a murderer?

And if so, did she have any chance at all of getting him to comprehend the real situation?

Several years back, when she'd been working as an assistant on one of the shows at her station, she'd heard a near miss rape victim describe how she got away from her captor. She got him to talk about his life, about why he was doing something so horrible, and ultimately, he let her get away.

Praying that a similar tactic might work for her, she said, "I've got a sister and I know how hard it would be for me if anything happened to her. I'm truly sorry that your brother died and I know everyone else is, too."

But instead of softening, the man shoved the gun into the small of her spine even harder.

"Do you think I give a shit that you're sorry? Do you think I even believe you, you lying bitch? You walked away with a couple of bruises, while my brother is dead!"

*I walked away with a couple of bruises?*

A few short moments later, it hit her. This crazy man was talking about the car crash.

Her hand went to her mouth in horror. "Are you saying that your brother was driving the other car?"

"Of course that's what I'm saying. You were too busy with the reporters to give a shit about my dead brother."

His bitter accusation made her stumble. He caught the back of her shirt in his fist before she fell.

"I swear to you," she said again, "the crash was an accident. And I did care about what happened to your brother. When the doctor told me he died, I was horrified. If I could change what happened to bring your brother back to you, I would."

"Bullshit! You're rich, you're famous, you think you're so important. You were probably putting on lipstick instead of paying attention to the road."

All of his accusations were false, but telling him the truth wouldn't help. Not when he'd already tried and convicted her in his own mind.

Her brain whirred as she tried to think of something—anything—she could say to sway him. Then he said, "I'm going to make sure you pay for what you did to my brother. And I'm going to use your precious little sister to do it."

She gasped, momentarily forgetting about the gun and swinging around to face him.

"You're the one who kidnapped April?"

"You might be pretty," he taunted, "but you sure aren't smart, are you?"

He thought she'd killed his brother. Of course he'd abducted her sister. April was the perfect means for revenge. April had said some guy grabbed her in the hospital's parking lot.

This was the guy.

Pure rage replaced fear as all of the fierce protectiveness Dianna had ever felt for April swelled up and filled her, head to toe.

"If you've hurt her, I'll—"

Her threat was cut off by the slamming blow of the gun against her cheekbone. The force knocked her against the rock and she might have fallen off the edge of the trail just like Sam if the man didn't grab her by the hair on her way down.

"If you haven't figured out by now, you can't do a damn thing to me," he said. "I'm the one who's in charge now. None of your money or fame means a damn out here."

His eyes held a strong glimmer of satisfaction. "So move the fuck forward or I'll shoot you right here and you'll never see your sister again."

Visions of April being hurt by this man and then another of Sam falling down the steep cliff assaulted her. Dianna's heart clenched with grief.

The guys on Sam's hotshot crew used to joke that he was superhuman, able to outrun a ball of flames in a single bound. Somehow she needed to keep believing that if anyone could survive a fall off the trail, it was Sam.

She could almost hear him telling her, *"Don't worry about me. Just concentrate on staying alive. I'll come for you. I promise."*

As the man pushed her farther down the trail, she tried to think what she could possibly offer this man that would make him back down. Practically, all she had was money. But even though she knew that nothing could ever bring his brother back, she still had to give it a shot.

"Let April go and I'll pay you whatever you want."

She heard harsh laughter behind her. "I knew you'd say that. Rich bitch like you probably thinks she can buy anything she wants. I'll bet you've never had to work an honest day in your life. Not like the rest of us."

"You're wrong about me," she told him, even though she knew he wasn't going to change his mind. "I've worked hard. Really hard. To provide a good life for my sister. That's why I understand how you're feeling."

He shoved the gun even harder into the soft spot beneath her ribs. "Your money won't bring Jacob back."

"Please, just let her go and I'll give you anything you want," she begged, wanting to make herself perfectly clear. "Anything at all."

"You stupid slut. I wouldn't fuck you if you were the last cunt on Earth. Now shut up and keep moving."

With his gun at her back, she had no choice but to continue moving down the narrow trail, farther away from Sam, but, hopefully, closer to her sister.

She wanted him to think she'd given up, but she hadn't. Not by a long shot. Every moment, she looked for an opportunity to escape. So when the narrow trail finally intersected a much wider dirt road, figuring it was her best chance to make a break for it, she went for a move she'd learned in self-defense class.

Kicking behind her, she nailed him in the kneecap with the sole of her shoe, then ran as fast as she could.

The sound of a gun exploding pierced her ears and she instinctively threw herself to the ground.

Quickly realizing the bullet had missed her, she scrambled to get back up, but before she could get back on her feet, his hands were yanking her hair and he was pulling her across the dirt.

"You tricky little bitch. You're just like your sister. Don't you dare fuck with me again or I'll make sure not to miss next time. Your fans might not think you're so pretty with half your face blown off."

He shoved her forward with his boot and she realized she was looking at a black tire.

"Get on the bike," he said, pointing to a dirt bike parked in the bushes just off the dirt road.

Finally accepting that the most important thing was to get to April in one piece—and praying the two of them would be able to come up with an escape plan once they were together again—Dianna straddled the leather seat while he shackled her arms and legs to the bike with sharp, thin chains that cut into her skin.

Although she tried to mentally prepare herself for his touch, she couldn't stop from shivering with revulsion when he got on the bike behind her and said, "You took my brother from me. I can't wait for you to watch me take your sister from you."

His body throbbed in a dozen different places, but Sam barely noticed. All he'd been able to think during his long fall was that he'd left Dianna completely at a stranger's mercy.

Up on the mountain trail with no supplies, with nothing to protect herself with, who knew what the crazy bastard would do to her, if he'd pull a gun and rape her?

Thoughts of losing Dianna threatened to overwhelm him completely, even though any hotshot worth his turn-outs knew how to keep going, even when a wildfire turned into a clusterfuck.

On the day Connor had been burned, he'd managed to get right back out on the mountain to fight the wild-fire, he knew he had it in him to ignore the sharp pains shooting through him head to toe. He needed to get back on that trail and save Dianna, goddammit.

Slowly activating one painful muscle group at a time, Sam pulled himself upright, letting lose a stream of guttural curses into the otherwise silent forest. It was almost as if the birds and animals knew something bad was going down and had decided to stay hidden until the danger passed.

Incredibly, he hadn't passed out. Fifty feet, at least, of crashing into boulders and tree stumps and thorny bushes and he'd felt every goddam thing. If it weren't for the mock-orange bush that had stopped his fall, he'd be as good as dead. He was going to plant a fucking grove of it when he got back to Lake Tahoe.

His pack was still strapped to his back—he figured it had probably kept his back from breaking—but the fabric was almost completely shredded. By the slight weight of it as he shifted, he guessed it was pretty much empty. He'd have to make do without his first-aid kit and the extra food, water, and supplies.

All Sam had left to work with was a pocketknife and a handful of flares that remained in his cargo pants' pockets.

Grabbing a thick tree trunk, he pulled himself upright, fitting the toes of his boots into crevasses between the rocks.

It was slow going up the mountain. His joints screamed in agony. The lacerations on his head and face stung as sweat dripped into them. With each painful bit of progress, he called on his years of extreme wildfire training, pulled from every deadly situation he'd ever made it out of alive.

Sam had risked his life a hundred times over for strangers. This time he was giving everything for the woman he loved.

Finally, his fingers hooked over the edge of the trail. So far, he'd been able to use the muscles in both his upper and lower body together, one compensating for the other when needed, but now he had to rely on his upper body alone to hoist himself up onto the ledge.

Closing his eyes, he took a deep breath and put himself deep in the zone, a place where pain was irrelevant, where all that mattered was that his body obeyed his brain.

Three, two, one—up!

Sam's biceps and triceps shook and his left shoulder hurt like a mother, but he got himself up on the ledge, belly down, and lay there until he caught his breath, then crawled on his hands and knees to solid ground, leaving a trail of blood and sweat behind him.

Pulling himself to his feet, he leaned heavily against the cool rock on the inside of the trail.

He was worse off than he wanted to admit.

One step at a time, one foot in front of the other, was how he was going to have to do this. At least their footprints were clearly marked in the mud. Thank God at least one thing was on his side.

The first quarter mile was the hardest. Sam felt like a newborn foal just learning to walk—stumbling, tripping, then picking himself up and trying again.

It was impossible to ignore the shooting pains through his right knee and the left side of his hip, so he gave in to them instead, letting the pain fuel his rage, along with his determination to find Dianna.

Finally, Sam picked up speed, managing to find his rhythm on the trail, even though he was moving a hell of a lot slower than he usually did. It helped that he didn't have a hundred-and-fifty pound pack. Without any sort of vehicle, he wouldn't overtake them, but he held tight to the hope that he wasn't too far behind.

Until he got to the dirt road and saw the tire tracks.

*Fuck!* The bastard must have stashed a dirt bike on the trail.

Sam could easily follow the tracks. But on foot, he didn't stand a chance of getting to Dianna nearly fast enough.

He needed help, but heading back to the Farm for re-inforcements and to call in the Rocky Mountain hotshot crew and police force was out of the question. Odds were Dianna would be dead by the time he hiked back the way they'd come.

Knowing he'd have to make do alone, Sam ran through the meager tools he had on him. The knife might come in handy later, but what about the flares? He still had four left.

Best-case scenario, the flares would simply send off a smoke signal to any passing aircraft. Worst case, they would ignite a forest fire.

As a hotshot, it went against everything in Sam to light a wildfire on purpose. Arson had always been his biggest enemy, but he couldn't waste any time feeling conflicted over the choice he was making.

He'd face a hundred arson charges if it meant saving Dianna.

Pulling the cap off of one of the flares, he bent down and lit a clump of dry brush on the edge of the trail.

Watching it burn and move across the mountain with

the wind, he hoped like hell that Will and the rest of the Rocky Mountain hotshot crew were canvassing these mountains hourly for wildfires. If the wind picked up, the flames would either ravage the forest in a matter of hours—or turn on him and catch him up in the fire he'd started.

Following the four-inch tire tracks up the dirt road on foot, he continued to light flares every half mile until he was down to his final one. Praying that someone on the local hotshot crew would read his smoke signal, he held one last flare in reserve.

Sam continued to make his way up the trail, his legs and lungs burning, sweat soaking his clothes, praying all the while that Dianna was still alive.

*Stay strong, sweetheart,* he silently pleaded. *I'm coming to get you.*

# CHAPTER TWENTY-TWO

WIND WHIPPED across Dianna's eyes, making them water as she held on to the handlebars for dear life.

The man was driving way too fast, the trees a blur beside them as he sped up the bumpy road. She kept sliding, first to one side, then the next, as she overcorrected. She squeezed her eyes shut against the trail dirt flying up from under the wheels, but she couldn't block out the image of Sam falling off the trail. It would haunt her forever.

Her captor pressed close against her, and even though he'd told her that he was disgusted by the thought of touching her, she could feel his hard-on pressing into her rear every time they hit a rough patch.

What if he changed his mind about raping her?

What if he'd already raped April?

Bile rose to her throat again, and along with the motion sickness she was feeling, she nearly spewed all over the handlebars.

*You're going to see April soon and then you're going to figure out how to get away from him.*

This mantra was all she had to cling to.

Her heart squeezed and she momentarily lost her breath as she thought about Sam being pushed off the trail. These past three days with Sam had been more than she could have ever hoped for. But they weren't enough.

She wanted a lifetime.

As the dirt bike wound up the trail, Dianna's hands quickly went numb and her legs and rear soon followed. She wasn't sure if it had been thirty minutes or two hours by the time he abruptly hit the brakes.

Her chest flew into the handlebars and she grimaced in pain as the man got off the bike, walking away without undoing the locks that held her captive on the dirt bike.

Dianna clenched and unclenched her hands to bring life back to her numb limbs until tingles started shooting up both of her arms. Blinking fast to clear the wet dirt from her eyes, she looked around at where he'd taken her. They were parked beside a barn on its last legs at the end of a long row of ratty old trailers. Surrounded by the metal boxes, it was almost like being a kid again, except for one big difference.

No matter how bad life in the trailer park with her mother had been, she'd never feared for her life.

"April!" she screamed just in case her sister was close by, but there was no answer.

And then the man reappeared, pushing April forward with his gun.

Although Dianna was overjoyed that her sister was still alive, she gasped at the state she was in. Her face was a mess of blood and bruises, her wrists were bound together with tape, and she looked horribly weak, like she might drop unconscious to the ground at any second.

"You found me," April said through wobbling lips.

Before Dianna could tell her sister how much she loved her, that she would have moved heaven and earth to find her, the man lifted up the gun and laid the barrel against April's skull.

"I didn't get to say good-bye to my brother," he said, his hands and voice shaking with rage. "You're not going to get the chance either."

Dianna frantically pulled at her chains, but there was no way she could get off the bike and save her sister.

Right before he pulled the trigger, April's gaze was steady, utterly unflinching, and Dianna read all of the love she and her sister had never been able to share with each other in her sister's beautiful hazel eyes.

Sam had been running too many miles, too fast without any water. His legs were starting to go and his chest was burning. With a stiff breeze sending the small fires he'd lit crawling up the mountain's mounds of dead brush, he was afraid this was about to turn into his worst-case scenario.

With no other option but to keep moving forward, Sam pushed through another tenth of a mile, his muscles and tendons screaming with every footfall. Minutes dragged by as he continued to put one foot in front of the other.

Hotshots were often called superheroes. But Sam had been doing the job long enough to know that they weren't. They were just average men who sometimes did extraordinary things. And like any other man on the verge of dehydration, he needed water.

Or he'd die.

And then, suddenly, he heard the sharp whirring of helicopter blades breaking through the silence of the forest. Using the last of his strength, Sam clambered up the tall edge of the cliff to try to make himself seen in the nearest clearing.

But the helicopter flew right past him.

All out of options, he lit his last flare and dropped it on the dry grasses a few feet away.

The seconds ticked by, the fire grew hotter, but Sam held his ground. And then, finally, the helicopter headed straight for him, his friend, Will, manning the controls.

With the open space too tight to land the aircraft, Will dropped the ladder and hovered above the spreading flames. Sam jumped up and grabbed hold of a step, commanding his weakening body to get the fuck up into the helicopter without blacking out.

Will was on his radio giving the Rocky Mountain hotshots the coordinates for the fires when Sam finally crawled inside. Usually, when wildfires were caught this early, it was only a matter of a couple of bucket drops to put them out. Sam hoped it would be the case this time, too.

And yet, even if the local authorities threw him in jail for arson, he wouldn't change what he'd done. Not when using the flares had been his only chance to get back to Dianna.

Will's eyebrows moved up toward his hairline when he put down his radio and saw the wrecked state of Sam's face, arms, and clothes that were soaked with sweat, dirt, and blood.

"Drink this," he said, handing Sam water.

As he drained the bottle, Will said, "I got a call from some guy at the commune. He said you and Dianna were heading off on this trail to look for her sister and asked me if I was planning to fly over this area today. What the fuck is happening?"

"Long story," Sam said, knowing he needed to conserve his energy. "Dianna's in trouble. Big trouble. We've got to find her. I've been following tracks from a dirt bike. How low can you fly?"

"Low enough."

"Fly as fast and as low as you can."

The chopper ate up the distance a hundred times faster than Sam had been able to on foot. A handful of minutes later, the tracks abruptly veered off the road into a thick grove of trees.

"I can't follow the tracks any farther," Will said.

"Find a place to drop me in," Sam instructed. "They've got to be close."

Through the thick tree cover, they looked down into a small trailer park.

"Damn it," Will said, "I thought all of these trailers had been cleared out last year by the Forest Service."

Just then, Sam saw a flash of color and movement. Yanking the helicopter's ladder back out, he secured it to the lip of the aircraft. "Get as close as you can. I'm going to jump."

Will didn't bother telling him he was crazy; he simply got to work positioning the chopper over a small hole between trees.

But as he prepared to descend, Sam's blood ran cold.

Dianna was chained to a dirt bike, and the man who'd shoved him down the mountain was holding a gun to her sister's head, only feet away. In the time it took him to get on the ground, both April and Dianna could be killed.

On the verge of fighting the hardest fight of his life, rage swept through every cell, every nerve.

He was going to save Dianna, even if he had to die to do it.

Time seemed to slow down as the man's finger twitched on the trigger. And then, suddenly, sand and dirt and pine needles were whipping into her eyes, and Dianna realized whirring helicopter blades were breaking apart the silence of the forest.

Without yet seeing him, Dianna felt Sam's presence and she was filled with renewed strength.

But before she could act, April took advantage of the man's distraction, kicking him hard in the balls, successfully knocking him off balance, the loud bang of a shot going wild and slamming into one of the trailers.

When keys fell out of his pocket, despite her obvious exhaustion and injuries, her tough little sister managed to grab them with her bound hands. Dashing over to Dianna, she got to work on undoing the chains around her right wrist.

But all Dianna wanted was for her sister to get away.

"Give me the keys and run!" she pleaded with April.

But April's stubborn expression said she wasn't going anywhere. "I'm not leaving you," she said in a gravelly voice.

But seconds later, seeing that the man was back on his feet, Dianna grabbed the keys with her free hand and tried again.

"Go!"

This time April started running, but she was too weak to outrun the man with the gun. His face furious, he grabbed her by the hair and dragged her into the forest.

Oh God. Dianna needed to get the final locks undone so that she could run after them and save her sister, but she could barely get her numb fingers to work.

And then, miraculously, Sam was beside her.

"He's taken her into the woods. We've got to save her."

Taking the keys from her and quickly undoing the locks around her left wrist and ankles, he untangled her chains with a steady hand.

"Run toward the clearing behind you and wait in the helicopter for us."

Without waiting for her agreement, he sprinted into the forest, following the two sets of footprints.

Dianna's limbs shook as she lifted one leg over the seat and held herself up against the handlebars. She trusted Sam to do everything he could to save April, and she knew he wanted her to be safe in the helicopter— just as she'd wanted April to run to safety—but there was no way she could sit back and wait in the wings while he faced down a truly crazed man.

Not when the lives of the two people who mattered most to her were on the line.

Moving as fast as she could on partially numb legs,

she prayed with every step that April was still alive. Running past the last trailer, into the thick grove of trees, her heart raced from a combination of panic and exertion. But what she saw in front of her made her heart nearly stop.

The man had shoved April to the ground, one boot on her skull.

But his gun was pointing straight at Sam.

Looking down the barrel of the gun, Sam knew he had only seconds to act, when he suddenly heard a familiar sizzle.

A flare.

He should have been furious that Dianna hadn't listened to him when he'd told her to get in the goddamned helicopter, but how could he be anything but amazed by her quick thinking? She'd always been the smartest person he knew.

The lit fuse flew past Sam's shoulder, nailing the man's chest dead center. The man's shirt caught on fire and he stumbled back.

Screaming in pain, the man jumped around the forest, leaving April wide open. Both Sam and Dianna dove for her, but Dianna was faster. Pulling her sister up off the forest floor, Dianna sank to the ground, cradling her sister's body in her arms.

Sam turned his focus back to the man who had almost taken everything from him, just in time to see the gun pointing at them. On a roar, just as a shot rang out, Sam launched himself at the man.

There was a sharp tug in his thigh, but he'd already been ignoring brutal pain for more than an hour. The new wound barely registered.

Tackling the man, they rolled over each other, the slope growing steeper and more precarious every few feet. Taking a quick glance at the forest, Sam realized they were on the edge of a precipice and picking up speed.

At the last possible second, he let go of his hold on the stranger, reached out with his good arm, gripped a narrow tree trunk, and held on for everything he was worth.

The man's hands slipped from around Sam's shoulders, his eyes widening with the sudden knowledge that he was going to die. Down, down, down he went, his screams for help echoing through the forest.

And then, his cries were suddenly broken by the sound of his gun going off.

Everything went silent.

It wasn't the first time Sam had seen someone die in the mountains. But it was the first time he wasn't going to head in to drag the body out.

Blood dripping from his arm, from his face, but mostly from his thigh, Sam knew he needed to pull himself up to safety. His vision starting to go, he hoisted himself onto a thick shrub he hoped would hold his weight.

He looked up the mountain to where Dianna was still sitting holding her sister, tears streaming down her cheeks.

She was safe. His job was done.

His brain and body could finally shut down.

# CHAPTER TWENTY-THREE

THE HELICOPTER landed on the roof of the hospital, and Dianna watched helplessly as Sam and April, both still unconscious, were rushed inside.

Desperate to stay with each of them—and to hear what the doctors had to say about their conditions— she was reluctant to submit to her own rounds of tests. No question, she was tired and scraped up. But mostly, she was afraid. Had the man hurt April during her three days of captivity? What were the extent of Sam's bleeding and injuries? After years of brutal firefighting, had he finally pushed his body too far?

The short helicopter flight had seemed endless as she'd tried to stop the bleeding in Sam's thigh by pressing one clean bandage after another against the open gunshot wound. But the bandages filled with blood almost as soon as she applied them.

Even when she'd watched the man push Sam off the trail, she'd been certain that he was still alive. But seeing all that blood, noting how empty of color his face was, how cold his skin, was the first time she'd ever been afraid that the man she loved was going to die.

If she could have, she would have given her life for his, stepped in front of that bullet and let it take her down. Instead, she'd watched from a distance, helpless in the background as she held on to her sister.

An hour after arriving at the hospital, the doctor attending to her held out a small white paper cup with four pills. Despite the unproblematic results of her scans and X-rays, he looked extremely concerned.

"Your body has had quite a lot to deal with this week, Ms. Kelley. It's time to give it some rest. These pills will help."

Dianna didn't take the cup. "What are they?"

"Anti-inflammatories and something to help you relax."

"No," she said firmly. "I don't want any sedatives."

She couldn't check out, even if exhaustion was coming at her from every angle. Not when the two people she loved most in the world were injured and unconscious.

The doctor frowned. "I'm going to leave them with your nurse in the hopes that you'll reconsider, which I strongly urge you to do."

But Dianna had no intention of taking the pills. After the doctor had left the room, she got up off the bed and went into the bathroom to splash some cold water on her face.

For the second time in a week, looking in the mirror was like looking at a stranger. Who was this woman with wild eyes and tangled hair?

And yet, again, the longer she stared, the more familiar the woman became. She'd buried herself beneath her "perfect" re-creation of Dianna Kelley for long enough. And even though she wasn't a wild woman, regardless of what she currently looked like, her journey through the Rockies with Sam had convinced her not to waste any more time playing it safe.

Life was precious. From here on out, she was going to risk everything.

Especially her heart.

Stripping off her hospital gown, she turned on the faucet in the small shower and quickly scrubbed herself, head to toe. She could have lived with the dirt and mud, with the tangles in her hair, but she desperately wanted to wash away her memories of the man who'd abducted her sister, of the way he'd pressed against her on the dirt bike, the feel of his hands around her neck, yanking her hair.

The standard hospital pump soap was as sweet smelling to her as any of the luxury brands she'd used over the years. It made her fresh cuts sting, but she was glad for it because it meant she was still alive.

Quickly toweling off, she finger-combed her hair as best she could. Her clothes were wrecked, but they were all she had, so she put the ripped and dirty khaki pants and shirt back on along with her socks and boots.

Three days ago she'd been in this same position, getting out of a hospital bed and getting dressed despite doctor's orders to rest. There was no way she could have predicted her reunion with Sam or their newfound love.

Moving back into the room, she picked up the phone and dialed a number she hoped was still in service. Thankfully, the warm voice she remembered picked up the phone.

"Connor, it's Dianna." Her heart was pounding hard at the news she was about to give Sam's brother. "Sam's been shot. I think you should come."

"Where is he?"

There was no hint of fear in her almost-brother-in-law's voice, but the MacKenzie brothers hid their emotions well beneath a nearly impenetrable armor of self-control.

"Vail General Hospital. The wound is in his right thigh." Her voice broke. "I'm so sorry. I shouldn't have agreed to let him help me find my sister."

She realized that she wasn't making sense, that Connor didn't know about April's disappearance, but she couldn't find the words to explain. Not yet.

"I tried to talk him out of going to Colorado," Connor

said. "I tried to tell him it was a bad idea to see you again."

She sucked in a shaky breath. Of course he would have cautioned Sam about coming here. Connor had been there to pick up the pieces. She hadn't.

"I didn't know that," she admitted. "But I understand why you did it."

"Forget about me. The only reason I'm saying any of this is to let you know that Sam wanted to go to Vail despite all of my good reasons to stay the hell away. He wanted to be with you, Dianna. Simple as that."

She was amazed to realize that it really was that simple. She and Sam were two people who wanted to be together. Who belonged together. Sure, it was messy. But it was real. And pure.

"I'm sure I'll find out what's happened soon enough," Connor added, "but the one thing I know for sure is that if Sam wants to do something, if he wants to help somebody, there isn't anything anyone can do to stop him. Even if we think he'd be better off going on without us."

She quickly realized he wasn't simply talking about all Sam had done to help her find April. He was also referencing what Sam had done to save Connor's life in Desolation Wilderness the previous summer.

"I'll take the next plane out." Their connection went dead.

Hanging up, as she stepped into the hall, her brain

took her back ten years, to the day that she'd told Sam she was pregnant and he'd quickly proposed.

*"I've never done anything because I have to"* was what he'd told her then. *"From the moment I saw you, I wanted you."*

She knew that Connor was right. Sam took care of people. Strangers. Family. Her. He would never change. And she didn't want him to. She loved him just the way he was.

Slowly walking over to the nurses' station, she finally started to notice how bruised and beaten her limbs felt.

Knowing she should be friendly and polite to the extremely helpful hospital staff, but not having an ounce of extra energy for a smile, she said, "I need to see April Kelley and Sam MacKenzie."

"Of course, Ms. Kelley," the woman said, obviously recognizing her despite her current au naturel look. "I'll take you to your sister," the petite woman said, standing up and coming out into the waiting room.

"I need to see Sam, too," Dianna insisted. "I need to know how he's doing, if he's going to be all right."

"I'm sorry, Ms. Kelley," the nurse said, "but I'm afraid I can't speak to you about his case."

"I know I'm not his wife," Dianna pleaded, putting her hand on the woman's arm, "but I have to be with him. He needs me."

The woman's brown eyes were full of empathy. "I can't guarantee anything, but after I take you to your sister I'll contact his surgeon and see if we can set up a visit."

"Surgeon?" The one word was hollow with fear.

She'd known he'd been hit by the bullet, but she'd hoped it had merely grazed the skin. Had his injuries been worse than any of them knew, especially given his terrible fall off the cliff?

Suddenly, she could hardly breathe.

The nurse took her arm. "I think you should rest, Ms. Kelley."

Knowing she had to pull it together or she'd be sent off for more tests, Dianna said, "I'm fine" in a steady voice. "And I appreciate your help."

The nurse pressed her lips together, clearly disagreeing with Dianna's self-assessment, but she continued to lead the way to April's room.

"You'll be glad to hear that your sister is doing very well. She was extremely dehydrated and a bit bruised on her face, but it looks like she'll be just fine."

"Thank you," Dianna told the woman once they arrived at April's door. "I'll wait here for news of Sam."

Nodding, the nurse walked back to her station. Stepping inside April's room, she saw her sister lying on the bed beneath a thick white blanket, her skin pale, her eyes closed. She looked so tiny in the hospital bed that Dianna's throat clogged with tears as she looked at the little sister she loved so much.

Moving to her side, Dianna covered April's hand

with her own and was surprised when she opened her eyes.

"Hi," April croaked.

Dianna picked up the cup of water beside the bed and put it to her sister's lips. After she'd drained the cup, she had to ask, "Did he hurt you?"

"Only right here, with his gun," April said, touching her cheekbone. "That was his big move, I guess," she said, looking at Dianna's matching bruises. "But I think he was waiting for you to really do something."

"Thank God," Dianna said, glad at least that the man hadn't raped her sister. "Don't ever scare me like that again, okay?"

"I hope I never do," April replied, her lips curving up in a small smile.

Her baby sister was beautiful, Dianna thought. A gorgeous young woman with her whole life ahead of her. She could do anything. Be anything. If only she'd believe in herself the way Dianna believed in her.

April sucked on her lower lip, just like she used to as a toddler. "Thank you for coming for me."

Dianna shook her head. "Are you kidding? Nothing could have kept me from coming to get you. Nothing."

April closed her eyes, the dark smudges beneath them mirroring the ones Dianna had seen beneath her own eyes in the bathroom mirror. Still holding April's hand, Dianna sat down on the chair beside the bed, planning to stay with her for as long as the nurses would let her.

"I never should have come to Colorado," April said finally, her words soft and regretful. Opening her eyes, she said, "If you hadn't come to meet me in Vail, you wouldn't have gotten in that crash. And then that guy wouldn't have . . ."

Her face twisted and her words fell away.

"Don't you dare blame yourself," Dianna said. "The crash could have happened anywhere. And I'm glad I went to the commune. I met your friends and heard about the work you've been doing. I was wrong to assume it was a bad place without checking it out first."

"I didn't exactly invite you up for tea," April acknowledged.

A small laugh escaped Dianna. The short burst of happiness felt amazingly good—and very unexpected given the circumstances.

Opening her mouth to let her sister off the hook the rest of the way, a sudden flash of insight held her back. She couldn't go on as she had before. Not if she wanted things to change. Besides, April didn't need to be coddled anymore. She'd always been tough, and managing to escape not once, but twice, from her kidnapper only proved her strength yet again.

"I heard you've been cooking and helping with children. I want you to know that I'm proud of you, April, but I think it's time you and I came clean with each other."

April's eyes grew big and Dianna was tempted to back off, but if there was one thing she'd learned during the past few days, it was to get everything out in the open.

"Why did you leave?"

The words were barely out of her mouth when she realized it was the exact same question Sam had asked her.

He'd been right when he said that she and her sister were more alike than she'd ever thought; they both ran away from people when they were scared.

Nodding, as if she'd expected the question, April rubbed her eyes before answering. Despite how thin she was, how fragile her body looked, Dianna couldn't miss the new maturity in her sister's pensive expression. The April she'd known in San Francisco would have immediately gone on the defensive.

"I overheard your PR staff telling you I was bad for your image."

Shocked, Dianna sucked in a breath, but before she could say anything April held up a hand.

"Please, let me try and get it all out, okay?"

"Okay," Dianna agreed, "I'll try not to interrupt."

April needed to tell her story, no matter how painful. For the first time, Dianna needed to listen. Just listen. Just as she should have listened to Sam so many years ago.

"I'd been wanting to get away for so long and I told myself it would be better for both of us if I just left. I thought if I was gone then you wouldn't have to worry about me anymore and I wouldn't keep disappointing you."

God, it was hard not to say anything, Dianna thought as she let April continue.

"I guess part of leaving was wanting to hurt you," April admitted. "It never seemed fair that our mother kept you and not me. I kind of hated you for it. For being better than me. For being more lovable. But once I got to the Farm and started making friends, they helped me see that I wasn't being fair."

April sighed. "Actually, what they really said is that I'd been acting like a spoiled brat. They helped me see that I was so busy trying not to be you all these years, I forgot to try and be myself." Her mouth quirked up in a rueful half smile. "I know it's hard to believe, but when I asked you to meet me it was because I was trying to figure out a way to apologize." Another quirk of the lips. "I really am sorry for being such a jerk all these years."

Even though she'd vowed to stay silent, Dianna couldn't help but say, "It didn't help that I immediately jumped down your throat, though, did it?"

"I guess neither of us invited the other person to tea, huh?" April joked.

Wanting to get everything out on the table, Dianna knew April wasn't the only one who needed to apologize.

"I blew it, too. I never should have tried to get you and Mom back together. I don't know what I was thinking. It was such a terrible idea."

April shrugged. "In a way, it was kind of good that you did that. It made me realize how shitty it would have been to stay with her." Looking at their hands, still threaded together on the bed, she said, "I never asked you what it was like living with her."

It was so tempting to make it sound normal, better than it was. But Dianna didn't want to lie anymore. Not to her sister. And not to herself.

"If I didn't hide some of her unemployment money every month, she and her boyfriends spent it all at the bar."

"Were her boyfriends horrible?"

"Some were okay, but others were," she almost shivered remembering, "scary. Once I started to develop they'd try to corner me, touch me. And she was always too wasted to stop them."

"No wonder you never wanted me to drink. Or date." Dianna put her free hand over her heart. "I know I was overbearing, but I was so scared of anything happening to you. I don't know if I can change overnight, but is it good enough if I promise to at least try to be less controlling?"

"You can't help it if you're a control freak," April said. "Once I met our mother, things became a lot clearer. I started to see why you've worked so hard for your job and house and security. You didn't want to be like her."

"No," Dianna said softly, thinking again of Sam and the baby they didn't have. "I didn't."

April squeezed her hand. "I really am sorry for all the ways I've hurt you, Dianna. Especially when you've done more for me than anyone else."

"You're my sister," Dianna said softly. "And I love you. I'd do anything for you."

"I love you, too," April told her, "but here's the thing. I don't want to be taken care of anymore. I need my own space to figure stuff out."

"I know you do," Dianna said. "I just wish we didn't have to go through all of this to figure things out."

April sucked on her lip again, her brows furrowed. "So, you were at the Farm?" When Dianna nodded, she asked, "How did you even get up there? Did you hike?"

"And river-rafted and climbed rocks and slept under the stars."

Her sister couldn't have looked more surprised. "You did all of that? By yourself?"

In an instant, all of her worries about Sam slammed into her. "No, I didn't do it all by myself." April had already been unconscious by the time Sam showed up. "I had help. Lots of help."

Dianna swallowed past the lump in her throat. "His name is Sam MacKenzie and I was engaged to him a long time ago."

But before she could tell her sister more about Sam's heroics, and about how they'd fallen back in love, a knock came at April's door.

A gray-haired doctor stood in the doorway. "I'm looking for Dianna Kelley." His expression was grave.

Barely feeling April squeeze her hand, Dianna pushed back her chair and stood up.

"Yes, that's me."

"I'm Sam MacKenzie's surgeon. I need to speak with you right away."

# CHAPTER TWENTY-FOUR

HER LIPS were numb. So were her hands. Oh God, Sam had to be getting better, not worse. He didn't deserve any of this, not when he'd been nothing but a hero.

Willing herself not to fall apart in the hospital hallway, she asked, "Is there a problem with Sam?"

The doctor raised his eyebrows. "Physically, no."

She had to blink a couple of times. "You mean he's going to be okay?"

The man waved one hand in the air and she suddenly realized he looked more irritated than worried.

"He's pretty beaten up and we had to pick a couple of shards from the bullet out of his leg. The problem is not his health."

"Then what's wrong?"

The doctor pinched the bridge of his nose. "He's

driving the nurses on his floor crazy asking for you. He's tried to get up and walk out of his room a half-dozen times. And he's refused to take any of the pain medication or sleeping pills he needs. I'm afraid we're going to need your help to get him to cooperate."

Dianna couldn't hold back a grin. Thank God, he sounded just like the Sam MacKenzie she'd always known.

And always loved.


Sitting up in the bed, the covers barely covering his hips, Sam pulled off his hospital gown and threw it on a chair. A nurse walked in the room and did a double take when she saw his bare chest.

"Was there something wrong with your gown?" she asked him, stuttering over every other word, her eyes never leaving his naked body.

"I need my clothes," he growled.

He had to get out of this bed, this room, and find Dianna. He needed to make sure she was okay. He hated being away from her, not knowing if she was in pain.

"Mr. MacKenzie," a young male doctor said as he stepped forward, "it's a pleasure to meet you."

He didn't have time for this bullshit, for meeting any more doctors who wanted to ooh and ah over his injuries. The bullet had barely grazed his thigh. He was fine.

"What happened to my clothes?"

The doctor chuckled. "They were pretty much shredded beyond recognition." Tapping on the chart he was holding, he said, "You'll be happy to know that you passed your CT scan with flying colors. No breaks. No ruptures. How are you feeling now?"

"I feel fine. As soon as I get some clothes I'm out of here."

The nurse looked helplessly at the doctor. The man shrugged, "I'm afraid we can't let you leave quite yet, but we can try to get you some clothes."

"I don't know if I can find anything that will fit him," the nurse said, blushing profusely as she gestured to Sam's muscular shoulders and broad chest.

"Dr. Keyes has a similar build. Why don't you go see if he's got an extra set of clothes he could lend Mr. MacKenzie?" Turning back to Sam, he said, "Before I go, could you tell me how you did it?"

"Did what?"

"Lived through your fall. You could have died a dozen different ways. But you didn't."

Dianna had needed him. He'd needed to get back on the trail so that he could save her and April—and marry Dianna. That had been his motivation, plain and simple.

"I had unfinished business to take care of." And a woman he loved waiting for him on the other side.

And then a woman walked in carrying a handful of clothes, but it wasn't the nurse.

It was Dianna.

Dropping the clothes, she ran to Sam, burying her head in his chest. He wrapped his strong arms around her and stroked her hair.

Even though she'd managed perfectly well by herself for ten years, she was no longer afraid to admit to herself that she needed him.

His strength. His confidence. His love.

When she was with Sam, she finally felt safe.

"I was so worried about you," she said softly. "Are you okay?"

He smiled into her eyes and she'd never seen anything more beautiful than his scruffy tanned face—cuts, bruises, and all.

"Never better. Why aren't you in bed? You've got to be exhausted."

She laughed. Here he'd been hit by a bullet and he wanted to know why she wasn't resting.

"This time you're the one who needs to rest," she said, pressing a soft kiss on his lips. "You've spent so long taking care of me and everyone else. Now it's finally my turn to take care of you."

"I'm fine," he insisted, but she wanted to make him understand.

"For so long, I told myself I didn't need anyone to watch over me, that I wasn't going to wait for some guy to swoop in and save me. But I was wrong. It's not about being saved, it's about knowing there's someone out there who will always have your back, no matter what."

She leaned in close to kiss him again. "You've always been the strong one, Sam. You've always been the one who had my back. This time, let me take care of you."

Cupping her face with his hands, he kissed her so sweetly, her lips were a direct line to her heart.

"How can a guy argue with that?"

Smiling, she said, "I told the doctors I'd work my special powers to get you to see reason."

"Tell them to throw their pills away. You're the only medicine I need," he said, before asking, "How's April doing? Have you seen her yet?"

"I was just in her room. She's going to be fine. And we talked, Sam. Really talked for the first time."

"I'm glad," he said, smiling. "I can't wait to meet her to tell her what a great big sister she has."

And then he grew serious again, a muscle jumping in his jaw. "Who was that guy on the trail? Why was he after you? Did he hurt you?"

As if on cue, there were two sharp raps on the door. The two police officers from the campground walked into Sam's room.

"Ms. Kelley, Mr. MacKenzie, if you don't mind, we've got some questions to ask both of you."

Dianna's heart jumped, but Sam's hand on hers helped calm her down. Never having been nearly as comfortable on the other side of the interviewer's chair, she wanted to get her part over with as soon as possible.

Speaking quickly, she summarized the situation as best she could for the cops. Talking about the stranger's revenge plot, she felt as if she were watching herself from a distance.

When she finished recounting her part of the story, the police turned their attention to Sam.

"So you admit to lighting the fires, Mr. MacKenzie?" one of the officers asked when he was finished recounting his part of the story.

Sam's steady gaze didn't waver. "Yes."

He'd already explained his reasons, that creating a smoke signal was his only chance to be seen beneath the thick canopy of trees. He didn't give excuses or make apologies.

Now more than ever, Dianna saw that he'd risked everything for her. His career and his life.

"Did the hotshot crew put the fires out yet?" Sam asked.

"Yes, but we're still going to have to write you up for arson."

"Understood."

The police closed their notebooks and stood up, but Dianna had no intention of letting them leave before she got her questions answered too.

"Who was he?"

The taller cop with the gray hair answered. "His name was Graham Taylor."

She could tell they wanted to leave it at that, but she, Sam, and April had all nearly died at his hands.

"What was that place he took me to?"

The officers looked at each other, the older one giving a quick nod to the younger one, who said, "A meth lab. We've been looking for him for the past few months, but all trails led to his twin brother. We were still gathering evidence and hadn't yet questioned either Jacob or Graham." Clearing his throat, he said, "I'm sure we'll be back in touch by phone in the near future."

Dianna sat down hard on the edge of Sam's bed when they were alone again, stunned by everything that had happened.

"I can't believe what you had to do to find me and April. I'll never forgive myself if you lose your job."

"I'd light those fires again, Dianna. If you were in trouble and it was the only way I could get to you, I wouldn't hesitate for a single second. I can get another job. But without you, I've got nothing."

And then Sam was running the back of his hand along her jawline, making her unable to focus on anything except the shivers running through her body.

"There are so many things I want to say to you right now. But the most important thing is that I love you, Dianna. I've always loved you. I always will."

She brought his hands to her lips and kissed his warm skin. "I love you, too. Always and forever."

His eyes were starting to close and she could see how hard it was for him to stay awake.

"I'm not going anywhere, Sam. I promise. Right now the most important thing you can do is rest."

She watched him sleep for a couple of hours, her heart full with happiness. While the past three days had almost taken everything she loved from her, miraculously, she'd come out the other side with more love than she'd ever dreamed possible.

Still holding Sam's hand, finally at peace, she closed her eyes and leaned her head back against her chair. The next time she opened them, she found Sam awake and staring at her, his blue eyes dark and passionate.

He held out his arms and she crawled up onto the bed with him, careful not to brush up against his thigh.

"Am I hurting you?" she asked, even though she had no intention of leaving him.

"The only thing that hurts is having you so far away."

His lips ran a trail of kisses down her face, past her earlobe, lingering at the sensitive spot on her neck.

"I'm pretty sure this isn't what the doctor meant when he said you needed to rest."

She felt Sam's grin against her skin. "To each his own. All I can say is I'm feeling better already."

His kisses felt so good and she wanted to sink into them and forget everything, but there were so many things she needed him to know.

Pulling away slightly, she was mesmerized by the gleam in his eyes that told her how much he wanted her. She was amazed all over again that he wanted her, just as she'd been at eighteen.

Of all the women he could have chosen, he'd picked her.

And she'd chosen him right back.

Only this time, they were actually going to get the fairy tale. The whole thing, not just the opening credits.

"I can't wait to hear what you're thinking," he teased, brushing a lock of hair out of her eyes.

At her silent question, he said, "Your brain is always going, always working, always questioning. It's one of the things I've loved about you from the start."

Her smile huge, she said, "I was just thinking about us. About our future."

She paused and looked at him to see if the word "future" had freaked him out, but his expression remained open and loving, a far cry from the shuttered, closed-up man he'd been through the first half of their journey to find April.

"Earlier, when April and I were talking, she told me it isn't my fault that I'm a control freak." He chuckled as she said, "But I've finally figured out that it's time for me to let go. Not just with April, so that she can live her own life, but with you and me. I don't know what's going to happen, Sam. I can't predict what's in our future. When I was eighteen, I was scared, so I left. But I'm not scared of risking my heart to you anymore."

Sam's mouth came down over hers with a kiss so sweet and filled with love that it brought tears to her eyes.

But there was one more thing she needed to know.

"What about everything you said to me? About needing to stay away from me because of what happened after I left?"

His black hole. How could she ever forgive herself if he ended up back in that dark place?

His answer was swift. Sure. "I'd risk a thousand black holes for the chance to love you, Dianna. Because not being with you will hurt me far more than anything else. Even falling off a cliff," he teased.

And then they were kissing again and her hand was making its way beneath the sheet when the door opened.

"I'd tell you to get a room," a nurse joked, "but I'm afraid even that's not going to help you around here."

Not feeling the least bit repentant, Dianna snuggled in closer to Sam. She couldn't wait to start their new life.

Together.

# CHAPTER TWENTY-FIVE

*Almost a week later . . .*

HAVING FALLEN into a deep sleep on the plane out of Vail, Dianna was still groggy as they headed to Sam's car in the San Francisco Airport parking lot.

And then they were standing in front of his old green Jeep and memories came rushing back, one after the other. Of Sam teaching her to drive a stick shift and laughing when she stalled in the middle of the intersection and cars from all four sides started honking at them. Of driving to one of Tahoe's small, deserted beaches and making out in the front seat, then pulling off their clothes and going skinny-dipping under a full moon.

She'd had so much fun sitting beside Sam in the Jeep. More fun than she'd ever had with anyone else. Not to mention pleasure beyond her wildest dreams.

"You still have the Jeep."

His dark eyes were full of heat. "I couldn't get rid of it. Not when it felt like my only connection to you."

"I'm glad you didn't."

Relaxing in the passenger seat, Dianna felt looser and lighter as the miles clicked by and they started climbing into the mountains.

That morning, April had headed back up to the Farm to reconnect with her friends and make some decisions about what to do next. Although it was hard to let her sister make the trek back up the mountain on her own, Dianna knew she had to let go and leave April's life up to April.

As expected, Sam recovered quickly from his injuries. After Connor had arrived at the hospital, everywhere Dianna went she overheard both female nurses and doctors talking about the "gorgeous firefighters" on the fifth floor.

Dianna would never stop feeling lucky that Sam was *her* firefighter.

After a long talk with her friend and producer, Ellen, they both agreed that Dianna wasn't ready to go back and host *West Coast Update* yet. Not without a long vacation first. So when Sam had asked her to go back to Lake Tahoe with him, she'd immediately agreed.

And then they'd gotten the good news from the Rocky Mountain police. The Forest Service wasn't going to press charges against Sam, the explanation being that the now-defunct meth lab he'd helped shut down was a far greater threat of wildfire than a handful of flares in the hands of a celebrated hotshot.

Feeling content as she held Sam's hand on the stick shift and looked out the window, Lake Tahoe had never seemed more beautiful. As a child, Dianna hadn't been blind to its beauty, but the only time she'd experienced all the scenic town had to offer was while dating Sam.

After their breakup, she'd avoided the Sierras whenever possible to avoid coming face-to-face with her memories. Now, she simply couldn't wait to spend some time rediscovering her childhood home with her true love at her side.

Once upon a time, there'd been walks through the forests, sitting on the beach and talking, roasting marshmallows in front of a roaring fire. Letting the warm breeze through the open window rush across her skin, she simply couldn't wait to continue her new life with Sam.

Sam could see that Dianna was exhausted. There were dark smudges under her eyes, and her collarbones were protruding slightly from beneath her shirt.

He was going to spend every hour, every minute for

the rest of his life taking care of her. Even if he had to go work for an urban station to live in the city, giving up wildfires would be worth it. Dianna was worth any sacrifice.

He parked in front of his rental house and Dianna woke up. Grabbing their bags, he suddenly saw his house through her eyes.

Basic furniture, white walls, a kitchen that stayed spotless because no one used it.

It wasn't that he didn't have enough money to buy his own place. Due to some good investments over the years, he had plenty. He'd even bought a plot of land with a killer view that was ready to be built on.

But he hadn't seen the point, not when he didn't have a family to share it with. He hadn't spent much time in his house apart from sleeping and eating. Wildfires had been his life and he'd been perfectly happy with that. At least he thought he was.

Now, he was ready for a wife. For kids.

But before he put their bags down his cell phone started ringing. He knew who it was and didn't want to answer it.

But Dianna wouldn't let him off the hook. "That's Logan, isn't it? There's a fire."

Silently cursing out his squad boss, he reached for her and pulled her close.

"Probably. But I'm not going to fight this one. I'm going to stay here with you. You need me more. I wasn't here for you ten years ago. I'm not going to make that same mistake again."

Her gentle kiss told him he was making the right decision, but then she surprised him by saying, "You don't have to prove to me that I come first. I already know it. Just as I know that being a firefighter means answering the call, no matter how inconvenient." Another kiss. "So go, Sam. With my blessing. You'll always have my blessing."

Sam had stuck by her through the hardest ordeal of her life. And she would stick by him for the rest of their lives, through every wildfire, no matter how long he was away, no matter how much she missed him.

And when he came home, there'd be love, laughter, and sharing. And plenty of hot sex.

Love at first sight had grown into a bigger love than she'd ever dreamed was possible.

Two days later, after enjoying a day on the beach with a great book, she was just about to make some dinner when she heard a car pull up in the driveway. Her heart started pounding and she threw the blanket off, leapt off the couch, ran out the front door, and threw her arms and legs around Sam while showering him with kisses.

"You're back," she said softly and his answering grin knocked all of the air from her lungs.

"I missed you," he said simply, cupping her face in his hands and kissing her, slowly, sweetly.

Her eyes were still closed when the kiss ended. Being with Sam again felt like a dream. The best dream she'd ever had. He pressed soft kisses to her eyelids, her forehead, her cheekbones, before finding his way back to her mouth.

"You smell like sunshine," he said against her lips.

He smelled like smoke and the clean sweat of a man who'd, yet again, smashed straight through the boundaries of human strength.

"You smell good, too," she said.

He chuckled, a warm, rumbling sound that made her toes curl.

"I'm pretty sure I need a shower."

But she didn't want him to go, so she brushed her fingers across his chin, the beginnings of a beard lightly scratching against her fingertips.

"You're perfect just like this. I always thought so."

She met his eyes and she was startled by the intensity in the blue depths.

"I knew you were mine from the minute I saw you, Dianna," he said softly. "Getting pregnant only speeded things up. I love you. I've always loved you. And I always will."

"I love you, too," she whispered. "Forever. Always." She pushed his jacket off. "Take me inside and make love to me, Sam."

His eyes flashed with desire so intense that her skin almost felt singed. "I've never been able to turn down a damsel in distress."

"I was banking on it," Dianna said before pressing her lips against his.

Turn the page for a sneak peek
at Bella Andre's

# NEVER TOO HOT

Available next month from
*Rouge Suspense*

# CHAPTER ONE

CONNOR MACKENZIE slid his rental car into the gravel driveway behind the old log cabin and was pulling the keys out of the ignition when the cheap metal key ring scraped against his palm. He swore as it bit into the bumpy, scarred flesh, skin that still felt too tight every time he flexed his hands or made a fist.

Still, today was one of the good days. All through the flight and the two-hour drive from the airport through winding back roads he'd been able to feel everything he touched.

The worst days were the ones where the numbness won. Days when it took everything in him to fight back the angry roars, when he felt like a wounded lion crammed into a four-by-four-foot cage in some zoo, just waiting for the chance to escape and run free again. To be whole and king of the jungle again.

His hand stung as he pulled off his seat belt and slammed the driver's-side door shut. He needed to get out to where he could see the water, breathe it in. Calm the fuck down. Get a grip.

This lake, deep in the heart of the thick Adirondack woods, would set him straight.

It had to.

He'd come from another lake, from twelve years in California's Lake Tahoe fighting wildfires. But he couldn't stay there another summer, couldn't stand to watch his brother and friends head out to fight fire after fire while he went to physical therapy and worked with rookies in the classroom, teaching them from books and trying not to notice the way they stared at the thick scars running up and down his arms from his multiple grafts.

Coming to Blue Mountain Lake had been his brother's idea. *"Dianna and I want to get married at Poplar Cove end of July,"* Sam had said. They'd been planning a big wedding for late fall, at the end of fire season, but now that Dianna was pregnant, their schedule had moved up several months. *"After all these years, especially with Gram and Gramps down in Florida full-time, I'm sure the cabin needs work. Might be a good project for the next few weeks. Better than hanging around here, anyway."*

Connor had wanted to camp outside the Forest Service headquarters until they agreed to sign his umpteenth round of appeal papers, the papers that would put him back on his Tahoe Pines hotshot crew. He'd been jumping through one Forest Service hoop after another for two long years, working like hell to convince the powers that be that he was ready—both mentally and physically—to resume his duties as a hotshot. Up until now they'd said there was too much risk. They thought it was too likely that he'd freeze, that he might not only take himself out, but a civilian too.

Bullshit. He was ready. More than ready. And he was sure this time his appeal would be approved.

But he could see what Sam was saying. Getting at the log cabin with a saw and hammer and paintbrush, running the trails around the lake and going for long, cool swims might do something to settle the agitation that had been running through his veins for two years.

Things were going to be different here. This summer was going to be better than the last, a sure bet it would be a hell of a lot better than the two that he'd spent in a hospital.

This summer the monkey that had latched itself onto his back, the persistent monster that had been slowly but steadily strangling Connor, was going to finally hop off and leave him the fuck alone.

Moving off the gravel driveway, Connor walked past the grass and through the sand until he was at the water's edge. He looked out at the calm lake, the perfectly still surface reflecting the thick white clouds and the green mountains that surrounded it, waiting for the release in his chest, for the fist to uncoil in his gut.

A cigarette boat whipped out from around the point and into the bay, creating a huge wake on the silent midday shore, and the cold water splashed high, up over Connor's shoes, soaking him to the knees.

Fuck.

Who was he trying to kid? He wasn't here for laughs this summer. He was here to push past the lingering pain in his hands and arms.

He was here to force himself into peak physical shape, to prove his worth to the Forest Service when he got back to California after Sam's wedding.

He was here to renovate his great-grandparents' one-hundred-year-old log cabin, to work such long, hard hours on it that when he slept he would outrun his nightmares, the god-awful reminders of the day he'd almost died on the mountain in Lake Tahoe.

He was here to be alone. Completely alone.

And no matter what he had to do, he was going to find the inner calm, the control that had always been so effortless, so innate before the Desolation fire.

Turning away from the water, he stared back at the log cabin. The words POPLAR COVE were etched on one of the logs, the name his great-grandparents had given the Adirondack camp in 1910. He forced himself to look for its flaws, for everything he'd need to tear down and rebuild this summer. The paint was peeling beneath the screened-in porch on the front where the storms hit hardest. Some of the roof's shingles were askew.

But even as he worked to be dispassionate, he mostly saw the precision detailing his great-grandfather had put into the cabin a hundred years ago: the perfect logs holding up the heavy corners of the building, the smaller logs and twigs that framed the porch almost artistically.

Eighteen summers he'd spent in this cabin. Ten weeks

every summer with Sam and their friends under the watchful but loving eyes of their grandparents. The only people missing were his parents. One time he'd asked his mother why they couldn't come too, but she'd gotten that funny, breathless, watery-eyed look that he hated seeing— the same look that she usually got when she was talking to his dad about his long work hours—so he'd dropped it.

He couldn't believe it had been twelve years since he'd stood here.

After signing up to be a hotshot at eighteen, Connor's summers had been full fighting wildfires. Any normal July 1st this past decade would have seen him in a west coast forest with a 150-pound pack on his back, a chain saw in his hand, surrounded by his twenty-man, wildland fire-fighting crew. But the last couple of years had been any-thing but normal.

Connor had never thought to see the word disability next to his name. Seven hundred thirty days after getting caught in a blowup on Desolation Wilderness and he still couldn't.

Still, even though he belonged in Tahoe beating back flames, as he stood on the sand, the humid air making his T-shirt stick to his chest, he felt in his bones how much he'd missed Blue Mountain Lake.

Heading back to his car, he grabbed his bag from the truck, slung it over one shoulder and headed for the steps off the side of the screened-in porch that stretched from one side of the house to the other.

Most of his indoor time as a kid had been spent on this porch, protected from the bugs and the rain, but open to the breeze. His grandparents had served all their meals on the porch's Formica table. He hadn't cared that his teeth had chattered on cool mornings in early summer while he downed a bowl of Cheerios out there. He and Sam had lived in T-shirts and swim shorts regardless of the cold fronts that frequently blew in.

One of the porch steps nearly split beneath his foot and he frowned as he bent down to inspect it. Guilt gnawed at his gut as he silently acknowledged that his grandparents could have hurt themselves on these stairs. He should have come out here in the off-season, should have checked to make sure everything was okay. But fire had always come first.

Always.

Something grated at him there, so he reminded himself that the bones of the log cabin were sound. He'd heard the stories a hundred times of how his great-grandfather had cut each one of the logs himself from the thick forest of pine trees a half mile from the lake. Still, time took its toll on every building eventually, no matter how well constructed.

Taking the rest of the stairs two at a time, ready now to see what other problems awaited him inside, Connor reached for the handle on the screen door.

But instead of turning it, he stopped cold.

What the hell?

A woman was dancing in front of an easel, swinging around what looked like a paintbrush, white cables dangling from her ears as she sang in a wildly off-tune voice.

Every few seconds she dipped into her paint and took a swipe at the oversized canvas.

He couldn't believe what he was seeing. Some strange singing, painting woman on his porch was the last thing he wanted to deal with today.

Still, he couldn't help but be struck by how pretty she was as she did a little spin before squirting more paint onto her easel and sweeping her brush through it. He was close enough to see that she wasn't wearing a bra under her red tank top and when she wiped at the damp skin on her neck and the deep vee between her breasts with a white rag, his body immediately responded in a painful reminder that it had been too long since he'd been with a woman.

He quickly filled in the rest of the sensual, unexpected picture. Curly hair piled on top of her head and held with some sort of plastic clip, cutoff jeans, tanned legs, and bright orange toenails on bare feet.

It took far longer than it should have for him to snap himself out of the haze of animal lust that was wrapping itself around his cock. Another time he might have walked in with a smile and charmed the panties right off her. But he hadn't come to the lake to get laid.

A woman had no place in his summer, no matter how well she filled out every one of the boxes on his checklist.

For whatever reason, the woman was trespassing.

And she had to go.

*　*　*

It was, Ginger thought with a smile as she mixed Cinnabar Red and Ocean Blue, a perfect summer day. She'd started it off with a walk along the beach, then took a bagel out to the end of the dock to munch while reading a sexy paperback, and now here she was painting like crazy on the porch.

The pop song streaming into her ears at top volume hit the crescendo of the big final chorus and she had to stop painting altogether to play air drums and sing harmony. She felt so happy, so carefree, and it hit her suddenly, powerfully that she could never—*never!*—have done this in her old life.

Oh, the way her ex-husband and their "friends" would have reacted if they could see her now. Her whole life she'd been perfectly buttoned up, overly coiffed and made up, and elegantly outfitted despite the fact that the tag on her clothes had always been in the teens rather than the single digits. Discounting the fact that her body refused to shrink even if she ate nothing but heads of lettuce, in every other way she'd been the perfect rich girl turned businessman's wife.

But not anymore. Not at Blue Mountain Lake.

She didn't have to be that woman here.

Sure, she was still doing a lot of fund-raising for the school's art program, but she loved knowing she was helping people. Besides, it had always been a rush to know that she was good at getting people to reach into their pocketbooks and do good. Great at it, actually. The joke back home—shouldn't she stop thinking of the city as home, already?—was that all she had to do was walk into a room full of millionaires and they'd start throwing money at her as fast as she could catch it.

Helping out at the Blue Mountain Lake schools had been a great way to get involved with the town, to not feel so alone as she started over. What the locals lacked in dollars they made up for in enthusiasm. And so although she'd come to this small town to focus on painting, she couldn't help but be swept up in her work with the kids and parents.

The day she'd moved into Poplar Cove she'd vowed not to waste any time looking into her past. She'd rather live in the moment. Take each day as it came. And everything would really be perfect, if only she had a . . .

The song ended and in the silence between tracks she could hear a mama bird announce her arrival to a nest full of baby birds on the underside of the eave. Ginger leaned forward to watch as a little head poked out of the nest and took food from its mother's beak in what looked like a kiss.

Another bouncy pop song started up, but Ginger pulled out her earphones. She wasn't in the mood anymore. She stared at her canvas, but instead of seeing the painting she'd been working on all day, she saw an image of the cute baby that had been playing on the beach during her morning walk.

The little girl had been positively gleeful as she jabbed a pink shovel into the sand, her sweet round cheeks and chubby little legs poking out of her pink polka-dot swimsuit. Her mother had looked tired, almost frazzled, and yet, as she watched her daughter play on the beach, perfectly content at the same time.

Her husband, Jeremy, had held her off for years. *"One day,"* was what he told her. *"When the time is right, then we'll see."*

By the time she'd realized the time was never going to be right, that his "one day" didn't work for her, she'd had to face up to the fact that the marriage didn't either.

Lately, she wondered more and more when it was going to happen. *If* it was going to happen. She knew plenty of women who had to do in vitro at thirty. Three years past that, Ginger sometimes wondered if her viable eggs were all drying up one by one.

But there was more. Because if she were in one of her foolish I-should-know-better romantic moods (which usually involved several glasses of wine), the truth was she still wanted a wonderful husband to have the family with. Yes, her first marriage hadn't been great. But that didn't mean the second couldn't be the love she'd been searching for.

This was perhaps the only problem about settling into a small town as a single woman. The available men (who weren't ordering from the senior menu) were pretty slim pickings.

She'd been set up by one of the local biddies with Sean Murphy, who co-owned the Inn with his younger brother, but there'd been no chemistry. Yes, he was a great-looking guy. Tall, dark, chiseled. But even though she'd enjoyed his company, she couldn't shake how much he reminded her of her older brother.

One day in the not too distant future was she going to have to pull up stakes again, simply for the chance to start a family?

She sighed. Maybe it was time to get a refill on her iced tea. It was pretty darn hot after all. And she had only thirty minutes left to paint before she had to leave for her shift at the diner. No point in spinning off in her head with what-ifs and worries when she should be enjoying the time to herself.

But just as she was about to put down her brush, the screen door to her left abruptly swung open.

She spun around to see a large man standing in the doorway, his face tight and grim, his eyes narrowed. Fear hit her square across the chest.

How long had he been standing on the steps? Had he been watching her?

She'd never met him before. He wasn't the kind of man she would have forgotten. So why was he looking at her like that, like he'd come to get revenge?

Oh God, her parents had told her this would happen, hadn't they? They'd told her it was crazy to live out so far in the woods. Her nearest neighbors were nearly an acre away, far enough that they wouldn't be able to hear her screams. Maybe, she thought wildly, the biggest problem about being a single woman in a small town wasn't having trouble finding dates, it was being murdered.

Ginger gulped in air, swallowed hard, tried to remember how to breathe. She gripped the paintbrush like a weapon despite the fact that she knew it wouldn't do a lick of good in beating back the wall of muscle staring her down.

"Who are you? What do you want?"

He moved all the way onto the porch, the door banging closed behind him. "What are you doing in my house?"

His house? What was he talking about?

Huge and nuts. Not a good a combination. She was in big trouble here. Too far from the phone to place an emergency call to a friend, or even the police. Was her only choice to try to bluff him with some tough-chick act?

She was toast.

Widening her stance, lifting the paintbrush as if it were a knife, she growled, "Get off my porch," just as the sun moved out from behind a cloud and landed on his torso.

She sucked in a sharp breath. She hadn't been able to see his arms and hands clearly at first, but now she couldn't take her eyes off them. His skin was a mess, beneath the short sleeves of his T-shirt, raised and bumpy, covered with red lashes and lines. In the glimmering sunlight streaming in through the porch screen, it looked fresh and raw and terribly painful.

"Oh my God, what happened to you?" She dropped her paintbrush and moved toward him.

If anything, his expression became even more fierce. "I'm fine."

She continued across the porch. He was obviously in shock. In denial about the pain he had to be in.

"You don't need to pretend you're okay. I can see your arms, they . . ."

By then she was only a handful of feet away from him, close enough to see the true damage. She swallowed the rest of her words as her eyes and brain finally made the connection.

She'd just made a terrible mistake. Yes, he'd been hurt. Badly. But it wasn't recent. They were old wounds.

His words were low and hard. "I was burned two years ago. I'm fine now."

She bit her lip. Nodded. "Oh. Yes. I can see that now. It's just when the sun hit you, I thought—" She should stop talking now; the hole she'd dug was already big enough. "I'm sorry. I didn't mean to make such a big deal about your . . . your scars."

The silence that followed her horrible words was long. Borderline painful. He must hate it when people freaked out over his scars and here she'd practically been wrapping gauze around them.

And of course, now she couldn't stop wondering how he'd gotten so badly burned. Even though it was none of her business.

Finally, he said, "I'm Connor MacKenzie. And this is my house. I thought it was empty. I just flew all the way from California. It should be empty."

His name registered quickly. At last, something that made sense. "Are you related to Helen and George MacKenzie?"

"They're my grandparents."

She breathed her first sigh of relief. He wasn't a serial killer. He was related to the cabin's owner.

"I'm Ginger. Why don't you come in." She tentatively

smiled. "Maybe we can start over and I could offer you a glass of iced tea?"

He didn't smile back. "How do you know my grandparents?"

Did he realize that every word out of his mouth sounded like an accusation? Like she'd screwed up all of his big plans when she didn't know him from Adam.

"I'm renting this cabin from them. Didn't they tell you?"

He stared at her for a long moment, and she got the uncomfortable feeling that he was trying to assess whether she was telling him the truth.

"No."

There would have been a time when a big, strong man of few words like this would have had her trembling and weak-kneed. She would have assumed she was the one in the wrong even when she clearly had it all right. Fortunately, a lot had changed in this past year. And she, frankly, wasn't in the mood to be pushed around.

"Wait here." Sixty seconds later she was back with the signed lease. "Here it is."

He took the document from her and as he read through it, she was able to take a good long look at him for the first time. Golden-brown hair, deeply tanned skin, thickly lashed eyes, a full yet masculine mouth and strong chin, presently covered with a half-day's stubble.

Now that she was no longer worried that he was going to attack her, on an elemental level, her body suddenly recognized his beauty.

His innate power.

Up close, not only was he strikingly handsome, but he was even bigger than she'd first thought. Between the wide breadth of his chest and the muscles flexing beneath his T-shirt, from the size of his biceps and the way his chest tapered down to slim, tight hips, she could feel her breath slowly leaving her body, quickly being replaced with something that felt—uncomfortably—like desire.

It wasn't until several long moments later that she realized he was staring back at her. His eyes were making a lazy path from her face to her partially covered breasts, then farther down to her hips and legs before slowly moving back up to her face.

Suddenly, she remembered what she was wearing. Or, more to the point, wasn't wearing.

She'd never go out in public without a bra, but here, in the privacy of her own house, she did as she wished. It was one of the things she enjoyed most about having her own place. The freedom to not only do whatever she wanted, but to wear whatever she wanted.

A tank top and cutoff jeans had never been part of her city vernacular. But here at the lake, especially when she was getting down and dirty with her paints, when the thermometer read eighty and the humidity was ratcheting up all day in preparation for a rainstorm, she liked the bohemian feel of cutoffs.

Not thrilled about flashing some stranger—even less thrilled about him taking any surreptitious pleasure from looking at her—she crossed her arms over her breasts to stop the peep show. But then she realized he hadn't given her the lease back yet, so she had to unfold one arm and reach for it.

The corners of the papers crumpled in his fist. Damn it, he'd already cut into most of her dwindling painting time for the afternoon. She wasn't in any mood for games.

Switching into a stern demeanor that had been known to make billionaires quiver in their Ferragamos when they "forgot" to give one of her charities the money they'd publicly promised, she said, "Now that you have your proof, I'd very much appreciate it if you'd give me back my lease."

But this man didn't quiver. He didn't shake. Instead his eyes continued to hold hers and she was almost certain she saw a challenge in the blue depths.

And wouldn't you know it, her heart started leaping around in her chest. She supposed it was some sort of instinctual response to the combination of his devastating looks and the threat that he clearly posed to her perfect summer on the lake.

"Lucky you," he drawled. "Getting this place all to yourself this summer."

She was caught off guard by the way his low, rough voice slipped and slid through her veins so seductively. How the hell had he managed to almost make her toes curl on the porch floors with nothing but a few words?

Up until now he'd been hard. Unyielding. Definitely not in a bargaining mood. But now that she'd not only staked but proved her claim, it looked like he'd decided to change tactics by stunning her with the full force of his sensual power.

Well, just because she liked what she saw (she'd have to be drained of all hormones not to), didn't mean she had any intention of touching. Which meant she was immune.

Mostly, anyway.

"You're right," she agreed, and even though she wouldn't normally feel the need to rub in her win over a virtual stranger, she couldn't resist adding, "It's breathtaking."

He looked out at the lake. "Not many views this good, even on this lake. My grandfather used to call it the million-dollar beach."

When he turned back to her his lips were curled up on one side in what might have been a half smile under other circumstances. But right at that moment it was colored more with a sneer than anything even remotely connected to happiness.

"I'm just wondering one thing. How did you know my grandparents were thinking of renting it when they didn't even remember to tell their own family?"

It was a sucker punch. Oh no, he wasn't going to get away with that. Because Ginger Sinclair was no longer afraid to call people on their shit. And this guy was fairly brimming over with it.

"Are you accusing me of something?"

The half-not-a-smile dropped. "Only if you've got something to be guilty about."

Jesus. What was with good-looking guys? Were they so used to getting their own way all the time that they thought they could say and do whatever they wanted, whenever the mood struck? Someone should have taken this one down a peg a long time ago. Looked like the job was all hers.

Twisting her mouth into that same half smile, half sneer he'd just graced her with, she said, "Well, since I've already been living here for eight months without your knowledge, it's clearly been a long while since you've had a chat with your grandparents. Seems to me I'm not the one who should have the guilty conscience."

She braced herself for his next parry, but instead there was that flash in his eyes again, not angry now, more intrigued. The way her pulse jumped confused her, made her head feel like it was spinning. What was it about this guy that had her body turning traitor on her?

It had to be the muggy weather. All the dancing on the porch must have depleted her electrolytes. She was dehydrated. That's all it was.

"You're right," he finally said. "I need to call them."

Ginger couldn't believe it. Was he actually agreeing with her? Well, that was that. Now that they'd cleared everything up, he'd go and leave her alone. Good.

She couldn't wait.

But then, she noticed the large bag at his feet, presumably full of his clothes. Clearly, he'd been planning on staying in the cabin tonight. Because he'd thought it was vacant. Which meant he didn't have any other place to stay.

Oh no.

She looked at his face again, immediately getting snared in his dark blue eyes.

Definitely no.

This log cabin was hers and hers alone. The cuckoo clock chimed four times over the fireplace in the living room and she was hit by a sudden rush of anger at her perfect day falling to shreds.

"Look, I'm sorry that you didn't know someone was living in the house, but I've got a twelve-month agreement, so you're going to have to find another place to stay." Tonight and thereafter, thank you very much. "And I'm afraid I'm going to be late for work if I don't leave soon, so . . ."

She looked at the door, making it perfectly clear that it was time for him to leave.

He nodded, picked up his bag and said, "Okay."

She was midway through releasing the breath she'd been holding when he added, "I'll come back tomorrow. So that we can figure out something that will work for both of us."

What? He was coming back?

She should have known a guy like this wouldn't back down so easily.

"I'll say it one last time. *I've got a lease through the summer.* Good-bye."

There. She couldn't have been clearer.

But he still wasn't leaving. Instead his eyes were scanning the cabin and then he was walking over to a log that held up the wall between the porch and the living room. Without warning, he slammed his fist into it.

She half screamed in surprise. "What the hell are you doing?"

Calm as anything, he used his fingertips to brush away the crumbled wood chips.

"See that?"

She swallowed hard. "You just made a hole in the log."

A perfect fist-sized hole. How strong did he have to be to hit it like that without even flinching?

"This rotten log is just one of the half-dozen ways this old house could come down around your head." He turned back to her, raised an eyebrow. "I'm sure my grandparents would be happy to give you a refund on your rent."

Her heart was still pounding from the shock of seeing him knock a huge chunk out of the log. But she was bound and determined not to let his scare tactics work.

"I'm not going anywhere."

"Then we'll talk tomorrow."

The screen door slammed shut behind him as he left. Ginger couldn't stop herself from moving over to the log to get a better look at it. And as she put her hand into the hole he'd left, she hated how Connor had made her look at the cabin that had been her refuge with different eyes.

With doubt.

*Rouge* is a new romance list from Random House, releasing new titles every month across a wide variety of genres including:

Want your romance with an edge of danger? *Rouge Suspense* is where drama and intrigue meet passion in the best in romantic suspense.

Come over to the dark side with vampires, werewolves and demonic bad boys in our paranormal romance line.

Like your heroes in britches? Find your own Mr Darcy in *Rouge Regency*.
Step into the world of Austen and Heyer with the best in sexy regency romance.

All our books are available digitally and now, for the first time, select *Rouge* titles are also available in print.

Follow us on Twitter @rougeromance

Find us on Facebook www.facebook.com/rougeromance

Or join the conversation at www.rougeromance.co.uk